Prodigy

Book II of The Shapeshifter Chronicles

Natasha Brown

Natasha Brown

Acknowledgments

I would like to thank my friends at the World Literary Café for all of their support and advice, without which, I would be utterly lost. And without Bev Katz Rosenbaum's editorial expertise, Prodigy wouldn't be what it is today.

I would like to acknowledge my friends and family, who have supported me through my ups and downs. You know who you are—you are an invaluable part of my life.

Chapter 1

Dense mist licked at Chance Morgan's exposed skin and at the tall evergreens that surrounded him. The moisture in the air condensed in his lungs, making it hard to breath. As he stared into the twilight, a dark shape lunged at him through the fog.

A fierce black bear pulled its lips back and displayed ivory teeth that held the promise of pain. Deep growls poured from its chest as its arm lashed out to claw him. Chance scrambled back against the rough bark of a pine, its abrasive coat biting at his bare skin. With nowhere to go, he held his arms up to protect his face from the oncoming attack. Chance closed his eyes and prepared for the end.

The black bear slowed and began to shiver and quake. It grew and shifted into a huge feathered raptor. Cinnamon feathers tumbled in layers down its body. The majestic bird extended its wings to their full breadth. Its yellow eyes flashed, focusing on Chance huddled in the dirt, and waited until he met its gaze.

Chance, you are not done with your education. There is more for you to learn if you are to be saved from your innocence. Remember, I will always be with you.

The thunderbird disappeared into the rolling mist and resonant chanting filled the air. The fog dispersed and revealed Chance's grandfather kneeling before a man's lifeless body. Niyol's hands hovered over the man's chest.

Chance stood helplessly by as a sapphire glow

radiated from his grandfather's palms. Light entered the still body beneath and following a burst of air, Niyol fell silent before collapsing.

Darkness consumed them.

"Grandfather!"

Chance bolted upright in bed, the gray sheets tangled around his muscular body. The numbers on the clock glowed red. Morning already. He groaned and dropped his head into his hands. *Grandfather, why are you doing this to me? Or am I just going crazy?*

He wasn't sure how much more he could take. He'd had the same recurring dream for so many nights it was beginning to wear him down. In each one, different animals attacked him, but it always ended the same way, with the creature shapeshifting into the thunderbird, his ancestor's form of power. The dream usually involved a message from his grandfather. At least it sounded like him. Chance knew it had to be his subconscious trying to tell him something. What, he didn't know.

The worst part of the dream was revisiting his grandfather's death. Maybe Chance deserved it. It was his penance for killing him. If Chance hadn't died saving Ana he would still have his mentor and teacher here to guide him. Instead, Niyol used all his power to return Chance back to life. Besides Ana, he was alone in his struggles. She was the only one he could talk to about what had happened. Because his grandfather insisted his powers remain a secret from everyone, including his parents, Chance was forced to lie and say Niyol had a heart attack while they were on a hike. The lies and secrets were exhausting. He wanted a break from it all.

Chance pushed his legs off the bed and freed himself from the sheets. Standing tall, he stretched his arms above his head, and his spine arched like a feline's. He thumped down to the floor and began his pushups.

A soft knock came from his door. With a pang of sadness, he remembered how often he had answered his grandfather's morning greeting.

He did another five reps and said breathlessly, "Yes?"

"You slept in. Dad's already at the shop and I'm heading in to work. Can I come in real quick?" Aiyana asked.

"Sure."

He rolled to his side and looked up when the door opened. His mother's long dark hair was pulled into a braid. A pair of yellow scrubs hung from her thin frame. She stepped cautiously into the room and her dark eyes swept the shadowy space as though she was searching for something.

"What's up?"

Aiyana's eyes met his and she smiled. "I was wondering what you had planned today. Were you going to look at any of those college brochures downstairs?"

"C'mon, Mom. I'm eighteen. I just graduated high school, I want a break. I'm not ready to hit the books, I'm gonna travel. You know I'm heading to Mexico to look for relatives. Don't you want to learn more about Grandma's side of the family? Once I save enough money, I'm leaving."

Aiyana frowned, walked over to the windows and

opened the shades. Light flooded the messy room, and exposed piles of dirty clothes on the floor.

"Okay, last time I ask. You're really planning on being gone for a few months?"

"Sure, why not? I promise I'll come home if I don't find anyone. But if I do, I want to hang out and learn more about where Grandma came from. Hopefully, she left some stuff around that'll lead me in the right direction. That's why I'm stopping by Grandfather's ranch. You still can't remember anything new? Where Grandma grew up?" Chance jumped to his feet and folded his arms across his chest.

His mother shook her head. "No. I don't really recall her ever saying much about her childhood. I know she helped raise her sister after her mother died and she never really talked about her dad but you already know that."

Aiyana took another lingering look at the whirlwind of clothing strewn across the room, and added, "You know, before you see Ana today you *could* take care of your laundry."

Chance grimaced. "Not a bad idea. But it's just—not fun."

"Well, I won't be with you when you're on the road. You need to know how to wash your own clothes, unless you're planning on looking like a bum."

"I won't get mugged that way."

Chance kissed his mother's cheek. "Don't worry about me, Mom. I can take care of myself."

"I know. It doesn't mean I won't miss you or worry."

Aiyana started for the door and glanced over her shoulder. "Love you."

"Love you too, Mom. See you later."

In a minute, the sound of the front door closing echoed through the house. Alone in his disorganized room, he took his mother's advice and gathered a large pile of clothes, trudging into the hallway. His eyes paused on the door across from him and he thought of his grandfather's tidy room. Everything left in its place as though some day he might return, as if he was just on vacation.

Chance still couldn't understand why his grandfather had kept so much from him. Why hadn't he told him he was a shapeshifter, too? Since Niyol gave his power to save Chance from death, he'd been reliving his grandfather's memories. Those memories had filled in some information but left Chance feeling lost and confused.

That stormy day on the mountaintop he had learned with certainty that there were other shapeshifters in the world. His cousin, Markus had shown up to kill him and absorb Chance's power. But in the end, Chance and Ana were the only ones left standing. At least before his grandfather died, he had ended Markus's life. It was Chance's only consolation as he stared at his grandfather's door. He swallowed the lump in his throat and forced his gaze away.

With his parents gone, Chance used the opportunity to speed downstairs. His feet barely touched the steps as he swung over the banister. Inhuman speed was one of the unique talents inherited from his ancestors, specifically, his grandfather. Chance combed his fingers through his hair, satisfied he hadn't dropped a single piece of clothing. Being alone in the house had its advantages.

After he dumped the armload of dirty jeans and t-shirts into the wash, he ran back to his room and got dressed. All the unanswered questions were pushed aside as he grabbed his keys and walked out the door.

A cool breeze cut through his thin cotton shirt, a sure sign Fall was gaining a finger hold. Chance jumped into his classic truck and with a turn of the wrist, brought it thundering to life. His heart squeezed in his chest as he thought of Ana's green eyes. She was only minutes away now, and he couldn't wait to return to her. Like the tide, he always found his way back. He resolved there would be a day he wouldn't have to leave her side.

Chapter 2

Eager to feel the last rays of summer, Ana went out the back door, breathed in the pine scent and called out to her younger sister, "Eva, I'll be back soon. I'm going for a hike."

A muffled response wafted out the kitchen window. "Kay."

Ana started down a worn path that curled through the evergreens behind their little blue house, and wandered into the private clearing she used for stargazing. Lately she hadn't gone alone; Chance usually joined her. There wasn't anything she enjoyed more than spending her time doing the thing she loved most with the person she loved most.

Ana enjoyed pushing her physical capabilities on a daily basis. After a lifetime of being forced to sit on the sidelines, she was eager to get out and do what she hadn't been able to before Chance healed her heart. Born with birth defects and a heart condition that prevented her from doing any physical activity, her health had deteriorated when she moved with her mother and sister to Clark Bend, Idaho. Now, while jogging, she had the comfort of knowing her heart wouldn't give out. Muscles in her legs that never had the opportunity to develop with exercise were now sore from use, but she didn't care. It felt good—it reminded her she was alive.

That same joyous reminder was also the marker of a painful loss. As she ran through the wilderness, she thought about how Chance had saved her from death using his amazing abilities. Even though she was angry with him at the time for putting his own life on the line to do it, she tried not to dwell on that fact because she knew Chance carried enough guilt. After all, his actions had led to his grandfather's death.

She leapt down an embankment, and jogged across the grassy fields. The wildflowers that had only weeks ago been splashed over the green landscape were disappearing, letting their seeds rest protected in the soil until next year. Squirrels foraged with more urgency, scurrying around the bushes and trees, sensing it was time to prepare for the oncoming change of seasons.

Ana watched a pair of finches dart through the sky and envied their world perspective. Dreams of flying had visited her almost every night over the last month and a half, since Chance had saved her. They were so realistic, in fact, when she woke in the morning she could swear she had actually flown.

A familiar spicy scent caught her attention and she spun around.

"You're getting better at that. How'd you know I was here?" Chance straightened from his crouch, walked up to her and kissed her neck.

Distracted, Ana shook her head and said, "I don't know. I can just always tell when you're near. Did you fly or drive here?"

Ana already knew the answer. Since Niyol died Chance didn't seem to want to shapeshift anymore. He didn't talk to her about it, except to say he 'didn't feel like it'.

"I drove."

She smiled and slipped her fingers into his hand. He turned away from her as he stared at the landscape, frowning. Ana noticed his hair hadn't been brushed, and she reached up to tuck some strays back into the fold.

"You okay? Had another dream?" she asked, concerned.

Chance squeezed her hand and said with a shake of his head, "You can always tell."

He moved ahead and led her away from the rising sun.

"I think it's time to start planning the trip. Maybe the dreams will stop or change once I get moving. Since Grandfather died, the dreams have been relentless. I know I'm missing something, but I just don't know what."

They stopped at a grassy spot beneath a large pine. Ana sat down and pulled him onto the grass beside her. She traced the planes of his hand, and turned it palm up to run her finger along his life lines. She still marveled at the fact he didn't have scars or rough skin, a trait he would possess as long as he shapeshifted. After phasing into another animal, he always returned to his true form. A form without injuries or sickness. If Ana had the choice or ability to lose the long scar that traveled down her sternum from her heart surgery, she wasn't entirely confident she would want to.

She lifted her face and looked into his eyes. "I'm coming with you, you know."

Chance's jaw clenched and he sighed. "Ana, I'm not sure that's such a good idea. What if I run into trouble? I don't want you to get hurt." He paused, leaned over and kissed her tightly pursed lips. After a moment, she gave in and returned the kiss. Then he added, "But I admit, I'd rather not be without you. It's painful to think about being apart."

Ana sighed and said, "I don't think I could bear it, either. Anyway, what if you do run into trouble? I want to help. Plus, not knowing if you were okay or not would just kill me."

"I want you to be with me every minute of every day. I hate leaving you to go home at night. But I also love you too much to put you in danger. I don't know what I'd do if anything happened to you."

Ana's face darkened as she whispered, "I do. And I won't let you risk your life for me again. I'd never forgive you. Once was enough."

She didn't like bringing up the fact Niyol wasn't around any longer to save him if he made a dangerous choice. She suspected this was the reason he was having the dreams. He needed to find his next instructor and mentor. Someone needed to teach him how his powers worked, what the limitations were and more about the world he had been sheltered from. There were gaping holes in his knowledge. It had become obvious just how dangerous his naiveté could be when his mentally unstable shapeshifter cousin had shown up, ready to kill him—and to take his power. Ana forced the image of Markus's twisted sneer from her mind.

Chance grimaced and picked at the pine needles on the ground. Ana let it go. She knew he would get cranky if she pushed it.

He breathed out and said, "Well, I suppose if you do tag along, you can see if Grandfather really did bury something for me on his ranch."

Ana shot him a wicked grin, pushed him into a lying position and pinned his shoulders down. "Oh, I'm coming with you, all right!"

Chance threw his arms up in mock defeat. "Okay, okay! I'd be crazy to say no to you."

He put his arms around her, and in a flash, he was pinning her to the ground, and growling in her ear. Her body quaked. Shivers raked her arms and neck. His face grew serious and he closed his eyes. He appeared to struggle to regain control over himself. When he reopened his eyes, she was waiting.

"With your heart condition gone, it's hard finding a reason to stop..." Reluctantly, he sat up and fixed his gaze on a small beetle trudging across the forest floor.

"It's nice not worrying about my heart stopping just from kissing," Ana said in a whisper and reached out to touch her finger to his lips.

"Yes, it is."

Suddenly, Chance was on his feet. "Up for a walk to the river?" He grabbed her hand and started off into the sunny fields. "Race you!"

Ana freed her hand and sprinted through the long grass. As she ran, insects flew away to safety, making skittering noises. Grass blades bent and broke as her swift moving form blew past.

A blur whizzed past her, and she shouted, "No fair using your powers! Cheater!"

Her toned legs flexed as she pushed her muscles to perform faster. Her eyes squinted against the sun's rays and she leaned into her run. In the distance, the river glinted like an exposed vein on the earth's surface as a sparrow watched the commotion from a nearby log.

Chapter 3

Chance's eyes watered as he stared unblinking at his laptop screen. Research was boring but he preferred it over hiking the trails outside his home. There were too many memories of Niyol here. He had avoided shifting since he'd transformed into the thunderbird for Ana. Using his powers only reminded him of his absent grandfather. Like salt in a wound, it hurt to think about his loss. Instead, he focused his attentions on finding his next teacher.

When Niyol had sacrificed himself, he'd given Chance his power, along with his memories. He'd discovered this immediately following his grandfather's death, when visions of Niyol's last minutes were revealed to him. Like watching a movie from the bottom of a glass, fuzzy around the edges with a clear center point, a handful of nagging questions had been answered. But, they were only replaced with new ones.

Afterward, Chance had pieced together information about his grandfather's past. After fleeing from his shapeshifting brother who'd killed their father, Niyol had traveled to Mexico. There he had met an experienced shapeshifter who gained his trust and became his teacher. In a vision, his name, Balam, was revealed to Chance.

Chance's grandmother was from Mexico as well, which was the perfect cover story for his parents, who understood his supposed need to go search for long lost family members. Only, it wasn't family he was really in search of.

Chance typed in 'Balam'. He discovered an online encyclopedia page with the heading, *A number of Pre-Columbian Mayan rulers bore the name B'alam*.

Chance skimmed through at least a dozen names. The word 'jaguar' was in all the translated meanings. *So Balam must mean jaguar!*

He clicked onto another page about Mesoamerican cultures linked with jaguars and his eyebrows rose. "Jackpot," he murmured.

OLMECS, JAGUARS, AND THE 'WERE-JAGUAR'

In surviving Olmec archaeological records, jaguars are never pictured naturally, but with a combination of feline and human characteristics. These 'were-jaguars' have been found as carved jade figurines or as carvings and paintings on altars.

The jaguar was believed to have the ability to pass from this earth and into the spirit realm. Shamans used them as spiritual companions to guide them to battle against evil souls.

JAGUARS AND THE MAYA

The Maya, whose territory spanned along the Yucatán peninsula and down the coast to Guatemala, were a literate society who left much documentation of their lives. The Maya believed the jaguar was able to cross between worlds. They associated the underworld or spirit world with night, which is when jaguars patrol the jungle. Jaguar pelts were worn only by the ruling class, and 'jaguar' became a part of their rulers' names.

After reading the page, Chance sat back in his seat and scratched his head. Everything seemed to fit: his name, his location and fact he was a shapeshifter. That could mean Balam was a descendent of the Olmec or Maya. Chance considered the possibility that there could be different families of shapeshifters across the world. If the thunderbird form was used by various shapeshifters in Native American tribes, it would make sense that different cultures of shapeshifters could have created their own important animal representations as well.

Although this research was interesting, what Chance really needed to figure out was how to find Balam. He hoped the answer lay in the buried box at his grandfather's ranch in Montana. When he'd dug Niyol's final resting place on their secluded property, he'd had a vision. He saw Niyol dig a hole and bury an intricately carved box. Chance knew the location well because it was their secret place. Niyol would take him there for evening bonfires whenever he visited the ranch. At the time it didn't mean anything to him but now Chance wondered if his grandfather wanted him to find the secret box that was entombed within the rocky soil in the clearing south of the homestead.

"Well, I guess it's time to start planning," he mumbled to himself. He grabbed a piece of lined paper from the top drawer of his desk. Numbers were scrawled across it in jumbled clusters. For the past two and a half years, he had worked diligently at a local auto body shop. He'd bought some parts for his own pet project, an old Chevy truck, but he also had a nice nest egg saved up. If his calculations were correct, it would easily cover the cost of gas and food for a couple months. But if Ana came along as she'd threatened to, then they needed to find some more resources.

His black cell phone lit up and started vibrating on the edge of his bed. Without hesitation, he reached over and answered. "Hey."

"How's the planning coming?" Ana asked.

"Okay. With my savings I think we can make a couple months on the road. But it'll be tight. Mom did say a while back she was going to give me some money from Grandfather's estate to help out with the trip, though."

"Well, thanks to Mom, I've had a couple of photography jobs. She can't help but brag about me to all the locals who come through the bank so I have a little in savings. There's also the check that Aunt Tera and Uncle Jace gave me at graduation. I haven't used any of it except for what I used on Eva's birthday present," Ana said.

"Good. We should be okay with money then. I just don't know how long of a trip this'll be. Grandfather gave me two years of training. I doubt that if I find Balam he'll be all, yeah here's the handbook, take care! Mom seems okay with me going away for a couple months while I look for Grandma's side of the family. I don't know how long I can stretch it out for."

Ana said in hushed tones, "I know what you mean. I'm not sure how to tell Mom I'm planning to go with you. Eva will be bummed."

"If you're coming along, you need to understand this won't be like a vacation. For all I know, we'll be searching in the jungle. We won't find Balam poolside at the Hyatt. We need to travel light. Get a backpack, the kind you can fit a lot of stuff into. Are you game?"

He could hear Ana's smile through the phone as she said, "Of course. I think it'll be exciting."

"It's time. I can't wait any longer. I'm going to call George up at Grandfather's ranch and let him know I'll be coming through next week...and that I'll have someone with me."

"So do you know where we're going yet? Any road signs in your dreams?"

"I wish. Not so easy. I know we need to head to the Yucatán Peninsula. But once we get there I just don't know. I hope Grandfather left me some answers buried in that box because otherwise we may wind up lost and I'll never find Balam. He's probably dead, anyway. Why can't any of this be easy?!" Chance's fingers curled tightly around the phone and the plastic creaked under the pressure, reminding him to loosen his grip.

"Hey, don't think so negatively. Let's just wait and see. Have faith." Ana's gentle voice calmed him. She was the only one who could do that. Chance's thoughts settled on Ana's words. Have faith. He supposed he would have to, because the sinking feeling in his gut made the hairs at the back of his neck raise. His instincts were clear. He was in danger.

Chapter 4

Ana stretched her feet onto the dashboard and let the sun warm her toes. She closed her eyes and took a deep breath. The passing fields and forests went unseen while the rumble from the van's engine served as white noise as she fell asleep.

After driving the first couple of hours, she had switched over to the passenger seat. Chance seemed more than happy to drive, even though it wasn't his precious truck. Days ago, they had decided to use Ana's van rather than Chance's Chevy truck. Although Ana's VW camper was brightly colored and loud as a lawn mower, it had the living space they needed for their trip. Equipped with a simple kitchen and table, it was also perfect for camping out, if necessary.

Ana was exhausted. Saying goodbye to her mother and sister had been emotionally draining. Eva didn't want to see her go, and cried as they rolled off the driveway. Her mom had stayed in the house. She was too angry at Ana for ignoring her wishes. Melissa didn't want her daughter to leave. Although months had passed since the doctors gave Ana a clean bill of health, Melissa hadn't trusted it, even though the evidence was clear. Ana was upset that her mother couldn't understand how important it was to her to go and explore the world now that her heart was healed. She decided she would call her tomorrow and try to smooth things over. Ana steadied her breathing and closed her eyes.

A catnap was just what Ana needed to relax and unwind. She was free. Free from the constraints of her health condition. Free from school and responsibility. She was finally free to do what she wished. The whir of the pavement below them served as a lullaby. While her mind let go and began to soar in her dreamland, a soft grin touched her lips.

Pine trees dotted the grass-carpeted valleys below as she glided in the sky. A warm breeze combed through her feathers, caressing the contours of her lean, light form. She was where she belonged. It felt good being so close to the stars and heavens. Soon, the soft, familiar feeling of flying began to fade.

For only a moment, she was unsure of where she was. Then, she recognized her nighttime observatory, her special place to gaze at the evening stars and the spot where Chance had revealed his most impressive form yet, the thunderbird.

She was as at home here as she was in her room, or possibly even more comfortable. Pines clustered together and swayed like a mother soothing a child. The open expanse presented countless glimmering stars. Her thoughts clouded and the dark angular shapes around her fell away. Now only a foggy gloom surrounded her and she grew anxious.

Where'd the stars go?

As confusion overtook her, a melodic sound calmed her nerves. Birdsong unlike anything she had ever heard filled the air. The gloom lifted and she was standing on a rocky shore of a lake with her toes in glacial water. A chill ran up her spine as a breeze blew past her.

I am here for you, Ana.

***

"My love. Time to wake up."

Ana jolted awake and she momentarily had the sense she was falling. Her hands flew out and gripped the closest things to her: Chance and the dashboard. Her surroundings were filtered through a sleepy fog. The sun was low in the sky, getting closer to the mountains in the west. Chance had her door open and was leaning inside with his hand on her shoulder. He snickered at her reaction and gave her a kiss on the lips.

"We're here."

"What? How long was I out for?" Ana stretched her arms and yawned. A fetid smell blew in from the open door and she quickly raised her hand to her nose, crinkling her face. "That smells *fresh*."

"Get used to it. This is a cattle ranch. Soon, you won't even smell it."

"Do you smell it?" she asked.

"Oh, yeah. No getting by my animal senses."

He held his hand out to her and she slipped out of the van. A soft breeze blew across the prairie. It picked up some loose strands of Ana's hair and moved them across her face, tickling her nose. After getting past the pungent whiff of cattle, she took in the ranch.

There was a large log cabin to their right and a thin

man was walking down the front steps to greet them. He had on a wide brimmed cowboy hat that dwarfed his small head and covered most of his gray hair. His worn leather boots scuffed the dirt as he walked.

"Chance, it's been too long." He held his calloused hand out to Chance, who gave it a firm shake.

"Hey, George. Nice seeing you. I see you've kept the place up. Looks good." Chance turned to survey the property. Ana thought it was to cover up his quivering cheek.

George's face grew serious and he toed the dirt. "Well, thanks. I do my best without Boss around. He knew this land better than any 'un. It's too bad he's gone."

They stood in silence for a minute. Ana watched the men out of the corner of her eye as they stood like statues, not wanting to crack. Chance's soft hand found hers and she gave it a reassuring squeeze.

"So, George. I'd like to introduce you to my girlfriend, Ana."

"Well, hello. I've heard about you." He punched Chance's shoulder playfully and winked at Ana. "Well, why don't ya' come on in, I've got some beef stew on the stove, and your bedrooms are all ready."

"Mmm, sounds good. I *am* pretty hungry," Ana said.

"Well, you may have a different opinion after a couple nights of it." George laughed. "It's my best recipe, but only one of a handful."

"No need to apologize. I'm no critic." She eagerly entered the house and took a deep breath, taking in the delicious smell of beef stew, which she considered a vast improvement to the aroma outside. George disappeared through a doorway into what Ana figured was the kitchen.

The cabin was homey and rustic, immediately putting her at ease. She recognized a familiar shape woven onto a tapestry that hung from the wall. The thunderbird. Ana reached out and touched it gently, the scratchy wool brushing her fingertips. Beside her, Chance tensed up, then retreated to the corner of the living room and gazed out a large, paned window.

"What is it, Chance?" Ana wandered over, slipped her arms around him, and nuzzled her head against his back.

"Smells like him here."

Ana breathed in deeply, recognizing Niyol's scent, a musky fragrance mixed with something else—cinnamon. She closed her eyes and was comforted. "Everything will turn out fine, I just know it."

***

With Ana's arms wrapped around him, Chance tried desperately to think that but instead, the same worrisome fear that had plagued him earlier crept into his chest and he scanned the horizon from the window. Finches perched in nearby branches, flit to the ground in search of food. A singular fence lizard crept along the wooden sill and stopped in a sunny patch to warm itself but kept its eyes on Chance's silhouette behind the glass…

Chapter 5

The sun had barely kissed the plains on the horizon when soft taps at Ana's door woke her. Not ready to meet the day yet, she squeezed her eyes tight and hoped the sound was only a dream. When the rapping at her door came again, she groaned and it swung open to reveal Chance, dressed and ready to go.

"You're not up yet?"

Ana yanked the sheets over her, immediately thinking about her bed head and disheveled appearance. "Give me a minute, I'm not presentable."

A loud snort sounded and then footsteps. He gently coaxed the sheets back down and looked at her. Chance smoothed her stray hairs, cupped her face in his hands and gazed into her eyes.

"Why are you so shy around me? Nothing can hide your true beauty." He leaned forward and touched his lips to hers. After a minute, he slowly pulled away from her, letting his fingers trace her jaw and neck.

Ana frowned, clearing her throat. "Nice try at distracting me. I'd like to believe you, but I know what I look like and it isn't pretty. You ready to head out already? Do I have time for a shower?"

Chance's face fell. It was clear he was thinking about the time he'd lose waiting for her to get ready. She reconsidered and said, "Oh, never mind. I probably don't need one. I won't even be able to smell myself with all of those cow patties out there. I'll just get on some jeans and run a brush through my hair. But can we get something to eat before we take off? I'm starved."

Chance grimaced once more but when Ana slipped out of bed wearing an oversized t-shirt and nothing else, he seemed to forget about his irritation. The bottom of the shirt brushed her legs mid-thigh and his eyes lingered on her bare skin. Ana folded her arms and waited for him to look up.

"Sorry." With visible effort, he forced his eyes away and studied the bookcase beside the bed instead. Ana slipped on a pair of jeans and momentarily questioned leaving the private room for a bright sunny pasture filled with manure. After pulling on a gray sweatshirt, she grabbed her brush and gave her hair a quick onceover.

"Okay, I'm presentable for livestock now."

Chance rushed to hold the door open for her. As they quietly wandered through the hallway, noises from the kitchen met their ears.

"Guess we aren't the only ones up," Chance said.

The smell of bacon and eggs filled the house and Ana couldn't ignore the thoughtful gesture from their host or her bellowing stomach. She glanced at Chance, who seemed almost disappointed he had to stop to eat. He wasn't one for patience.

"Hey there, kids. I heard you so I thought I'd make a proper breakfast." George winked at Ana and added, "Another recipe I do well. That only leaves griddle cakes, sausages and hash browns. The only things I know how to cook. I've always said, if you're gonna do something, do it well."

As Ana sat down, George put a plate of food in front of her. It smelled delicious. The eggs were still steaming from the griddle and a large pile of hash browns were flecked with crunchy bits of bacon.

"Looks good. Thanks, George," Ana said.

"Breakfast of champions. Protein, best thing for ya'."

"Oh, George," said Chance, eyeing the steaming food, "I left that paperwork on the coffee table in the living room. Mom wanted me to tell you how much we appreciate you continuing to manage the ranch. There's no one we'd rather take care of the business." George nodded, leaned against the counter and struck his feet out in front of him.

Chance joined Ana at the table and wolfed down a plate heaped with eggs and hash browns. She watched as his food disappeared, then ate as much as she could before Chance's impatient stare made her set her fork down.

"How 'bout we get going?" Chance grabbed both their plates, rinsed them in the sink and set them on the drying rack. "George, we're going to take a look around the property. Would you mind if I took Tallulah to drive 'round the outskirts?"

George nodded in response. "She likes a gentle hand."

"I remember. Grandpa taught me how to drive her." Chance stared out the kitchen window, leaned against the counter and added, "Don't worry about entertaining us today. I know you have work to get back to."

George gave Ana a wink before turning out the back

door.

Chance palmed the keys and tugged on her hand, practically dragging her outside. The fragrant smell of cattle was hard to avoid but it didn't bother her as much as it had the day before.

"So, who's Tallulah?"

With a smug grin, Chance led her toward a large barn. The red stain had worn through to reveal gray wood grain beneath. Although weathered, the structure still appeared sturdy. She didn't realize just how big it was until she stood before it.

Chance opened up the large doors and walked inside with Ana close behind. In the dim, dusty light, a pair of pale eyes stared back at her. If a truck could have a face, Tallulah had heaps of character. She was painted dull blue but patches of rust stretched down her length. The bumper and grill almost looked like they were smiling at her.

"Meet Tallulah." Chance patted the hood and then disappeared into a stall. Moments later, he reappeared holding a shovel. He dropped it into the back of the truck and slipped behind the wheel.

The Ford 150 rumbled to life and he edged it out of the barn. Ana jumped inside and shut the door with a loud metallic bang. They drove past the house and continued along the dirt road in silence. Ana watched the prairie out her window. The flat landscape remained unchanged for another ten minutes until he slowed and turned off onto a path in the scrub that sported a faint set of tire tracks.

The neglected path sloped down and the surroundings became increasingly wooded. Chance drummed his fingers on the steering wheel in rhythm to the squeaks and thumps of the truck as they sped over the uneven ground. Every spring in the bucket seat poked into her and she braced her feet to absorb some of the impact.

Ana thought about her mother and the muscles in her throat tightened as her sadness welled up again. Melissa wouldn't even give her a hug goodbye. She didn't require her mother's approval, but it hurt just the same.

"I should really give Mom a call when we get back to the house. I hope she's not still mad at me..." Ana said and glanced over at Chance, who was silent and absorbed in his own thoughts. It was clear driving wasn't what was on his mind...

***

Chance's eyes blurred as he stared off in the distance, thinking about his grandfather. Those last moments had been haunting him since that fateful day. His surprise and joy when he discovered Niyol was a shifter as well had evaporated when Ana's life line turned into a wispy thread. His thoughts went to the vision of his grandfather in wolverine form battering the bobcat, his ruby red maw and claws wet with Markus's blood. Forced to shift and heal, their adversary had tried to scurry free as a prairie dog, but instead, he was pressed into the ground by Niyol's forceful attack. The rattle of the old Ford truck was reminiscent of Ana's sputtering heart and he felt his throat close up. Swallowing hard, he let out a shuddering breath. His grandfather's voice echoed in his head. *No, Chance, wait*, were the last words he'd spoken.

"Hello? You listening?" Ana said, clearly agitated.

"Oh, sorry. Was thinking about Grandfather." Chance glanced over, surprised. He'd almost forgotten he wasn't alone.

She winced after a particularly big pothole and asked, "How much farther?"

"Sorry, we're getting close," he said as he let up on the accelerator and reached over to hold her hand.

The truck climbed the top of a bluff and they caught one last view of the landscape before they descended a slope into a small field. A wall of evergreens greeted them as the ground leveled off. Chance turned parallel to the trees and parked before an outcropping of rocks that rose from the earth like ancient fists.

Before Ana could reach for the door handle, a tinny creak sounded and suddenly her door flung open. Chance held his hand out and helped her from the rigid seat.

As he went around the back of the truck, Ana wandered around the large boulders. He watched her disappear from view, set his hands on the tailgate and stared down at the yellow blades of grass at his feet as they waved in the breeze. As he thought about his grandfather, he reached over, and seized the shovel from the flatbed.

He started off in search of Ana. Her familiar scent curled through the air and he followed her tempting perfume up a hill away from the trail. Past a rocky slope, he caught sight of her stretched out on a large log hewn in half, soaking up the sun's rays. A blackened pit encrusted with stones lay feet away from her resting place. So many nights were spent with his grandfather in that very spot, at the mouth of a bonfire.

It had been years since they had visited this place together. When Niyol had come to live with them, he'd left everything else behind. It had been too painful for him to continue to live in the same place he'd lived with Chance's grandmother after she died. Once Chance met Ana, he understood the pain of living life without another. And that understanding had driven him to save her rather than live in a world without her.

He rubbed his temple with his thumb and brushed his hair back as he moved silently to her side and watched her chestnut locks rustle in the breeze. It was then he realized something. "Hey, how'd you know where to go?"

Ana's eyes flipped open in surprise. "Oh, you got me that time. What do you mean?"

"This is where grandfather buried the box. This is our spot."

"Oh, I don't know, I just felt like exploring. I saw this sunny spot and thought I'd wait for you." She sat up and shielded her sparkling green eyes from the sun.

He kissed her forehead and let his fingers trail along the contours of her face before walking a few feet away, shovel in hand. Chance found the spot in his grandfather's memories and after one last glance at Ana, he started digging. The soil was dry and mostly made up of gravel, but that didn't faze him. He continued at a back-breaking pace, sending out tiny sparks as metal impacted stone. Finally, a loud, hollow thump rang out.

Chance's brows furrowed and he flung the shovel aside. He was on his hands and knees in no time, clawing at the dirt.

"Hey, take it easy, you'll hurt yourself. Slow down."

Ana's words of concern had no effect on him. He continued until, with a grunt, he pulled a carved wooden box from the earth. It was no larger than a loaf of bread and appeared to have been resting in its grave for quite some time. Dust and gravel clung to it like barnacles on a pier.

Chance joined Ana on the log. Silent and still, he stared at the box until Ana cleared her throat and said, "Are you ready?"

His hands shook as he brushed free the debris from around the edges. He grasped the lid and pulled. Chance wanted to savor the moment. He assumed his grandfather had buried this box for him. There could be anything in it. However, what he wanted or needed most were answers. The death of his mentor and teacher had been devastating, and had only raised more questions. Since the moment he'd awakened to discover Niyol had died saving his life, he'd felt alone and a little afraid. Any connection to who and what he was had been severed.

Chance glanced over his shoulder. His eyes combed the landscape, looking for anything out of place. Ana watched him and he gave her a reassuring smile.

The lid of the box was crusted shut. Even though he had the strength to force it open, he did not want to damage it. After some gentle coaxing, its mouth opened and the contents breathed fresh air for the first time in who knew how long.

His heart pounded in excitement as he flipped the lid open and exposed some folded paper. Chance set the wooden box on his lap and picked it out. He flattened it on his lap, and recognized his grandfather's familiar scratchy writing. He cleared his throat and read aloud,

Dear Chance,

If you are reading this letter, I have passed from this earth and you are a shapeshifter like our ancestors before us.

Watching you grow from a child has been an honor. I have seen your enthusiasm for the natural world. Your understanding of animals is clear. I am not surprised you have our ancestral gifts.

I hope I was able to teach you before my passing. If not, I am sorry. You must have questions. I will leave them to someone who knows more than I do. But I will try to explain my choices to you.

My father was a shapeshifter and a shaman, following in the family line. My two brothers and I wished very much to be like him. One by one, my older brothers displayed shifting abilities. It is beyond my understanding but in rare circumstances when the power is awakened, it creates a hunger—a hunger for more power. Madness poisons the heart, and any memory of love dies. My eldest brother's soul was poisoned. He hungered for more power so he took it from my brother and our father. It was my good fortune that saved me from his hunger, for he knew nothing of my own gifts, which had only just kindled.

I ran and tried hiding from him and any others who would seek my powers. My feet took me south to Mexico, where I met my teacher. It was there I met your grandmother, Balam's daughter. When I saw Itzel, my heart spoke to me. She was my new world. For a time I was trained by Balam, a wise instructor. I soon realized the power that was growing within me was also a beacon to other shifters.

My devotion for your grandmother was too great. I did not wish to attract the attention from the soulless. All I wanted was to grow old with my love. Balam reluctantly let us go, and gave us a large dowry so that we could purchase the cattle ranch and live a quiet life. I promised him that if any of my descendents had the gift, I would train them for a time and let them make the choice to continue their education, an education taught by him.

Chance, I am sorry I am not here to help guide you through your choices. It is a big decision and one that will affect your life forever. It should not be taken lightly. I know the choice you make will be the right one for you.

I believe in you and in who you are. I know your heart. It is kind and true.

If you choose to seek your great-grandfather, you must go to the ruins of Ek' Balam in Mexico. You will not find him. He will find you. Trust is hard to earn from other shifters so one must be careful.

I will be with you always,

Niyol

The letter crinkled in the wind. Chance gripped it

tightly in his hands as he stared at his grandfather's scrawled signature. He glanced up at Ana. Strands of long brown hair scattered across her face in the breeze and she mouthed, "Wow."

"My great-grandfather? Balam's my great-grandfather? I can't believe it." He rubbed his temple. "I guess this whole time I've been telling the truth to Mom. I really am going to Mexico to look for family. Man, I'm not sure I can take any more surprises from Grandfather."

Ana rested her hand on his leg and offered him a sympathetic look. She pointed at the box and said gently, "Chance, look, there's more."

He muttered under his breath, "What now?"

While he folded the letter, he dropped his gaze and saw something gleam in the light. He pocketed the note, dipped his fingers inside the box and pulled out a dark green pendant. A face stared back at him. The jade jaguar grimaced menacingly as it swung from a worn leather cord.

"Balam," he said in a whisper.

"Huh?"

"Balam means jaguar. I wonder..." He hung the necklace around his neck. The Navajo bear heartline pendant tapped against its new companion.

"Oooo, don't forget these." Ana withdrew some gold coins from the box and slipped them into Chance's hands.

They were the largest coins he had ever seen and they certainly weren't machine punched or Mayan. The design pressed into their rippled surface seemed more European, with the clear outline of a king and queen.

"I guess I won't have to worry about money anymore. Wow. Grandfather was trying to look out for me even after..."

Chance leaned forward, and Ana embraced him, guiding his head to her chest. The beating of her heart echoed in his ear and a tear dropped down his nose. He squeezed his eyes shut as his sorrow overtook him.

I wish you were here with me, Grandfather.

After a few minutes he pulled away and placed everything back into the box. As Ana stood up and retrieved the shovel from the dirt, Chance palmed a rock he found near his feet. With a yell, he threw it out across the grass, frightening some nearby ground squirrels into their holes—all but one, who stood on its back legs and barked a warning.

Chapter 6

"What are you more upset about—the fact I didn't listen to you, or that you think something will happen to me?"

Ana held her phone to her ear and stared at the wall. Chance was in the shower, so she'd figured now was a good time to check in with her mom.

After a minute, Melissa's hushed voice answered, "Both. I just don't know what to say to you right now."

Tears welled in Ana's eyes and her lip trembled. "Mom, please. You always said you wanted me to have a normal life like any other healthy kid. Well, now that dream's come true and I want to live my life without regret. I'll be safe. And I'm with Chance. He'd never let anything happen to me."

In the past, Melissa had never been able to withstand Ana tugging on her heartstrings. Ana wanted things resolved between them and hoped she would be forgiven. How could she truly enjoy herself on the trip if she knew the relationship with her mom had paid the price? She waited for her mother's response anxiously.

Melissa sighed and said, "If you're heading through Denver why don't you give Dr. Wilson a call? Maybe he can fit you in. Bet he'd like to see you again and take a listen to that miracle heart of yours."

Relief rushed through her. She knew things would take time to be set right again, but this was a step in the right direction.

"Thanks, Mom. I'll see if he can fit me in. But we'll probably only stop in Denver for a day or two before taking off to Mexico."

"You're still planning on driving there? I don't like the sound of that, baby." Melissa's worry was evident through the phone.

"We'll be safe. No one will mess with me while I'm with Chance."

"You keep saying that, but I'm not so sure. I didn't just watch you overcome your health issues to lose you to a Mexican gang. I was just watching the news and it's getting dangerous going off the beaten path down there. Marcy at the bank was just talking to me about that."

Ana treaded lightly, knowing she could land herself in more trouble with her mother if she didn't respond seriously.

"But we aren't going to those areas. We're looking for Chance's family in the Yucatan," she said. "It's safe there."

"I don't know Ana. I'll pay for you to fly home when you get to Denver. Please, baby?"

"I want to see the ocean, Mom. I don't have any stamps in my passport. I want to see the world. I love you, but you have to let me go. I promise I'll be safe. Listen, we'll be leaving in the morning to head for Colorado. I can give you a call when we get there."

Melissa groaned and said, "I'd appreciate that. But will you think seriously about coming home? Or maybe pick up some mace or something. I'll look up Dr. Wilson's number and send it to you. Oh, and say, when you head through Denver, will you give Beth a call? She was over the moon when she heard the news about your heart. Bet she'd really like to see you."

Ana had plenty of happy memories of her mom's best friend, Beth. She'd been her babysitter growing up and was practically a part of the family.

"Sure, I'll call her." Ana heard some whimpering in the background and asked, "What's that?"

"Oh, well, how 'bout I put your sister on? She'll tell you."

Muffled giggles and a thump made her hold the phone away from her ear. Then her sister's sweet voice burst from the receiver. "Ana? You there?"

"Hey, sweetie. How're you doing? Miss me?"

"Um, yeah. Guess what?" The pause was only momentary before Eva launched ahead and said, "Mom got me a puppy!"

Ana was surprised. Her mom had never let them have any animals. She'd said it was too much work and she didn't want any fur around the house.

"Really?" she asked incredulously.

"Lily is *so* super cute. And super tiny. And did I say cute?"

"Mom let you get a *dog*? I've only been gone a day!"

"Yeah, well, she knew how lonely I was without you. And she said it would help teach me how to take care of someone else. She says I'm a big sister now."

Yipping sounds in the background met Ana's ears and the jealousy she'd felt a moment earlier began to loosen its grip on her. How could she be upset because her sister was lonely? She was glad Eva had something to focus on and she knew just how much she had wanted a pet.

"What kind of dog is it?"

"We went down to the shelter and I picked out a yellow lab mix. I really liked this teacup poodle but Mom said that Lily wouldn't get eaten by the coyotes, so I chose her."

Ana chuckled. "So who's cleaning up after her?"

"Ew, that's the nasty part. Mom said she wouldn't get a dog if I didn't promise to do the cleanup."

"Well, have fun with that. I've got to get going, sweetie. Tell Mom I love her," Ana said. She slipped her toes out in front of her and stretched with the phone in her hand.

"'Kay and say hi to Chance for me. Love you."

Before Ana could reciprocate, there was a click on the other end of the line. *I guess puppies outrank sisters.* At least she didn't need to worry about her sister feeling alone back home.

Arms wrapped around her as she was dipped sideways off the chair and Chance's face lowered over hers. She let out a squawk and heard her blood pounding in her ears. He coaxed her chin back and dropped a line of kisses down her neck. Goose bumps rose on her arms and chills rocked her body. While he stared into her eyes, he lifted her upright and gave her shoulders a squeeze.

Ana blew her breath out slowly, trying to calm her nerves. "Got me that time. Didn't know you were there."

Chance grinned a little too brightly and said, "You're getting hard to surprise."

He scratched his wet hair and sent a shower of water droplets onto her.

"Nice. I'm going to get you back, you know. You won't know it's coming either. You'll be doing your thing, and then, *bam!*"

Chance's brow lifted and an amused smirk slid across his face. He pinched his lips shut and turned away from her for a moment. Talking to the wall, he said, "How about now? I'm not expecting it."

Ana jumped up and swatted his shoulder. In one deft motion, he reached behind him and spun her around his body until she faced him. She was surprised to see he was serious. "So, everything okay back home? You're sad."

She was only momentarily surprised at his observation. He was so attuned to her moods.

"Well, I think everything's going to be okay. Mom wants me to call my old cardiologist when we get to Denver. I told her I would, but I don't see the point. I just wanted to make her happy." Ana shrugged and said, "Also, Mom just got Eva a puppy. She never let us have one before."

"What, you think she's trying to make you feel bad or something?"

"No, that's not her style. It's nothing. I think she's just trying to make Eva happy. Oh, and Mom went on and on about how unsafe it is to drive through Mexico. But I don't think there's anything to worry about. I've got you with me."

Chance remained quiet for a moment. She had expected him to side with her but now she wasn't so sure.

"Your mom might have a point."

Ana withdrew and sat down on her chair again. She brushed her hair in silence while trying to decide how she felt about Chance's new position. She shook her head and reminded herself it was because he loved her.

His hand touched her shoulder and she set her brush down. His soft words breezed past her ear. "I'm sorry, Ana. Never mind. How 'bout we talk about it when we get to Denver? You know how I feel about you. Just want to keep you safe."

She reached up to touch his hand and said, "I know."

"You okay? About your mom and all?"

Ana nodded. "Yeah, I think so. I'm relieved she isn't as upset with me now. Just sucks it had to be like that to begin with anyway."

A loud creak came from the kitchen, followed by some footsteps. George came around the corner. He pulled his hat off and smiled.

"Gosh, it's nice having company round. Y'all interested in beef stew tonight?"

Chapter 7

The broad night sky stretched over their heads as they lay in the flatbed. Parked just outside the barn, a brisk seasonal wind brushed past them, chafing their still bodies. Chance grasped Ana's fingers in his hand and felt her healthy rhythmic pulse just below the surface.

He knew how important stargazing was to her and after the call to her family, he figured an evening under the stars was in order. Through the dark, he could see a soft smile play at her lips.

After more thought, Chance was beginning to think Melissa was right. Ana may not be suffering from a heart condition any longer but that didn't mean her life wasn't just as fragile as it always had been. She didn't have the power to heal herself if she got hurt, unlike Chance. He knew he had an edge on anyone who wanted to harm her. Well, maybe not *anyone*. They hadn't discussed the fact that there were other shifters around. But soon enough he hoped to be training again, building strength and gaining new abilities.

His painful memories of his grandfather had kept him from shifting, but he decided it was time to get back to work. He glanced at Ana and after laying a quick kiss on her cheek, hopped up and flipped over the edge of the truck.

"Chance?"

"It's been too long since I've shifted," he called out.

He threw his shirt into the back of the Ford and heard Ana squawk in surprise. She quickly responded and worry was evident in her tone. "Just don't shift into something George will want to shoot."

Chance chuckled while he unzipped his jeans and kicked his shoes off. "No worries. I think I'll stick with an owl. No peeking." He put his clothing into a lumpy pile near the Ford's tire and heard Ana giggle nervously.

Butterflies fluttered in his stomach as he sat down on the cold, prickly earth and focused on an old, familiar form. He realized the last time he took the shape of the nighttime guardian was before Niyol had died. His mind relaxed and he envisioned the wide yellow eyes, nutmeg feathers and sharp talons. It took a moment for the blue mapping, a glowing crosshatch of lines, to ignite around the regal silhouette. At age sixteen, his shapeshifting powers had manifested while he watched squirrels scavenge around the forest behind his home. Each species had a unique pattern that he needed to familiarize himself with to be able to shapeshift into its animal form. As he focused on the owls sapphire mapping, he realized that its dim glow wasn't as bright as it once was. Wary, Chance tried to harness the static energy around him and pull it inward. It reacted as if he was paddling through a river of peanut butter.

"Chance? Anything wrong?"

"No," he answered quickly.

He clenched his fists and the veins in his neck throbbed. The strain gave him a headache, which made it even harder to focus. Determined, he made one last push and felt the extra boost he needed to make the final transition.

Feathers rippled down his chestnut skin as his body tingled and shrank, changing in shape. His vision was suddenly sharp in the darkness. Pivoting his head around, he spied a mouse scurrying along the edge of the barn. He stretched his beak open and snapped it shut. He was awkward at best as a bird—he preferred being a mammal to anything else—but Ana's warning was realistic. A bullet between the eyes as a cougar, bear or fox was extremely probable on a cattle ranch.

He stretched his wings and allowed the breeze to comb over his feathers. With very little effort, he lifted off the ground. In the first moments of flight, his heart squeezed and he teetered while getting used to flying again. After a few minutes, he tilted his wings and let the air currents carry him upward. Although he was never entirely relaxed soaring above the ground, he had to admit it was amazing, an entirely different way of seeing the world.

His keen eyes focused on Ana lying below. She was winding her long dark hair around her finger. Her expression was almost melancholy as she tracked his flight through the sky.

Even though he would rather be lying beside Ana, he couldn't bring himself to come down yet. He didn't want to think about how hard it had been to phase into the owl. It shouldn't have been that challenging. Shifting into a smaller animal was easy, or it used to be. How long had it been since he last shifted? He thought back to when he took the thunderbird form for Ana after Niyol's death. It had been particularly challenging to do. Since then he'd avoided shifting and had only tried a couple times in the last two months. Each instance had been hard, and he was unsure what that meant.

The cool breeze pushed him downwind and he flapped hard to fly back over the truck. His wings were growing tired, but he wanted time to think in private. Voicing his concerns to Ana would be admitting there was a problem.

Was he having issues because he missed his grandfather so much? Was it because he blamed himself for Niyol's death? If he hadn't saved Ana, his grandfather would be alive, but he himself would have lost his reason for living. *It's still your fault.*

A thought teased at the corners of his mind. *What if I'm losing my powers*? That singular and terrible fear kept him flying for another twenty minutes, trying to hold onto every moment. He clung to the hope that Balam would know how to help him. Because if he couldn't, he wasn't sure what would happen to his powers.

Chapter 8

Ana gripped the steering wheel and craned her head as she read the passing road signs.

"We're getting close."

Chance quietly watched the passing scenery out the window. Rolling prairie had accompanied them along their entire trip and now warehouses and industrial buildings cluttered his view. He was pleased to see the Rocky Mountains weren't hidden behind the surrounding cityscape. They rose tall and proud, as if they were ancient sentinels protecting the inhabitants below.

Ana kept her eyes on the road and said, "We should get a hotel. But I don't think we should stay downtown— too noisy."

Chance glanced over at her and noticed a rosy blush touch her cheeks. He entwined his fingers through hers and kissed each fingertip. "Money is no object. Where do you want to stay?"

"All right, Mr. Moneybags. There *is* a place I've always wanted to stay. It's in the foothills, a bed and breakfast. I think you'll like it there. It's close to Red Rocks."

"Red Rocks? Sounds familiar."

Ana pointed toward a series of peaks in the distance.

"Right there in the front range of the Rockies. Above the city of Morrison, there's an amphitheater built into the red rocks. Wait till you see it. Mom took me to a concert there once. It was amazing. The acoustics are fantastic, and the view is out of bounds." Ana slipped some loose hairs behind her ear and craned over her shoulder to change lanes.

"Sweet. Sounds nice." He paused. "Hey, doesn't Denver have a pretty decent zoo? It could be a good opportunity to map some new animals. What kind of beast should I add to my collection?"

Ana's eyes darkened and she avoided looking over at him.

"What's wrong?" He asked, sensing her mood shift.

"Let's not talk about beasts. Reminds me of Markus. Something I'd rather forget."

It had only been a couple months since she'd been abducted and dragged up to a mountaintop to die by his cousin. Her heart had stopped, but not for long. Chance wouldn't let her go without a fight.

"I'm sorry, I—"

"S'okay. But, no more talk of beasts."

He nodded in agreement and remained quiet. He instantly regretted his innocent comment.

***

They headed west toward the mountains and the setting sun. White clouds glowed against the orange sorbet twilight. Commuter traffic engulfed them and they trudged at a slow pace until they reached the foothills. The radio's music filled the silence.

Taillights on the road ahead of her glared like angry red eyes. She tried to keep the painful memories at bay but they haunted her.

A sour smell made her flinch and she realized it was only a memory, the memory of the beast that threw her into the back of the van. Markus in his distorted werewolf form was an image that would forever be ingrained in her mind. Goose bumps rose on her arms and she suppressed the tears that threatened to spill out. She mentally scolded herself for letting his ghost upset her.

She refused to give him power over her. He was dead. Niyol had killed him. *You are strong, Ana. He can't hurt you anymore,* she reminded herself. He was gone but there wasn't a day she didn't think of him. She hadn't told Chance because she didn't want to upset him. She wondered what had made Markus so dangerous and worried that the same thing could happen to Chance. An insatiable hunger had gripped his cousin and it was one Markus hadn't been able to control. He'd craved power and taken it. In his sinister pursuit, no one was left unhurt. The only one who hadn't survived the attack was Niyol.

Ana clenched the wheel and took a shuddering breath to calm herself. They were still here. Despite the fact she was still angry with him for giving his life to save hers, she was thankful to be alive. And to be sitting beside him.

She knew the loss of Chance's grandfather was like a wound that wouldn't heal. It was festering and she worried that his anger would turn against him. As if he knew she was thinking about him, he turned and met her eyes. No, there wasn't evil there. Only love.

She shook off the sad thoughts and reached out to

him. He grasped her hand in his and lifted it to his lips. His hot breath on her skin kindled a fire and its warmth spread throughout her body.

A passing road sign snapped her back to reality. "Oh, that's our exit!"

She whipped her hand back and navigated them to the off ramp. The foothills ran alongside them now and shielded the craggy peaks of the Rockies. Large pointed stones jutted up behind the darkening ridge and she pointed them out to Chance.

Soon, they were driving along a one-lane road. Small shops and stores lined the street. Ana turned at one of the two traffic lights in town and guided them into a quiet neighborhood. She pulled up in front of a Victorian home with a wooden sign hung amongst some boxwood, proclaiming it a bed and breakfast.

Chance and Ana climbed out of the van and stretched. Ana's legs were stiff and she felt as though her vertebrae had fused together. She reached her arms above her head in a stretch.

"Come on, Grandma."

"What did you just call me?" Ana spun around and swatted Chance with the back of her hand. His muscles tightened at her touch and she imagined his chiseled body beneath his long sleeved shirt.

Chance grabbed her hand, tugged her close and nibbled her ear. She was startled at how much he sounded like a bear. She wouldn't have been surprised to see a furry paw nestled at her side. She smacked his shoulder before turning down the walkway.

Chapter 9

"Well, we have a room with two twins," the woman behind the desk said as she tucked some loose hairs into her bun. Her eyes roamed subtly over Chance's body and she blushed very slightly and adjusted a set of reading glasses on her nose.

Chance pulled his wallet out and handed her a credit card. "That should work, right, Ana?"

Ana nodded and then glanced around the formal sitting room. She turned and sat on a sun-bleached claw foot sofa. Striped blue wallpaper made her vision blur and she rubbed her eyes, realizing just how tired she was from driving. The weight of her head was too much so she dropped it back and stared up at the ceiling. A creeping philodendron's leaves hung down the wall beside her and the soft ticking from the grandfather clock nearby gave the room a heartbeat.

Chance's face stared down at her and she realized she must have closed her eyes for a moment. Grinning, Chance lifted her off the couch, handed her the key and said, "So, how 'bout you go check out the room and I'll get our stuff? It's upstairs on the right—the Angler's Room."

"Sure." Ana gave him a light peck on the cheek and watched him dart outside. She turned and clutched the thick mahogany banister. Glad to have some support as she went up the steep stairs, she coaxed herself to the second floor, where she scanned the door labels.

At the end of the hallway, she spotted the Angler Room. She slipped the key into the lock and with a jiggle and push, she entered the bedroom. It was too dark to see so she flipped the switch and a vintage table lamp lit up, saturating the space with a soft yellow glow. She dropped the key onto a nearby nightstand and sat on one of the beds while her fingers outlined the pattern of the quilt beneath her.

If she weren't so tired, she would have focused on the fact she was sharing the same room with Chance for the first time. Instead, a wave of exhaustion overcame her and she lay down.

Minutes later Chance breezed in, carrying their bags. He dropped them with a thud and closed the door.

"You all right, Ana?" He sat down on the bed and rested his hand on hers. "My love?"

Ana said with a groan, "I don't know what came over me. I'm just so tired from the long drive. Not even hungry or anything."

"Roll over. I'll rub your back."

With great effort, Ana turned onto her stomach, pulled the pillow under her head and closed her eyes. Warm hands pressed down on her back and the tension in her spine released. The enjoyment of having him touch her soon dissolved into unconsciousness.

***

Ana squinted as she adjusted to the sunlight pouring into

the room from an open window. Confused, she bolted upright and the sheets tumbled down around her waist. A fishing net and an old fly rod hung from one wall and a strange flowery scent mingled with a musty odor. She crinkled her nose in disgust. The covers on the bed next to her hung onto the floor and pooled in a heap.

"Chance?" she called as she slipped her feet to the wood floor and stood up. A cold chill curled her toes. *Where are my pants?* Her eyes fell on a pair of wadded-up jeans on her bag. The tip of a white sneaker stuck out from under her bed.

A door behind her opened, Ana spun on her heel and pulled down the bottom of her shirt. Chance stood in the bathroom doorway with a towel around his waist and a toothbrush in his mouth, his bronze skin glistening with droplets.

"Good morning," he said, laughing, clearly amused by her embarrassment.

She scurried over to her things, snatched up her wrinkled jeans and slipped them on in a hurry. Now that she didn't feel on display, she was able to focus. "What happened? I don't remember going to bed...or taking my clothes off."

Chance stared at a mounted trout that hung on the opposite wall and a deep blush traveled from his cheeks to his ears. He pulled the toothbrush from his mouth and disappeared into the steamy bathroom. Ana heard the water running and a couple minutes later, he came out wearing a shirt, jeans and a sheepish expression.

"You fell asleep and I didn't think you'd be

comfortable with your jeans and shoes on." He paused to run his fingers through his hair. "I didn't look. Uh, well, not too much."

Ana couldn't believe she didn't remember anything. She hadn't been that tired since her heart condition. Her stomach gurgled and she bit her lip uncomfortably. "Did we eat dinner? I am *starved*."

Chance seemed relieved at her response and strode across the room to kiss her nose. "I ate three protein bars from my pack. I didn't want to leave you, so yeah, I'm with you there. Starved. Get a whiff of those pancakes." His nose lifted and his eyes sparked. She couldn't detect anything past the musty potpourri odor but she knew all too well that his sense of smell was far more elevated than the average man's.

"Go ahead eat and without me. I'm hungry, but I need a quick shower. After that long drive yesterday, I'm not feeling myself. I'll just catch up with you after." She picked some clothing out of her bag and shut herself into the bright yellow bathroom. After grimacing at her own reflection, she turned on the shower and dropped her dirty jeans and shirt to the floor. She stepped in and the hot water ran down her body, taking with it the grime and aches of the previous day.

***

Chance stared at the closed bathroom door for a minute before he flopped onto the stripped surface of his bed. He figured he'd go ahead and wait for Ana and go down to eat with her when she was done. Impatient to a fault, he stared at the ceiling and followed the cracks from one side to the other. When he finished studying the contours of the room, he jumped upright and wandered over to the window. A couple was loading their luggage into their car outside.

He felt strange. But he couldn't identify exactly what he was feeling. He let his senses open up and was saturated with various noises and smells. An orchestra of sound rushed in and threatened his balance. To steady himself, he dropped to one knee and rested his hand on the sill.

Desperate for fresh air, he opened the window and took a deep breath in an attempt to clear his head. He closed his eyes. The couple was bickering about the route they were going to take. There was a whiff of coffee in the air. A squirrel chattered in a nearby pine tree. Its nails scratched the trunk and sent tiny pieces of bark down to the street below.

There was nothing to cause alarm. He opened his eyes and scratched his head. Maybe it was nothing. He turned his thoughts to something else that was troubling him.

He had found little sleep or rest during the night. His grandfather's death—all their deaths—filled his dreams. Dread filled his soul like a poisoned well. Niyol's voice was urgent and insistent. *Chance, remember...remember.*

Remember what? He had no idea what the dreams meant. It felt like he was missing something, he just didn't know what.

He was sure he was on the right path. But Niyol wasn't

here to advise him now. Had he done the right thing taking Ana with him? Maybe Melissa had been right about driving to Mexico. What if it wasn't safe? The biggest question of all, the one that kept him up at night: what if there were other shifters out there hunting for more power? What if he wasn't strong enough to protect them from harm? He hoped his grandfather was leading him in the right direction. If he couldn't find his great-grandfather, Balam, what would he do next? Shapeshifting was in his blood. It was a part of him. He couldn't imagine giving it up. However, for love, maybe.

He realized the water from the shower had shut off and he prepared himself for the discussion at breakfast. No matter what Ana thought, he knew it was in his best interest to map some new animals if he could. After the challenging shift into the owl at his grandfather's ranch, he feared he was losing his powers.

The bathroom door opened and a billow of steam poured into the room. Ana was brushing some knots from her hair and said, "Oh, you waited for me? I'll hurry up. I have just one more tangle to get through."

"No problem. I can wait."

She snickered and shook her head. Maybe it hadn't been the best choice of words. She knew him too well.

Chapter 10

Ana switched off her phone and slipped it into her jacket pocket. Chance sat across from her, stuffing pancakes into his mouth without any sign of slowing. The entire time she had been on the phone, he had crammed one after another into his bottomless stomach.

"Bleck. Mom just won't give up. Can you believe she actually tried making me an appointment with my old cardiologist? Thankfully they didn't have the time to fit me in."

"Really?" Chance said with his mouth full.

"Yeah. I think she's starting to get how important it is to me to see the world. Now that she understands I won't just turn around and come home, she asked me to book a flight to Mexico instead of driving there. Man, she just won't give up."

Chance's brow wrinkled as he said carefully, "She just cares..."

"Oh that's right, she reminded me to call Beth."

Ana pulled her phone out and dialed the number she had written on her paper napkin. After a quick conversation she filled Chance in on the plans. "Beth said she's around tomorrow and that we can stop by anytime."

Chance nodded and gulped down a big swig of orange juice. "Perfect. That leaves today open. What should we do? Are there any cultural points of interest you can show me?"

"Well, I guess we could go to the zoo today. Maybe we can ride the carousel."

Chance's eyes widened and he smiled excitedly. He grasped her hand in his and said, "Anything you want."

He lifted her fingers to his lips and kissed them one by one. Warmth spread from her hand up to her cheeks until she noticed the owner of the bed and breakfast watching them from the kitchen doorway. Hastily, she adjusted the collar of her shirt and blushed.

"Well, what are we waiting for? Let's get going." Chance jumped up, his breakfast long forgotten.

Ana's hand felt sticky after Chance let go so she dipped a cloth napkin in her water glass and cleaned it off. He stood and watched her as he fidgeted with his phone. After giving him a warning glare, Ana pushed her chair away from the table and joined him as he eagerly led her to the front door.

"You are too much, Chance." She sighed and pulled her keys out from her back pocket. As she walked into the morning sunlight, his warm breath tickled her neck and sent chills down her spine. His soft words soaked into her skin. "I'm sorry. You know how impatient I get."

A pair of finches fluttered around the yard in what seemed like a game of tag. Their excited chirps made Ana laugh as she continued on to the van.

Before she could climb in, Chance was there looking at her from the passenger seat.

"You should be more careful, Chance. What if someone saw you move like that?"

His expression grew serious and he nodded in agreement but remained silent.

***

He knew she was right. His grandfather had been the voice of reason for so long. *Patience, Chance.* He could still hear the words in his head because Niyol had said them so many times. When they pulled into the parking lot, an array of smells saturated his nose. It was mid-week, but the zoo was surprisingly full.

"Man, busy place."

"Oh, yeah. They started renovating years ago, and have gone from one improvement to another. I can't wait to see what's new." She slipped out of the van.

Chance sauntered around the vehicle to meet her. His hand found hers and they snapped together like two magnets as they started through the wooded lot.

As they approached the entrance, Chance's breathing quickened and he involuntarily squeezed Ana's fingers. She glanced at him out of the corner of her eye, gave him a strained smile, then shook her head and chuckled. "I get it, you're excited. Behave yourself, though."

"I wouldn't do anything in public." With that, he pulled her to the ticket counter.

Calls, chirps and hollers came from all corners of the grounds. He could smell each and every animal, various forms of species from around the world. His senses began to overload.

A large peacock stood just past the entrance and

stared at him, posed with its impressive array of eyes fanned out in full display. It cocked its head and ventured closer, then caught sight of Ana and shook its plume.

Chance smirked and said, "He likes you."

He handed their tickets to the man at the turnstile and they walked in through a crowd of families. The faces of little children around him perfectly reflected what he was feeling: excitement and joy.

They walked down a series of steps just as a little girl squealed with glee. She clung onto her stroller for support with one hand and planted her free hand on the glass of the mongoose enclosure. The small mammals were scurrying about, protectively clutching food in their tiny claws and spinning in circles.

A deep rumble up ahead caught Chance's attention and he practically dragged Ana to the lion enclosure. She mumbled an apology to a couple they cut off as they brushed by.

A large male lion lay out on a rock sunning itself, making a vain attempt to ignore the crowd. The tip of his tail flicked, then his mouth opened and a pink tongue curled out in a big toothy yawn. A dark, shaggy fringe surrounded its huge head and Chance was entranced. It was hard not to reach out with his mind to map the animal, but he stopped himself.

Ana watched the large feline and asked him quietly, "Are you going to map him?"

In response, he led her away and up the path toward the zebra habitat. "It takes a lot of energy to map an animal. I may only have enough to do one today and I want to be sure of what I choose."

Ana squeezed his hand and said, "Niyol would be proud of you, being so patient."

Chance nodded, but he wasn't entirely sure that was why he was holding back. What if he tried to learn an animal's energy mapping and couldn't? The memory of the last time he'd phased into the owl stuck in his mind. He didn't know what was up with his powers but they weren't behaving like they did before his grandfather died.

"Well then, let's go window shopping," Ana joked.

She led him down a nearby path. A large building was just ahead and a wooden sign read, 'Felines'.

Chance's tan cheeks lifted into a grin. "Perfect."

"Come on. They've got a Snow Leopard. It's so beautiful." Ana tugged open the heavy glass door.

"I thought your favorites were birds?"

She stuck her tongue out at him playfully. "They are. But cats are starting to grow on me."

They wandered through the darkened corridor and stopped to gaze at the pale leopard, its fur milky white, with dark spots patterned across its lanky body. Chance marveled at its long tail and thick undercoat. An animal built for cold weather, its natural home was the impressive peaks of Tibet, the Himalayas. The wild cat skulked up to the glass and stared at Chance, then Ana. A group of children came running in front of them and called out, "Mommy! Look at the tiger!"

Their mother came up, pulling a wagon behind her. "That's a Snow Leopard. Isn't it pretty?"

Chance and Ana continued to walk through the building. The other enclosures were empty so they decided to look for their occupants outside. As they rounded the brick wall, Chance sensed movement and stopped to allow his eyes to focus. A dark shape leapt to a large branch behind the metal fence. Yellow eyes traced over him, and rested on his throat.

As shocked as he would have been getting plunged into ice water, Chance's vision blurred. The familiar feeling of a memory washed over him...

His grandfather's thoughts and voice echoed in his mind. *"I'm not ready—it's too hard."*

Chance realized that he was standing in the dark and enveloped by dense jungle. The night was still, and he could smell moist groundcover and other unfamiliar flora.

He saw through Niyol's eyes, which were fixed on a high point in the trees. Chance noticed two reflective orbs staring back at him. Having the keen senses of a shapeshifter, he made out the form of a huge onyx feline. Suddenly, the jaguar leapt down to his grandfather's feet.

He was nose to nose with the beast, which curled its lips into a sneer. The large brown saucer eyes stared into his own, unblinking. Chance felt his grandfather's fear bubble up and he started to shake.

The large cat turned and shifted into a man. He began to walk away from Niyol as he said into the darkness, "Your fear poisons you."

The memory dissolved as quickly as it had come and he was surprised to find Ana planted in front of him, her brow wrinkled in a frown.

"Chance? Are you okay? Were you mapping the jaguar?" she asked uncertainly.

Chance rubbed his eyes and blinked hard. "No. It was another memory of Grandfather's," he said and glanced up at the cat, who had since stretched out onto the branch in its cage and shut its eyes for a nap. "Before I only suspected Balam's special form, but now I know for sure."

"A jaguar?"

He pinched his lips together. "Yeah."

Chance was nervous. Balam didn't have the same quiet, accepting aura as Niyol's. He seemed far more serious and stern. He was probably just missing his grandfather and anxious about having a new teacher. But he wished he hadn't seen that Mayan apocalyptic movie before they left Idaho. Scenes filled with violent warfare contradicted the research he found on the Maya that said they were a relatively peaceful and intelligent people, although he was still worried Balam would be stern and intense.

"Ready to go on?" Ana rubbed his arm, then let her hand drop down to meet his.

"I think I'm done with the cats. I already know cougar form." Chance answered.

"Don't I know it." Ana snickered. "Let's find something new."

They continued on and nothing appealed to him. Polar Bears were interesting and dangerous, but he already knew grizzly bear form. Otters and seals were cool but they weren't on his short list.

"I think you'll like Tropical Discovery."

"Oh, yeah? What's that?"

In response, Ana pointed ahead to a large building and sped up. They passed through the heavy doors and into a misty, humid environment. A large tank was just ahead of them, filled with stingrays, turtles and tropical fish. Next to the tank, a young boy hung upside down from a bronze snake statue and giggled as his parents snapped a photograph.

Plants hung from the walls, which appeared to be made of stone, and the sound of running water and children's voices echoed all around. He noticed openings in the walls covered with glass. Movement inside drew him closer. Eyes stared back at him unblinkingly, set into dark scales camouflaged by the wood chips and lichen.

"It's cool, but..."

Ana's brow wrinkled and she ducked in close to whisper, "What?"

Chance scratched the side of his head and said, "I've never shifted into anything other than a mammal or bird. I'm not sure about reptiles, amphibians or fish. I may not be able to. I don't know."

Ana wrapped her arms around him and gave him a squeeze. She was always there for him, ready to comfort and encourage him. Thankful to have someone accept him for who he was, he also felt the weight of the responsibility to protect her.

"Well, you may not be able to *now*, but who says you won't? So, the question is, what do you *want* to learn? What animal's abilities are important to have?"

She always knew how to cut to the point. What would be of benefit to him? He had a few large and powerful animals in his repertoire but he could use some more.

Chance nodded and offered Ana a dark smile. He caught her scent, something that always stirred his senses. She turned and walked into a dark cavern. His eyes lingered on her body, moving lithely into the shadows. When had she become so graceful?

After he ensured no one was near, he flitted to her side as she watched bats cling to the rocky, cavernous ceiling. Eager to find an animal to map, they walked on, moving from exhibit to exhibit. They were nearly at the end when he saw a large group of kids huddled up against a large glass tank. He almost passed it by because he thought it was just more fish until he noticed a large stone at the bottom of the tank. Little fingers danced around in front of it; the children were trying to entice the inhabitant to move. Standing closer, he realized the stone had a face. Lumpy and knotted with a wide beak-like mouth, its round eyes peered out at him.

He looked down through the water and saw only an obscured shape below. Bored and with little response from the snapping turtle, the children ran off into the next room. Chance squatted down and inspected the still creature. Three rows of spikes lined the muddy shell and led up to the curved, open jaw.

"I wouldn't want my hand to be his snack," Ana said with a shudder as she joined him.

Chance shook his head in disgust and stood bolt upright. He tightened his hands into fists, and clenched his jaw until his teeth protested under the pressure. "Am I going to find *anything* worth my time?"

His frustration was getting the better of him. All his anxiety twisted into a knot and radiated out from the center of his chest. Ana took his outburst in stride, slowly rose from the floor and laid her hands just below his collarbone. His body reacted almost instantly, growing calm at her touch. His tightened tendons and muscles released their fiery stance. He let his chin settle on the top of her head and he pulled her into a tight embrace that blocked out everything around them.

"I love you," Chance said into her dark brown tresses.

"I love you, too. Now, come on. Let's just have some fun looking around. The Komodo Dragons are just around the corner." She grabbed his hand and led him away.

Determined not to be a killjoy, he took a deep breath and allowed himself to get dragged through the rest of the humid building. When they walked out the double doors, the moisture that settled on his exposed arms evaporated almost immediately in the dry air. His eyes took a moment adjusting to the light before they followed a trail of people up to the picnic area.

Even though Ana was trying to be inconspicuous, his predatory senses were alerted. She was monitoring him. She held onto him tightly and he could tell she was worried. There was no reason for her distress - he was fine.

"So, can I get that carousel ride?" she asked softly.

"Of course. This isn't all about me. Lead the way."

They walked casually through the zoo, stopping to

gaze at the larger enclosures and strolled with families in the sunshine. He attempted to stop thinking about which animal to map and focused instead on the beautiful girl by his side. Her green eyes sparkled like emeralds in the light and her hair tumbled over her shoulders in loose waves.

"So, what animal do you want?" Her voice rose in excitement.

"Um, I'm not sure…"

It wasn't like her to persist like this. He glared at the pavement and watched a squirrel with a piece of bread jammed in its mouth.

"No, I mean the carousel. Which one?" Ana pointed ahead at the large, colorful ride.

"Oh, sorry. Doesn't matter. You pick and I'll go next to you."

They filed past a large crowd of people just off the ride, paid for their tickets and walked onto the platform. Peacocks, tigers, zebras and bears lined up in a silent, joyful parade under the mirrored ceiling. Organ music played as children rushed past them and clamored up onto the various animals.

Ana's eyes widened and with a squeal, she darted forward with Chance right on her heel. She climbed onto a cassowary and he jumped onto the black leopard beside her, leaned over and kissed her on the lips. The ride started and they began to move up and down. Ana's eyes closed as she let her arms drop free. While she revisited childhood memories, Chance noticed the bags under her eyes. He wondered if she was still tired even after their long sleep the night before.

After the ride, they walked toward a picnic area and he stopped. "Ana, how've you been feeling? You seem tired. Have I been pushing you too hard?"

Her brow wrinkled and she rubbed her cheek. "Well, I guess I'm a bit tired. It's probably from the traveling. No big deal though, and no, you aren't running me ragged. But I am *really* hungry." The aroma of burgers and fries filled the air and she glanced over to a building with smoke rising from its air vents.

"Lunch. Right. I could eat."

They settled on a grassy lawn with their meal. Peacocks and squirrels monitored the area, ready to scavenge any food offered willingly or unwittingly from the multitude of children sitting in strollers and at picnic tables. Chance watched Ana wolf down her food, then eye him as he finished his second burger.

"Want another?" He laughed at her.

She puckered her lips and batted her eyes, blushing. "Guess I didn't get enough breakfast."

"Let's do it."

After clearing through her second meal, she patted her stomach and groaned. "Oooh, maybe I shouldn't have."

Ana walked slower following lunch and she seemed even sleepier. She gave him a heavy lidded smile, which initially made him chuckle, then drew his concern. Without being obvious, he let his thumb drift up to her wrist as he held her hand. Her heartbeat was healthy and rhythmic, nothing like it once was.

They paused in the gorilla and orangutan building, sat

against a carpeted wall to rest and watch the animals interact. After sitting for a couple minutes, Chance chuckled and scratched his arm. "They certainly are entertaining."

No response. He looked over and Ana's head was nearly touching her shoulder. She was asleep and counting sheep. So much for taking time to search for a new animal to map. He needed to take her back to the bed and breakfast for a rest. He would have been disappointed if he wasn't so concerned for her health.

He pushed himself off the floor, leaned over and brushed her cheek with the back of his hand.

Her eyes fluttered open and she yawned as she stretched out her arms and arched her back. "Sorry about that. The food put me out. Where to next? Elephants?"

"Home."

He offered her his hands and lifted her off the floor in one fluid movement. She nuzzled her face into his chest and took a deep breath.

"No. We're here for a reason. We're here for you."

Chance brushed stray hairs from her face and said, "No, my only reason for being here is you. And now we need to go so you can rest."

A shaft of light poured across them from the nearby door, which was flung open by a man with a toddler on his shoulders. Chance entwined his fingers through Ana's and led her outside. If he didn't think she would protest, he would have picked her up and carried her to the van but he knew he was just being overprotective. Instead, he settled for walking with his arm around her waist.

As they neared the entrance of the zoo, Ana stopped. "You shouldn't leave without learning a new form. Really—pick something, I'll wait."

The large lion enclosure was to his right. He could nearly hear their breathing. He closed his eyes and imagined himself as a king of the jungle, complete with thick regal mane and muscular build, ready to take on anything. Or anyone.

Tired from their day, he had already given up on the idea of mapping a new animal, but decided to give it a try.

Ana sat down on an empty bench and he wandered over to the rail. The lions were no longer out in the sun but resting in the shade near the glass of the building next to him. He turned and swung open the heavy wooden doors. The darkened room had large plate glass windows that looked out to the habitat. A couple of women were sitting on a bench and feeding their kids snacks at one end of the exhibit. They were involved with what they were doing and didn't even look up when he walked in.

A male lion was stretched out in the cool shadows. Chance squatted down beside the jungle cat and closed his eyes to relax. *Okay, Chance, you can do this.*

He called on his blue core of energy. Like the last time he shifted, it was sluggish, almost dormant. Its glow was a fraction of what it once was. A tug of war waged between him and his powers. Perspiration gathered on his forehead as his focus increased.

Chance looked at the lion. It stared at him as though it

were waiting for something to happen. He caught sight of a wisp of indigo thread near its eye. Faint traces of blue lines glimmered just below the surface of the yellow feline's fur. His eyes strained as he tried to grasp it in its entirety but just as he thought he caught it, it faded away.

Damn.

He shoved himself up and punched the glass. He just couldn't understand what was going on. It was starting to freak him out. If only grandfather was alive. He would have some advice for him, he was sure of it. Instead, Chance was forced to go find his great-grandfather. Someone he knew nothing about.

Defeated, he turned from the glass and tried to calm down. He didn't want Ana to see him so upset. Then he would have to explain his loss of power. Hearing the words aloud would make it real and right now, he didn't want to admit it to himself. He was afraid.

As he walked out into the daylight, Ana stood up and said, "So how'd it go? Ready to head out?"

Chance forced a grin and kissed her on the lips. It took effort to keep his voice light and positive as he said in response, "Great. You ready for your nap?"

With that, he led her out past the entrance and into the parking lot, trying desperately not to wonder, as he walked, if he'd ever be able to shift again...

Chapter 11

They woke to a darkened room after a much needed nap. This time Ana remembered where she was. She cleared the gravel from her throat before speaking. "Chance? Let's go get some food. I'm hungry."

The bedside table lamp switched on and she covered her eyes. She felt Chance's warm touch as he gently lowered her hand away from her face.

"Don't cover your eyes. I was just dreaming about them."

Heat radiated from her cheeks when his breath tickled her neck. She had dreams of lying tangled with his muscular body but she was frightened. There was no one she was more comfortable around than Chance, but when it came to physical closeness she was unsure of herself. She was inexperienced in romantic matters. It wasn't fear of being rejected that frightened her, it was the fear of the unknown.

She averted her eyes as she recalled what her mom had said to her before they left on the trip.

I know you love him, baby. And God knows he's head and shoulders above your dad, but don't make any hasty choices you can't take back. I'm not saying I regret having you, baby, because you are everything to me, but please be careful. Love is intoxicating, I remember. Just be true to yourself...always."

A tear formed and curled down the contour of her

cheek. Chance saw it immediately and wiped it away.

"What's wrong?" he asked, his brows furrowing.

"I was just thinking about how much I love you. And how much I trust you." Ana lifted herself up and let her bare feet settle on the wood floor. Chance sat beside her and remained quiet. His arm rested against hers and where their skin touched, electricity built. She stared at his muscular hands resting on his knees and noticed them twitch before he let one slide over to her leg. Her breath caught in her throat. Finding courage, she met his shining hazel eyes and discovered the same anxious excitement mirrored back.

A loud knock sounded on the door, shaking them out of their trance. "Hello?" a woman's voice called out.

Chance glared at the door, stood up and walked to it. He opened it a little, blocking the proprietor's view into the room. "Yes, hello, Grace."

"Oh, sorry to disturb you. I was wondering if your room's beds were made. I didn't mark it off."

Ana marveled at Chance's kind tone when she knew just how agitated he was. She could almost hear him clench his teeth while he spoke through his smile. "Nope, you got us. The beds are made. You caught us on our way out. Time for dinner."

"Oh? Well, there's a good Mexican restaurant in town, and there's a diner, too, if you like burgers," she added helpfully.

Ana wondered if Grace was really so forgetful, if she was nosy or if she'd simply wanted to see Chance's handsome face once more. Well, she couldn't blame her if it was the latter.

"Thanks. We'll see you at breakfast," Chance said and shut the door. "Well, you ready to eat?"

Her stomach rumbled and she covered her belly in embarrassment. "Oh, I guess so. I'm starved."

She bit the inside of her lip and avoided looking at him. Chance seemed to have brushed off the interruption and she felt his eyes trace over her. Heat flushed her cheeks as she thought about what would have happened if there hadn't been a knock on the door.

"You're keeping up with my eating habits. That's no small feat."

Ana shook her head and reached for her shoes. The tinkling of metal made her look up. Chance grabbed the keys off the side table, slipped on his jacket and gave her a broad grin. "Ready, my love?"

She stood up and stretched, and Chance went to the closet to retrieve her coat. Holding it out for her, he gingerly enclosed her in the warm cocoon. He fumbled with her zipper and drew it up slowly, letting it rest at the nape of her neck. They entwined hands and ventured from the Victorian house and into the darkened night.

Chance slipped behind the wheel, fired up the loud, rumbling engine, and started rolling down the street. "I miss my truck," he said, frowning.

Ana snickered while buckling herself in but stopped suddenly when a stray dog came trotting out into the street. The tires locked up as Chance pressed his foot on the brake. Chance's arm caught her as she lurched forward.

"You okay?" he asked, his eyes wide.

She sat back up and nodded as she watched the stray stop to look at them. Its steel eyes stared in through the glass, scruffy gray fur stuck out in tufts and it appeared to be in serious need of a bath. A dry leaf fell from its tail, startling it, and it moved across the road and around a parked car.

"Let's try that again."

They drove the short distance into town and found the Mexican restaurant. Ana was amazed at her appetite and a little embarrassed as well. She cleared her plate and even felt a little hungry when she was done.

They stepped outside and watched a stream of cars go by, heading up the mountain. A gust of wind blew past them. Ana held her jacket shut and tried to secure her hair behind her ear.

"Hey, weren't you telling me about those red rocks? Is it open now? Can we go up?" Chance regarded the dark shape of the hills to the west.

"That sounds like fun. Sure, it's just a couple minutes away."

Ana drove them out of town to a paved road that wound around huge pieces of stone jutting from the ground like worn, broken bones the earth could no longer contain. Scrub and brush filled in the empty space. As they wound along the one lane road, they saw the city glowing below. The rumbling yellow van passed through a tunnel carved out of the red rocks and she remembered back before Eva was born, when she would yell out the window every time they drove through, hoping to hear her own echo. She entered a large gravel parking lot and pulled up the emergency brake. It groaned in protest and the van rocked back, settling in place.

"Ready?"

"Can't wait. Show me around."

They locked up and walked to the top of the amphitheater. Row upon row of seating tumbled down the rocky enclosure built into the earth. High peaks of stone arched above them to their left and opened up for a perfect view of the cities below. Points of light glowed from the homes and streets of Denver, illuminating the horizon. Ana tipped her head back, expecting to spot a carpet of stars but found only a blank canvas. Cloud cover kept it from being a perfect night.

Disappointed, she sighed and looked at Chance. She could see his features through the tenebrous night and he was staring raptly at her.

She dipped her chin down, hoping he hadn't seen her awkwardness in the dark. His fingers traced down her forearm and to her hand. He led her down the stone steps and paused at a row near the top. They sat down and Ana leaned against him as he wrapped his arm around her.

"I'm sorry there aren't any stars out for you," he said into her ear.

When she turned to respond, his lips met hers in a strong embrace. She let out a soft cry of surprise and he curled his arm tighter around her waist. His free hand cupped her face and she felt his hot breath travel down her neck and back up to her ear. Soft, tender kisses engulfed her heart in flames, and it raced in excitement.

***

Ana's warm body pressed up against his made Chance unfocused, lightheaded. He buried his face against her neck and breathed in the floral scent from her hair. Since the moment they'd met, she had filled his dreams and thoughts every waking moment. When he was near her, he longed to hold her, touch her. He didn't have much experience with girls. When his powers developed as a teenager, he'd lost all desire to be around anyone who couldn't understand him. That left only his grandfather, whom he'd preferred to be around above everyone, until he'd met Ana.

Just below his fingertips, the fluttering pulse of her heart made him recall the time he would have pulled back instead of persisting. He was still getting used to her strong, healthy heartbeat. Her ragged breathing ignited a fire, a need he had been pushing away. He cupped his hand behind her head, leaned in and lowered her onto the wooden planks of the bench. Her eyes widened and then relaxed.

A gust of wind whipped over Chance's body, combed through his dark hair and lifted up his jacket. Soft fingertips drifted up his spine, sending a ripple of pleasure down his legs. He licked his lips, leaned in and whispered, "I love you, Ana."

Even in the murky dark, he could see her eyes open. Strands of long chestnut hair framed her almond shaped face; she was his own enchanting siren.

"Chance, I love you, too, more than anything," she choked out.

Crack—Boom! Chance lifted himself up, but kept his body over Ana's, tight and ready to spring. Everything was suddenly illuminated by a powerful burst of light. The rocky enclosure was bathed in a bluish flash. A wet drop slapped him on the cheek and then another struck his back.

Ana laughed beneath him and raised her arms up. Chance groaned. *Of course. Something always gets in the way.*

Just as he was about to help her up, he was hit with a familiar sensation. His muscular arms locked in place and his awareness became fuzzy as an unpleasant vision entered his mind, one he had experienced before.

Niyol was in the form of the wolverine and pummeling a bobcat with repetitive blows to the face, which forced the cat to tip to its side, blinded. The cat morphed into a defenseless prairie dog. Markus.

When the prairie dog turned to escape, his grandfather's thoughts echoed through his mind, *Go ahead and run—I'm faster than you.*

Markus's furry form scurried a couple feet before Chance felt his body dive into it, smashing it into the ground. He picked up the limp animal with his powerful jaws, and shook it fiercely. He dropped it to the dirt and leapt into the air, diving down onto the small creature. It trembled and disappeared.

His instincts triggered and his attention shifted.

Where's Chance? His gaze moved upward as he searched the landscape. Chance saw himself through his grandfather's eyes, leaning over Ana. He saw his body give a subtle jolt as his hands hovered over Ana's lifeless form and a sapphire glow emanated into her chest, radiating from his hands.

He heard his grandfather's voice call out. "No! Chance, wait!" His grandfather returned to his human form and ran toward him. "Wait!"

His grandfather's memory faded, flickered and continued. Niyol was now crouched over Chance's lifeless body with his hands hovering over Chance's chest, and chanting rhythmically. Soon the deep voice faded and he watched a blue light generate from his grandfather's fingertips and shoot into his still body as Niyol's thoughts faded into a soft whisper until there was only silence.

As Chance watched these memories play out in his head, Ana lay stretched out, giggling in the rain, completely unaware of what Chance had just experienced. He sat up, his senses in a soundless vacuum, as though he were trapped in a glass room. His hands remained lifeless at his side as he stared over the city and at the lightning strikes flashing through the inky night.

Chance hadn't been prepared for such a painful flashback and couldn't understand why it had happened. More raindrops tapped around him, and he recalled the lightning that terrible day, when it had allowed him to achieve the thunderbird form. The electricity in the air had given him the boost he needed to shapeshift into his ancestor's form of power. Another clap of thunder sounded and the hairs on his arms rose. In the same moment, a pitchfork of lightning struck out, and everything fell into place for him. Of all the three death scenes, one was quite unlike the others. It could only mean one thing.

It explained so much. The relentless dreams and the sense he was in danger...

Ana lifted herself onto her elbows and asked, "What'd you say?"

Chance scanned the landscape around them to check every nook and cranny with his eagle-like vision. He jumped to his feet and held his hand out to her. "Nothing—just mumbling to myself. C'mon, let's get out of the rain."

She stood and wrapped her arms around his shoulders, lifted herself onto her toes and gave him a kiss. Cold, wet drops plastered their faces and the rumble of thunder sounded over their heads. He grasped her hand in his and led her back up the stairs and out of the amphitheater. She threw the keys to him and he unlocked her door and helped her in. Rain dripped off the end of his nose while he stared into the rocky crevices of distant peaks. He jumped into the van, fired up the deafening engine and drove off. Ana was still buckling as she asked, "Where's the fire?"

It took a lot of self-control but he breathed out slowly and calmed himself down. He didn't want her to know. She wouldn't be able to do anything about it anyway. He was the only one who could protect her. With great effort, he forced a smile while slicking back his wet hair.

"Aren't you cold? We need towels and maybe a warm shower."

Ana seemed hesitant for a moment. She could always seem to tell when he was being deceitful but then she shrugged and wrung out her hair. He got them back to the bed and breakfast within five minutes and ushered her inside and up to their room. After he shut the door behind them, he flipped the lock and scoffed at himself. *A lock won't stop him.*

"Want the first shower?" He opened the bathroom door, flipped on the light and started running some hot water.

"Sure. Let me grab a nightshirt first," Ana called out from behind him.

He scooted out of the way as she came into the tiny room and set her things down on the toilet seat. Chance shut the door behind him and waited a minute to ensure she was in the shower before he whipped out his phone and called the airline.

They needed to leave as soon as possible. If Markus was still alive, he wasn't going to wait long before trying to kill them again. And there was no way in his current state he could protect them without some help. He needed to find Balam.

Chapter 12

The sound of shuffling and a zipper brought Ana out of her deep sleep. A shadow fell across her face. She blinked and propped herself up on one elbow.

"What's going on?" she croaked and cleared her voice.

Chance was standing over her with a guilty expression, the strap of his travel backpack in his hand. He was dressed in jeans and a black t-shirt and his hair fell across his eyes in a way that made her stomach flutter.

"Don't be mad, but I've made some plans. We're checking out. After breakfast we still have time to go by your mom's friend's place—then we're off."

Ana rubbed the sleep from her eyes and sat up in bed. She pulled her hair out of its messy ponytail and shook it loose, aware of his eyes following her every move.

"So are you going to tell me more about our plans? Or is it a surprise?"

He leaned over, grabbed a pair of jeans from her backpack and tossed them over to her. "Sure, you could call it that. How about you get dressed? I'll get your things together and we'll head down for breakfast."

She yawned and stretched. Trying to work against him would be too tiring. She had learned he'd do whatever he wanted to, anyway. Her toes touched the floor and curled on the chilly surface. A cold draft went up her long nightshirt when she stood up and she bent over her bag.

"Can I at least choose my own clothes?" She stuck her

tongue out as she passed him, a bundle of clothing clutched against her chest.

In the bathroom, she got ready as quickly as she could before sounds of movement outside the door drew her attention. He was getting anxious.

When she came back out, she found her bag on her bed, opened and ready for the rest of her things. Chance had their room door propped open with his backpack. He sat with his arms back, in a clear attempt to appear casual on one of the beds, which had been haphazardly made.

When her bag was ready, he offered to carry it and threw both packs over his shoulder. Chance poured down the flight of stairs like water sweeping through a river and set their things near the b-and-b's front door. He waited and walked with her into the dining room where breakfast was waiting.

Her stomach grumbled when she caught sight of the crepes and orange juice. After she'd had her fill and Chance had shoved the last crepe in his mouth, he stood and said, "Why don't you call your mom's friend while I settle up with Grace? Let her know we're on our way."

He leaned down and gave her a gentle kiss on the cheek. His warm breath and the sweet smell of strawberries mingled with his spicy scent completely filled her senses.

Ana called Beth to let her know they were on their way. At the front door, before she could reach for her bag, Chance's rugged hands beat her to it. "Why don't you get the door?"

"Grace sad to see you go?" Ana asked as they walked

down the path from the bed and breakfast.

Chance snorted and said, "I think after the amount of breakfast I ate over the last two days, she was happy to see me go."

He loaded their things in the van while she climbed behind the wheel. Ana turned on the ignition and surfed the radio stations, searching for one she liked. She watched him arrange their bags through the rear view mirror and noticed him searching around.

"Lose something?" she asked between verses of a song she was humming.

His head snapped up in surprise and his nostrils flared while he sniffed the air. "You smell that? Wasn't sure if a fry escaped back here or something."

After scanning around the back and standing up on the bumper to search through the bench and under the table, he jumped down and gave her a wink.

As Ana drove east, away from the mountains, excitement built as she wondered about Chance's surprise. She smiled at him and noticed his strained expression. He got stressed over the smallest things, she thought.

Green, grassy fields, touched with yellow, surrounded them as she exited the highway and onto a quiet road. She turned down a gravel driveway after ten minutes. A large metal shed stood alone against the stark landscape except for a navy Ford Explorer parked beside it. Ana pulled up next to the home, got out and scanned the property.

Muffled barking echoed nearby and grew louder and

louder. A yellow lab scrambled out from under the front porch and ran over to her. It stood on guard for a second until Ana called him closer. "Tricky! Hi, buddy! Come here."

The yellow lab lurched at her feet, wagging his tail, and rolled onto his back. Chance came around the van and said, "I wasn't sure if I needed to protect you there for a second. Looks like the only danger you're in is getting smothered by puppy love."

"This is Tricky, my best bud. The dog I never had."

Chance squatted down and held his hand out for the lab to smell. The dog paused in mid-wag and stared wide-eyed at him. Chance kept his eyes down and then a wet tongue licked his exposed arm, leaving a slimy trail.

Ana cooed and said, "Aw, such a tough guy, Tricky!"

"Ana, is that you?!" a woman's voice called from behind the house.

Chance stood up, trying to ignore Tricky, who was pressing his muzzle against his hand.

Ana called out. "Beth?"

A short woman with shoulder length blonde hair walked around the white building and pulled off a pair of work gloves. Arms outstretched, she embraced Ana and then turned to Chance with a grin on her face. She tucked some loose blonde hair behind her ear and introduced herself. "Hi, I'm Beth. I can see Tricky has a new best friend."

Chance rubbed the drying dog saliva off his arm and extended his hand to her. "Hey, I'm Chance. Nice to meet you."

Beth led them to the house, talking all the while. "I've already heard a lot about you, Chance. Did Ana tell you I used to babysit her? Oh, and speaking of Ana…" She spun on her heel and reached for Ana's hand before continuing. "I hear a miracle has occurred. When Mel told me the news, I did a little jig in the kitchen."

Ana laughed, and said, "Pretty great, isn't it? Which is why I'm able to visit you now and go exploring instead of sitting in a hospital room. This is way better."

They went inside and sat at the kitchen table while Beth started a pot of coffee and asked Ana all about her mother and sister.

While they talked, Ana noticed Chance checking the time and fidgeting with his phone.

Ana decided to say something when Beth left to get her camera from the other room. "What's up? What are the plans? We aren't late for something, are we?"

He drummed his fingers on the table and slid back in his chair. "Yeah, we need to get outta here and head to the airport in twenty minutes. We're flying to Cancun."

"What?!"

Beth breezed back into the room. "What's this about Cancun?"

Ana stared open-mouthed at Chance.

"Well, I thought, why drive down in your van when it sounds like it could blow a seal any day. Let's just get down there and have some fun." He stood up, walked around the table and held his hand out to Ana.

Ana considered that her mother may have had something to do with it, but she didn't care anymore. She thought about sitting beside Chance on a plane flying off to a place she had only dreamt of. Her heart sputtered in excitement. His hazel eyes stared down at her as he waited for an answer.

"I'm game. Sounds like fun," she said and accepted his outstretched hand to stand up. The tension slipped from his face and he beamed at her before giving her a kiss on the lips.

"My, that does sound like fun. If you weren't up for it, Ana, I was about to jump in," Beth said, lifting her camera up and snapping a quick shot of them both.

"Oh, but what about my van?" Ana stepped back with her hands on her hips.

"We'll just leave it in the airport lot."

"How long will you kids be gone for?" Beth asked.

Chance and Ana met each other's eyes and shrugged vaguely.

"Well, I'm not about to let you waste your money like that. You can keep it here. I've got enough space. Plus, maybe I can lure your mom out for a visit. She can drive it back home for you."

Ana recognized the gleam in Beth's eye. She was probably imagining a fun girl's weekend, which would result in Melissa getting fixed up with 'the perfect guy'. Beth always had some mischievous plan up her sleeve. Even if well-intentioned, it usually ended in apologies later.

"Well, let's take a couple more pictures for memory's sake and we'll load up my car and I'll drop you kids off."

Being at the other end of a camera wasn't Ana's

favorite thing so after a round of pictures, she strolled out to her bright yellow van and opened the hatch. Chance and Beth followed her over and soon they transferred all of their belongings to Beth's Explorer.

On the way to the airport, Ana called her mother to explain their new plans while Beth spoke up in the background. "Girls weekend coming up, Mel. Get ready for some fun!"

"What is Beth talking about?" her mom asked on the other end of the line.

"Beth wants you to fly out for some trouble and then drive the van home." Ana smirked at their chauffer through the rear view mirror.

"I suppose I could leave Eva with Tera," Melissa said distractedly, then added, "Well, I'm glad you're not driving all the way down to Mexico—thank Chance for me. I hope you have enough money for the trip. Let me know if you have an emergency. I'm still your mother. I worry. A lot. Please check in with me often and tell me when you're coming home when you figure it out. Wear your sunscreen and most of all, have a great time, baby. I love you."

"Love you too, Mom. I'm so excited. It's more than I ever could have asked for." Ana stared directly at Chance. A wave of emotion overtook her and she ended the call abruptly and wiped her eyes with the edge of her shirt.

With a healed heart, it felt as if the world had opened up to her and the possibilities were limitless. Out her window, she saw the tent-like white peaks of the airport in the distance and her heart fluttered with excitement.

"We're almost there, kids. Can you hide me in your bags and take me along?"

Ana laughed and checked her carry on bag for her passport and identification. Satisfied she had everything, she reached for Chance's hand and noticed him grow pale and glance in the back.

"We should have everything."

His eyes darted back to her as he combed his fingers through his hair and nodded. "Right."

Chapter 13

The engines roared and they lifted off the ground. Chance clutched Ana's hand and fixed his attention on the glowing red 'No smoking' sign above his seat. He kept telling himself that as soon as they were safe in Mexico with Balam, he could relax. Although when he thought about Balam, he got even more anxious. *What if I can't find him? What if he's dead? What if he doesn't want to be found?*

Chance closed his eyes tight and attempted to push his fears away. He couldn't afford to freak out over this. It was in his best interest to keep a clear head. How could he protect Ana if he was unprepared? He pulled a map from his blue backpack and laid it on his lap, pressing the seams down. The paper crinkled at his fingertips and he fixated on an area circled in black ink.

Briefly glancing at his watch, he realized they would get to Cancun early in the evening, which wouldn't provide enough time to get out to the ruins. They would have to find a hotel in the city and then find out about a tour for the following morning. It would have to do.

"Whatcha looking at?" Ana rested her chin on his arm. The smell of her hair distracted him and he got caught in the light dancing off her green eyes.

"Oh, um, I'm just figuring out the plan."

"I see. We aren't driving off into a dark jungle tonight, are we?" she asked, frowning.

"If you weren't with me, yeah, I'd be tempted. But that wouldn't be safe with you around."

She pushed back, folded her arms in front of her chest and rolled her eyes. "I'm not totally defenseless."

"Against me you are," he said and kissed her jaw line until the edges of her lips curled up, despite her clear efforts not to have that happen.

Through the entire flight, he attempted to relax. He closed his eyes and recalled the words his grandfather would use to calm him, knowing they would only temporarily dam the swell of nerves before they broke free. Around and around, thoughts tumbled in his mind like clothing in the wash cycle: Markus alive, *swish*, Balam and the unknown, *twist*, protect Ana from harm, *writhe*, the unexplained decrease in his powers, *smack*.

Ana, as always, seemed aware of his emotional state as she placed her hand gently on his arm, remained quiet and allowed him space to meditate. When the gleaming ocean came into view out the window, Ana pressed her face against the Plexiglas. She smiled so wide that her eyes watered and a single tear fell.

Her happiness cracked his rigid exterior and he wiped the tear from her cheek. While he stewed in his own emotions, Ana seemed to be living every moment like it was a gift.

"I never thought I'd get to go to a place like this. Never thought I'd live to see it myself," she murmured.

"I'm glad we came here together."

Although, deep down, he wished he hadn't brought her...

***

They stepped outside into the sunlight and Ana stopped, closed her eyes and breathed in the warm tropical air. Chance brushed up against her arm as he walked up beside her.

"Come on, let's get a taxi."

No sooner had he spoken than a cluster of men approached with their arms outstretched, trying to guide them to their drivers. Chance walked forward and Ana scurried close behind and said to the men, "No, gracias."

"Ana, do you speak Spanish?" Chance stopped and stared at her.

"Freshman through junior year with Mr. Blake. I know a little."

"Well, baby bird, time to fly. Negotiate a deal. Oh, and let them know we need a hotel."

Words jumbled in her mind. A sentence formed as she glanced to a man at her side. She grew more comfortable as she realized how eager the taxi drivers were to bridge the gap and make a sale and quickly negotiated a deal to be driven to a local hotel.

Their bags were whisked away into the back of the vehicle and they were ushered inside with some other travelers. A couple from Germany and a family from De Moines filled the back seats.

Before long, they were speeding on the highway and Ana's stomach began to tumble in circles. Her light lunch on the flight was churning around now. She wasn't sure how long she could hold off the terrible pain in her belly.

Beside her, Chance stared out the window and observed the city around them. The driver dropped off the German couple at a small hotel on a busy street, and continued south of the city.

The children's excited voices rose from the back seat as they drove down a long road and through the jungle to emerge near the beach. The sky glowed indigo as the sun set behind the trees. A large hotel blocked the ocean view and the stomachache Ana had been battling subsided for a moment, only to be replaced with butterflies. The driver pulled up to the entrance and the family pushed past them with apologies.

"This place looks nice. Should we see if they have a room for the night?" Ana asked Chance.

"Sure, why not? Just ask the driver to wait for us, just in case."

They slipped out of the van together. Ana got the driver's attention and did her best to explain they were going to see if there was a room available while Chance hung back.

Friendly, smiling faces greeted her as she walked into the expansive entry and she felt her face flush as she took in the grand surroundings. Large, oversized plants spotted the lobby. A huge fountain flowed into a reflective pool that led outside to a patio where guests were sitting and relaxing and holding colorful drinks that made her mouth water.

Ana walked up to a man at the front desk. He beamed welcomingly at her and she ventured ahead with her request.

"Yes, miss, I will check for you."

After a moment, he gave her a kind smile and said, "We have a room available on our deluxe plan. This includes your meals and drinks and is only one-hundred a night, per person."

Ana swallowed hard. *"Muchas gracias. Un momento por favor."*

She waved to Chance, who was leaning against the van. He pushed away from the vehicle and joined her. "What's up?"

"They have a room and it includes everything but it's two hundred for the night. Can we afford that?" She did the math in her head. She only had a thousand left. Although it was more money than she was used to having, she could tell at this rate she would be out of money in no time. She didn't want him to have to pay for everything. It wasn't fair.

"Don't worry." He ran his fingers through his hair. "Let's do it for tonight and hopefully we won't have to pay for another hotel as long as we find Balam. Remember, grandfather left me gold. We have a safety net."

Ana glanced up at the tiled ceiling and her shoulders sank. "Yah, but Niyol left that for you, not me."

Chance's soft fingers touched her chin and traced her jaw. His serious gaze held her attention. "Listen, you're a part of all of this now. I would be here anyways. Grandfather considered you part of the family and so do I."

Humbled and touched, she wasn't sure what to say in return.

"Here, take this and I'll go let the driver know we're staying." He handed her his passport, a folded handful of money wrapped around a credit card and placed a kiss on her cheek before he went back outside to the taxi.

They were checked in quickly and Chance returned, carrying their bags. The man behind the desk waved over a valet and handed them their passports along with the room keys.

"Thank you Miss. Hughes and Mr. Morgan, we hope you enjoy your stay with us."

They were led through the grounds of the hotel and Ana marveled at all the beautiful flowers. Easily the size of her hand, their petals rippled in the breeze like colorful skirts. Tall palm trees arched above the rooftops of the brightly painted buildings, and their fronds whispered as they brushed against each other. The valet led them around an orange, two-story building beside the pool and up a flight of stairs. He held his hand out for a key and Ana obligingly handed it over so he could let them into their room.

The door swung open, revealing a sun-drenched space with flowing curtains and tiled floors. She caught sight of the ocean out their balcony and ran to the sliding glass door. After she let herself outside, she leaned against the railing and closed her eyes. Emotion unlike anything she had ever felt overtook her. Happiness bubbled up, making her eyes damp. The sounds of music, children and laughter filled the air, along with the high trilling calls from birds. The breeze whipped her hair around her face and tickled her nose.

"Completely worth it." A deep voice whispered beside her.

"What is?"

Chance's hand slipped over hers. "It's worth every penny to see you this happy."

His warm breath tickled her neck and she turned and met his lips in a kiss.

He muttered into her ear. "Well, we may not have this opportunity again. What do you want to do first? Beach, pool or dinner?"

She frowned. Such a hard decision. It was her first time visiting the ocean. She couldn't wait to feel the sand between her toes and dip her feet into the wet surf. It was an experience she had always dreamt of. A deep rumble came from her stomach.

"My stomach's been bothering me since we landed. Maybe I should eat dinner and see if that helps. Hopefully I'm just hungry."

Chance grew serious. "Are you sure? Let me know if you need me to track down some Tums or something."

"I'm sure I'll be okay. C'mon let's have fun."

Ana opened her bag on the bed and pulled out a spaghetti strap dress and a pair of sandals. She locked herself in the bathroom and stared at her reflection. After a long day of travel, her hair was frizzy and the jeans and tank top she picked out in Denver no longer seemed suitable for their location. She changed, brushed her hair and washed her face.

Chance had changed into a pair of shorts. He was just buttoning up a short sleeve shirt when she came out of the bathroom. He let out a low whistle, walked toward her and slipped his hands around her waist. "Beautiful. Perfect."

She held the collar of his shirt, lifted herself up onto her toes and gave him a kiss on the lips. His spicy scent played at her nostrils and she wondered how he could smell so good after a long day of travel.

They packed away their things, put their valuables in the room safe and walked out carrying only their key.

"I can't believe we're really here. Can't believe *I* am," she said as they strolled along the pathway up to the main building.

Chance squeezed her hand in response. A large iguana lay stretched out on a broad porous rock and watched them walk by without moving its head.

"Oh," he exclaimed, "let's stop up front and see if there's a tour or something."

Chance strode through the spacious entry to the large marble desk. "Excuse me," he asked the concierge, "are there any tours to Ek Balam for tomorrow?"

The woman's fingers fluttered to smooth her hair back and said, "Ek Balam? Are you sure you don't want to visit Chichen Itza or Tulum?"

"No, thank you. We have been waiting to see Ek Balam."

"Yes, of course, sir. I can arrange that for you. Is it just yourself?"

Ana stepped forward, joined Chance and said, "For

two."

The woman nodded and began typing into her computer. After the short delay, they walked off with two tickets for the next day's tour of Ek Balam.

They followed other guests to the dining hall. The smell of food filled the air and Ana's empty stomach groaned. They grabbed plates and loaded them with different colorful foods.

Ana felt a little guilty as she looked down at the heap of spaghetti, mashed potatoes, steak, salad and pizza. They found a free table near some windows and sat down. Neither of them spoke as they cleared their plates. She marveled at Chance's ability to shovel so much food into his mouth as quickly as he did without making a mess of his face.

"Oh, well."

"What?" Chance asked as he took a big swallow of his soda.

"I was hoping to eat some traditional food. I didn't come to Mexico to eat American. I mean it was good and all, I was so hungry, but I dunno."

Chance stretched his arms above his head, flexing his muscles, then let them drop to his side as he answered, "I hear you. Don't worry, I bet we'll have lots of chances to eat local."

Ana regretted eating so much dinner. Her stomach felt bloated as they left the restaurant. But she realized her belly hadn't gotten any bigger since her appetite had increased.

"Ana, you hear that?" Chance asked with a straight

face.

"What?" She strained to listen. All she heard was the sound of soft music, birds chirping and the sea.

"It's calling you—the sea."

"Well, you've never seen the ocean either..."

"Yeah, but you never thought you'd live to see it."

He pulled at her hand and they ran ahead. Ana couldn't help giggling as her sandals slapped against the paved walkway. The darkened sky glowed indigo and the horizon glimmered as the day exhaled into night.

The gray path ended, dipped down into the sand and appeared as though the beach had swallowed it up. Ana slipped her shoes off and held them in her hands. With a quick sidelong glance, she leapt forward. Her toes sank into the gritty sand. Just below the cool surface, warmth trapped from the heat of the day pressed against her skin. She stood still and burrowed her feet down.

Chance kicked off his shoes and stood beside her. "You want to feel the ocean now?"

Ana nodded in silence and stepped out of the hole she had made. They walked to the dark water and let it lap over their toes.

"Are you happy?" he asked.

"This ranks in the top ten moments in my life. And you're a part of most of them."

He leaned down and brushed his lips against hers. The warmth from his fingers spread through her thin dress. She wouldn't have been surprised if he left handprints on her back.

She winced and doubled over from a sharp pain in her

abdomen. The blissful moment quickly ended as she clung to her side.

"Oh, ouch."

Chance's hand met hers, and his eyebrows furrowed with concern. "What's wrong?"

"My stomach. Let's go back to the room."

Without flinching, he swung her into his arms and carried her all the way back, hoping this wasn't a sign of things to come.

Chapter 14

Chance was roused from a restless sleep early the next morning. Birds began singing their song even before the sun crested the horizon and the soft footfalls of hotel employees echoed in his ears.

He checked on Ana, who lay still by his side, exhausted from her long night of stomach pain. Worried about her well-being, he threatened to call a doctor but she assured him she was okay, it was probably just her lunch that hadn't sat well. After the drama subsided, he ran down to the bar and got her some soda water, which helped, and allowed her to fall asleep. All night he lay half-asleep, checking her temperature, making sure she was on the mend. Having her warm body curled up by his side would have been enjoyable if he wasn't so concerned for her health.

He slipped from the bed, leaving her undisturbed. He checked his watch. It was just after five in the morning. The bus tour was scheduled to pick them up at eight. After he glanced once more at Ana nestled in the sheets, his shoulders slumped. They would have to reschedule, he thought, disappointed.

He darted into the bathroom and turned on the shower. Hopefully it would relieve his stress, because thinking about delaying one more day when he was so close made him crazy. The hot water that soon coursed down his body loosened his tight muscles considerably.

A soft tap on the door alerted him. He flicked off the shower and reached for his towel.

"Chance?" Ana's soft voice whispered.

"I'm sorry. I didn't mean to wake you. Do you need to use the bathroom?"

He drew the towel across his body briskly, wrapped it around his waist, leaned over and snatched up his dirty clothes. He hooked his finger around the doorknob and pulled it open to see Ana in her wrinkled sundress. If he hadn't felt badly for her, he would have chuckled at her appearance. But even with bags under her eyes and tousled hair, he considered her the most beautiful woman he had ever known.

She took one look at him and laughed behind her hand. "Your hair."

He reached up. Wet strands stuck out all over his head. As he slicked it back, a rivulet of water streamed down his spine.

"How are you?" he asked, frowning.

"Well, I've felt better but I think with a shower and a *very* light breakfast I'll be okay."

"You sure? Don't want you pushing yourself."

"My turn to take a rinse." Ana pushed past him and kissed his cheek as she went by. No doubt about it, she was stubborn, just like him.

He dressed and put his toiletries into his backpack while she was in the bathroom.

Ana emerged with a towel wrapped around her body and head, appearing a world better. The bags under her eyes were gone and there was a smile on her lips.

Chance suggested she get her belongings ready. "I'm going to run up to grab some breakfast for us and maybe some fruit and water for the road."

When he returned, he found her clothed and nearly packed. All her things were folded in neat piles on the bed. "Ugh! I've got my essentials packed, but now I'm trying to get my dirty clothes back in. How'd you do it? Roll them?"

Chance chuckled and sauntered over, setting an armload of food and water bottles onto the bed. "I dunno. I guess I used the cram-them-in-with-brute-force method," he said as he offered her a plate with fruit and yogurt. "A light breakfast, as requested."

They sat on the bed and ate in silence. Chance was too excited to talk. When they were done, they grabbed their things and headed out into the morning sunlight.

It was approaching eight in the morning when Chance strode up to the front desk to talk to the same woman who had arranged the tour for them. When she saw him, she beamed. "Hello, *señor*. How may I help you?"

"We need to check out." He pulled out a handful of money as she printed their bill and kept his eyes outside, searching for their tour bus. Then, hand in hand, he and Ana walked out into the sun and waited for their ride.

The large palm fronds nearby rustled in a soft breeze. Chance breathed in a lungful of humid tropical air and let it seep out slowly. His skin drank in the sun's rays and quickly grew hot to the touch.

A white van drove up to the hotel entrance. The passenger door opened and a man stepped out and

101

grinned at them. "*Hola*. Are you waiting for the Ek Balam tour?"

Ana touched Chance's arm and he glanced nervously at her before answering. "Yes, hello. I'm Chance Morgan and this is Ana Hughes. We're ready to go."

"Welcome. Please take a seat and we will be on our way." The man opened the side door and waved them inside. Another couple was sitting in the back and smiled at them as they climbed in and set their backpacks down.

The man shut the door and jumped into the passenger seat. He lifted a microphone to his lips and turned to face them. "My name is Miguel, and I will be your guide today. This is our driver, Joseph, and he will get us safely to the ruins of Ek Balam." His dark eyes sparkled as his round cheeks lifted into a joyful grin. It appeared that he truly enjoyed his job.

The van glided along the curvy drive until they turned onto the highway. Miguel continued in an almost singsong voice. "We will be going to the ruins of Ek Balam today, which is not as visited as its more popular cousins, Chichen Itza or Tulum. Let me first begin to tell you about the Mayan peoples," he said and paused to look at each of them. "The Mayan civilization lived and thrived in the Yucatán Peninsula for around three thousand years until their sudden collapse in the ninth century. No one knows why this happened.

"The Maya had their own writing system, and it is now believed they may have even invented writing in Mesoamerica. They also had a deep understanding of mathematics, which allowed them to chart the stars and planets far better than anyone else at that time."

He paused to wink at Ana, who rubbed her chin against her shoulder and shyly kept her eyes down. "This allowed them to create a highly accurate calendar. The sky meant many things to the Maya. They followed the seasons by watching the stars and movement of the sun and they thought the night sky was a window to the supernatural. They believed the universe was divided into many layers and that the crust of the earth was a thin layer separating the living from the spirit world - the Underworld, or *Xibalba*. The Maya thought the doorways to the Underworld were through caves in the earth. The last level was the heavens, where the gods lived."

Miguel paused, patted his brow with a white cloth and tucked it into the front pocket of his shirt. Chance glanced out the window at the wilderness darting by his window. Although he was interested in learning more about the Maya, he was having a hard time focusing on what their guide was saying. Too many thoughts were bouncing around his mind.

It didn't look quite as lush as he had imagined or as green as he remembered in Niyol's memories. But then, Summer was over, clearly, the rainy season hadn't started yet.

Ana slipped her fingers through his and he stared at her thin, pale, delicate hand. He gave it a squeeze and hoped he wasn't putting her in harm's way.

"The Maya were once thought to be peaceful but we know that is not wholly true. They were known for warfare as well and some think they were barbarians from the bloodletting and sacrificial ceremonies they held. It is important to understand why the Maya did this.

"They valued life, and this is why they offered blood and human lives to the gods. This is possibly why they waged war. Kings would take opposing rulers captive, torture and kill them for sacrifice to the gods. It was believed offering up blood would give you divine powers."

Chance shared a glance with Ana and ventured to ask, "Did the Maya think people and animals were linked or had special powers?"

Miguel beamed at him in response, clearly pleased to have an interested audience. He nodded and answered. "*Si*, the Maya believed that every person had an animal companion spirit. When you were born, the same soul was placed in an animal's body. They believed that some could transform into their animal companion. A king had the animal companion of the jaguar and so wore jaguar pelts. It was a sign of leadership. There was even a jaguar god of the underworld. Because jaguars walked at night— the time of the dead—they could travel from the earthly plane to the spirit world. Does that answer your question?"

Chance swallowed and nodded. "Yes, thanks."

Ana's grip tightened on his hand as she whispered to him. "That's so cool."

For another couple hours they drove into the center of the peninsula and deeper through the jungle. Chance watched out the window as he listened to Miguel speak, trying to catch sight of anything interesting. He stared at the pavement when he realized there wouldn't be any ruins visible from the highway.

Ana's fingers traced the lines of his hand, which made him relax into his seat. He wondered how she knew what to do to calm him. He was thankful she was with him. Right now. One minute he wished she had stayed home and the next, he was happy she was by his side.

The van slowed as they turned off the highway and Chance slid forward to try to get a better view. As they drove along the narrow road, he felt blood rush through his tense body and he pinched his lips together.

Ana's eyes sparked with excitement. "Almost there."

On the heels of her comment, Miguel switched on his microphone and turned to his passengers. "We will be at Ek Balam momentarily. We will park and then you will get to view this beautiful city with your own eyes. I will give you a tour and then you will have time to explore by yourself. You will have the freedom to explore the grounds, unlike the tourists at Chichen Itza, but please do not wander into the forest. There may yet be more ruins to find in our jungles but we wish for our guests to stay safe."

The couple in the back seat started shuffling around, gathering up their things. Chance lifted his backpack onto his lap. Ana did the same and rested her cheek to the sack as she hugged it.

"How are you doing? You feeling okay?" Chance asked, noting faint bags under her eyes once again.

She shrugged and grinned weakly. "Yeah, I'm okay. Just a little tired after the long night."

"Let me know at any point if you need to rest."

A muffled chiming noise came from her pocket and she extracted her phone. After she glanced at it, she slapped her hand to her forehead. "Oh, I never called Mom. Looks like I've missed a couple calls from her. I'm not getting good reception here. I'll try texting her when we're done with the tour."

The driver pulled onto a short driveway and into a small parking lot. Miguel jumped from his seat and opened the sliding door for his passengers. Ana stepped out first and Chance followed close behind. They flung their backpacks over their shoulders as their tour guide held his hands up and said, "You may keep your packs in the van if you wish. The driver will remain with the vehicle."

"Oh, no thanks. We prefer keeping our things with us." Chance replied.

The other couple climbed from the van, stretched, and slipped their cameras around their necks. Miguel clapped his hands together and bobbed on his heals. "Are you ready to learn about Ek Balam? Let us go!"

He had them wait for a few minutes as he went to pay for their tickets and returned ready to lead them, beckoning them forward. Chance noticed there weren't many people around, only a few tourists and locals milling along the trail.

The peaceful quiet was interrupted by Miguel's cheerful voice. "It is a pleasure to introduce you to Ek Balam, otherwise known as the Black Jaguar city."

Chance's spine tingled as the words soaked in. Miguel

led them along a dirt path tinged orange from the clay soil. Tall, wiry trees rose above them, providing patchy cover from the ascending sun. Its rays touched Chance's skin, kissing it with warmth yet the heat didn't feel stifling, as he'd expected.

"Excuse me, Miguel. I heard it was supposed to be really hot inland."

Without turning, their guide said, "Oh, yes. During the summer months, it is quite hard for most tourists to bear. It's away from the ocean breeze. But you are visiting us at the perfect time—in between the hot and the rainy seasons."

As he followed behind Ana, Chance sensed the wildlife around them, watching from behind the trees and bushes, peering at them as they passed by. "The Mayan people's most respected tree is the Ceiba tree. If you look up you will see the umbrella shaped crowns. Their fruit has a fiber in it like cotton that was used to make clothing. It is also used as a medicine plant, and is considered to have a connection to all three levels of the universe: the heavens, home to the gods; earth, where all living things exist; and lastly, the underworld, where the dead roam."

Miguel gestured to his side and some broad leafy trees. "And these are Copal trees. The Maya use their resin as incense in ceremonies and rituals. It is very sacred to them. Maize was also very important. You may know it as corn. Although it cannot be found at the ruins now, the surrounding villages do still grow it. It has always been an important food source to the Maya, and

Mayan folklore says the gods created us out of maize. Here we are."

As they emerged from the forest, they passed by a broken stone wall and into a grassy section. Large structures rose ahead of them and Chance marveled at their condition.

"This is the outer wall, which was not thought to be protection, but was built for ceremonial reasons. You will also see the 'white roads' that lead into the city. The Maya traveled at night to avoid the heat, so they created roads made of crushed shells and limestone that glowed white in the dark." Miguel walked past the low wall and into a center clearing.

"Many of the buildings were first built around three hundred to one hundred BC. At the city's population height, somewhere around nine hundred AD, it mysteriously shrank to a tiny fraction of what it was in the post-classical period, like so many other Maya cities. No one knows why. It is a mystery."

Miguel pointed to a set of buildings and said, "These are known as 'The Twins'. Two mirroring temples. And to the center, we have the oval palace."

Chance was disappointed. Nothing Miguel had pointed out looked familiar. He'd been waiting—hoping— to recognize something from one of his grandfather's memories. Panic set in as he considered the possibility he had led them in the wrong direction. *What if we're in the wrong place?* But his grandfather's note had specified Ek Balam.

While their guide spoke animatedly about the once

great Mayan city, Ana's soft voice carried to his ears. "Don't worry, Chance. We'll find him. Try to enjoy yourself."

Her lips grazed his shoulder and he glanced down at her, his own eyes meeting her sparkling green ones, and his anxiety subsided. "We are in Mexico. Mexico, Chance."

He nodded and dropped his head. Noises from the jungle engulfed his senses. Miguel's accented voice faded away, replaced by chattering sounds from nearby monkeys and percussion from the leaves and foliage. With each breath he took, the living habitat around him sighed in rhythm. He felt his grandfather with him in that moment, encouraging his meditative state.

A familiar floral scent breezed past his nose and he lifted his head. Ana's back was to him as she followed behind their tour guide. Their small group began climbing up a tall series of steps. The pyramid-like structure rose high above the trees. Chance darted to catch up, and took only seconds to join Ana. He placed a kiss on her warm shoulder.

"This is the Acropolis. It is one of the tallest pyramids in the Yucatán. Ek Balam flourished for around one thousand years, when most other Mayan cities only peaked for less than ten years. This was an important Mayan epicenter. As we work our way up—" Miguel panted and continued "—you will notice thatched roofs, which protect the stucco sculptures from the rain and sun. It is rare to find stucco sculptures. These are intact because over a thousand years ago, when Chichen Itza became such a large important cultural center, the Maya buried the Acropolis to preserve it."

Miguel led them under an awning and into the shade. His mouth opened into a bright smile as he bobbed on his heels. "This is the tomb of Ek Balam's greatest leaders. It's known as 'The Throne' and the jaguar altar. The doorway is an opened jaguar's mouth—you can see the teeth there." He pointed proudly.

Large rounded white stones pointed upward, and appeared just like a gaping maw. Hieroglyphs were carved into the pale stone that surrounded a dark doorway at the center. Chance's eyes caught on winged figures that stood on pedestals and he pointed them out to Ana.

Miguel noticed and said, "You will see Mayan winged warriors, or guardians, protecting their king. They are a rare find. Archeologists haven't found many Mayan angels."

Chance let his eyes comb over the vines and trees that encroached the long deserted city while they slowly moved up the stairs. Finally they reached the top that overlooked the vast jungle.

"On a clear day you can see Coba and Chichen Itza from the top of this tower. You may also notice trees covering mounds throughout the jungle. They are unexcavated ruins."

As the tour concluded, their guide invited them to explore alone. Ana and Chance stayed at the top of the pyramid and sat on the steps, side by side.

"Now what?" Chance said. "I almost thought it would

be easy. Like I would have a memory or Balam would step out of the jungle and introduce himself."

His shoulders dropped as he flicked a pebble with his finger and watched it tumble down the stone steps.

Ana squinted in the light and pinched her lips together. "I'm not sure. But, I don't think you should give up after one try. I know we're close. We're closer than we were in Idaho."

She stood, wiped dirt off her backside and started down the stairs. Glancing back at him, she cocked her eyebrow and asked, "You coming? Let's see about getting some *real* Mexican food. I don't know about you but I could eat."

As soon as she mentioned food, his stomach growled hungrily. "Yeah, that sounds good. Guess thinking on an empty stomach won't get me far."

Ana went down the steps two at a time, and Chance sped past her, laughing when he got to the bottom. It took her a few minutes to catch up and they walked back down the path to the entrance of the ruins. The parking lot only had a few cars in it and they stopped to glance around in an effort to spot any locals.

A young man around their age was just stepping away from the ticket booth in the direction of the road when Chance jogged ahead and called out. "*Señor*, excuse me!"

The dark haired man turned to face them and Ana scurried forward with a shy expression. He grinned apprehensively back at them and his cheek dimpled. Chance listened as Ana spoke easily in Spanish. He was impressed with how quickly she'd settled into the job of interpreter. Although she wasn't fluent, it was obvious she had an ear for language. She had no difficulty asking about finding authentic Mexican food. With a modest wave of the hand, she indicated him and said, "*Dónde podemos conseguir comida Mexicana auténtica?*"

Chance watched as the stranger's eyes lingered at the neck of his shirt. Ana seemed to notice as well and she touched the jade jaguar pendant that hung around his neck. "*Estamos buscando familia. Un hombre que se llama Balam.*"

The man nodded and said, "*Hola, mi nombre es Dario. Vengan conmigo.*"

Ana said to Chance, "His name's Dario and I told him we're looking for a man named Balam."

Chance and Ana introduced themselves, shook his hand and he started walking, waving at them to follow.

"He wants us to follow him. Shouldn't we tell Miguel we aren't sticking around?" Ana asked as she scanned the entrance and parking lot for their guide.

Chance indicated the white van they came in. Their driver sat under a tree near the vehicle, eating his lunch.

Ana called out to their new acquaintance. "*Un momento por favor*, Dario."

Chance walked Ana over to the resting driver and waited as she communicated to him their plans. At first, he seemed to be confused, but then he looked over to Dario, who was waiting for them at the edge of the lot and he gave a single nod.

As they jogged to catch up with Dario, Ana said under her breath, "What about later? A place to stay?"

"I saw some hotels not too far back in that town we passed. We'll just get a taxi or pay someone to take us there. But hopefully we'll find Balam instead." Although Chance was starting to doubt they would ever find him.

When they got to Dario, he turned around to give another dimpled grin, but this time it was directed at Ana. Chance was relieved that she seemed oblivious of his attention. Dario mumbled something Chance couldn't understand and started down the gravel road. His lanky body moved ahead of them at a quick pace. Chance stared at his back while they walked behind him and he opened up his senses. Besides the sounds of the birds and bustling wildlife, he sensed nothing to alarm him. He decided they must not be in danger and let worry fall to the wayside.

After about fifteen minutes of walking, Chance checked in with Ana, who had kept up with his pace the whole time. Her fingers gripped her backpack as she leaned forward in a rhythmic walk, but she looked pale. "You holding up okay?"

A ring of sweat encircled her forehead and her muscles flexed with effort. Her emerald eyes crinkled as she cleared her throat. "I dunno. I thought I was hungry earlier, but I think my stomachache is coming back. Maybe water will help."

She reached behind her and slipped a water bottle out of the mesh side pocket of her pack.

Dario noticed they stopped, turned around and walked back to them. He said something to Ana, who responded and rubbed her stomach. Their conversation ended and he touched her elbow with a sympathetic frown.

"He says it's just a little further and that his grandmother's a healer. She should be able to help me," Ana said when Chance looked at her questioningly.

After another ten long minutes of walking—more slowly now—some narrow roads and modest buildings came into view. Dario pointed ahead once more. Chance hoped they were close because Ana wasn't holding up very well.

Their guide turned down a dusty road and his pace picked up. A gathering of people came into view and soon Dario disappeared into the crowd. They were all clothed in white and Chance noted that none of the men or women had on shoes. As they welcomed the newest arrival into the fold, words of greeting were exclaimed and then a hush fell as they noticed the two unfamiliar faces.

Chapter 15

Ana's stomach rumbled nervously as she stepped back toward Chance, who moved forward to block her from view. Although she was the one with bilingual skills, she was happy to let him take the lead in this new situation.

The assembly stared at them and Ana felt like a shiny pimple at the end of a nose. Dario reemerged and said a few words and the sea of people stepped forward with hands outstretched.

"*Hola, muchas gracias.*" Chance stammered as a particularly jovial man slapped him on the back.

Ana had never been surrounded by so many welcoming strangers before. She felt awkward, standing around in her travel clothes in an ocean of white and cream. Her cheeks flushed as she realized they must have come while they were celebrating a special occasion. Hands touched her back and she turned to find a pair of chocolate brown eyes staring up at her. A little girl stood with her face turned up in wide-eyed fascination.

She whispered a greeting to the child, who giggled and slipped her soft delicate fingers into Ana's hand. They were led into a clearing and Dario walked up to an old woman and whispered in her ear. Her eyes combed over Ana, then Chance, and hesitated at the pendant around his neck.

When the woman walked up to them, Ana was struck by her creased hazel eyes and the purity reflected back at her. Waves of charcoal hair wove around the older woman's head. Her dark, wrinkled skin was supple up close, not leathery as Ana would have imagined. The elderly woman said something that didn't sound quite like Spanish.

Stomach cramps revisited her, and memories of the previous night gave her cold sweats. The woman noticed Ana grasp her side.

"Where is your pain?"

Unable to stop holding her breath, Ana pointed at her abdomen. The elderly woman touched Ana's forehead and promptly walked off.

Chance wrapped his arm around her and asked, "Is it getting worse, Ana? We should've stayed at the hotel. I knew you weren't better. Do you think they have a doctor around here?"

"No, I think help's coming." She grimaced while clinging to his shirt.

Minutes later the old woman's familiar face settled in front of her, and she held out a cup filled with a cloudy drink.

Chance took the cup from her hands. "What is it?"

He sniffed at it and eyed the elderly woman while Ana asked the question again, but this time in Spanish. The woman kept her gaze on Ana and said, "It will help your stomachache. It is medicine—it will make you feel better. Please." She guided the cup to Ana, who clutched it tightly.

"I don't know, Ana. Who is this woman? We don't even know what's in the cup." Chance peered at the drink with a frown.

Ana lifted the cup to her nose and took a deep breath. The citrus-y smell seemed harmless enough, but there really was no telling. Not unless she drank it. Ana stared at the deeply lined face of the elderly woman before her and made a decision. She would trust her. Without hesitation, she lifted the drink to her lips. Lemon flavored water washed through her mouth and she gulped it down fast. The wave of liquid hit her churning stomach acids and she could almost imagine the licking flames of a fire being put out. She emptied the cup and handed it back to the woman, who patted her hand.

"Are you okay? You'd tell me if you felt worse, right?" Chance moved in closer, protectively. He wrapped his arms around her and she leaned against him for support. Ana nodded, sank into his warm body and let the drink take effect. To her relief, over the course of a few minutes, the pain subsided.

"Good? Yes?" the woman asked in Spanish.

Ana nodded. "Much better. Thank you so much for your help. My name is Ana, and this is Chance."

"I am Grandmother Sanchia." Her eyes traced their faces and she said to Ana, "I am glad you are well."

Ana faced the plump woman. "How did you make..." She paused, unsure what the word for remedy was and said, instead, "Drink."

Sanchia's chin lifted with pride and she spoke so fast, Ana's mind reeled. Half of what tumbled from the woman's mouth, Ana barely understood. From what she gathered, the woman's mother was a healer and had taught her everything she knew. The town had no doctor, but she was called on to provide natural remedies for the sick. However, this was only a small amount she was able to understand. Ana must have worn a puzzled expression, because Sanchia stopped rattling on and then grasped her hand. A frown crossed her face and she appeared confused for a moment. Then she said, with excitement in her voice, "I will show you. But first, you eat."

Banana leaves heaped with tamales, beans and potatoes were handed to both her and Chance. Amazingly, the stomachache that had plagued her along the walk was only a distant memory now and she was ready to eat.

She was overwhelmed by the generosity and kindness of the strangers. Although she didn't know them, she was beginning to feel at ease. After a sideways glance at Chance, she saw the sentiment mirrored in his face. They sat down beside each other on the ground like the locals were doing, and began to eat with a little encouragement from Sanchia and a few watchful women. Ana's eyes slid shut as she tasted the first mouthful. Had Eva been there with her, she was confident she would have begged for the recipe now that she was a budding chef. The tamales fell apart at her touch, and steam billowed from the meaty center. Before she knew it, she had cleared her plate. Ana blushed when she noticed she was being watched. A group of elderly women were giving her toothy smiles and laughing as they patted their bellies. Horrified, Ana set her plate on the ground and let her hair fall around her face so she could hide from her audience.

Despite her shyness, she murmured in Spanish. "Thank you for the delicious food."

Sanchia beamed in response and rose to her feet, her toes gripping the dry earth. Her raspy voice said a word Ana recognized. "Come."

Ana was curious and a little apprehensive. She glanced over to Chance, who was just finishing his plate of food and was having a conversation consisting of sign language and choppy Spanish with a man who was fascinated with his jaguar pendant. She leaned over and said, "I'll be right back. Sanchia wants to take me somewhere."

Chance's eyes narrowed but a second later he nodded and watched her stand up to leave. "Be careful. Don't be long unless you want me making a scene."

The short, stout woman turned and walked past the celebrants. Ana tried to keep up, but Sanchia was deceptively fast. She reached the edge of the gathering and squinted in confusion. Where did she go?

A throat cleared and Ana was surprised to discover the elderly woman hidden in the wilderness off the road. "Come."

Ana hesitated, unsure if she should follow. She gave one last look at the party and stepped into the greenery where she discovered a narrow, worn path. As she moved along the trail, the glow of the sun obscured and shadows slanted across the wilderness. "Hello? Grandmother Sanchia?"

She took a few steps more and saw Sanchia's hunched silhouette at a tree. Ana wandered a little further. Sanchia lowered herself down and her hands fluttered around a plant that grew close to the ground.

"For stomach pain." Sanchia grasped at Ana's arm and straightened up. A smile crept across the older woman's lips. Then something scratched against Ana's hand as green leaves were thrust into her palm.

Sanchia pressed her thumb into her palm in a crushing motion and said some words Ana wasn't familiar with. From the gestures and the words she did understand, it was clear the instructions were to crush and drink with water and lemon.

"Thank you," Ana said.

They were only a short distance from the gathering so she could hear stringed instruments and melodious voices rise in a beautiful chorus. Sanchia shuffled past her and up to a tree. She unwound a red cloth belt from her waist and hung it from a branch. Ana couldn't understand what she was doing but didn't want to ask. When no explanation was offered, she shrugged and followed the woman back to the party.

Ana looked at Sanchia and the people around her. It was clear they lived extremely modest lives. Ana thought about her home in Idaho. It truly felt as if she was a world away, but she saw the happiness on the faces of the locals and was touched. As they made their way past what seemed like an entire village of people, they walked into a clearing where a beautiful altar stood. Each of the four uprights were wound with aromatic flowers.

Sanchia started speaking so quickly in Spanish, Ana wasn't sure she understood everything, but she did understand this was a wedding celebration. The couple had been joined earlier. She was standing in front of the wedding altar, each point of which was important. North had red flowers; east yellow; south, purple; and west, white.

Ana touched the native flora bound to the ceremonial altar and breathed in each flower's scent. The woman was pleased and began introducing her to everyone they passed. Hoots and hollers came from the road and soon music filled the air. A group of men, young and old, were playing instruments and singing as they strode around the party.

A scruffy dog skirted around the boundaries of the gathering, sniffing the air. Ana found a dirty tortilla on the ground and threw it to the stray. The creature watched the yellow disc land, but kept its attention on her. As she and Sanchia walked back to where Chance sat, the dog trailed along the edges of the wilderness, its wide eyes glued to Ana's every movement. She studied the animal briefly, and decided it wasn't anything to worry about. She had already seen countless dogs roadside on their drive through Cancun and the small towns.

"Chance, did you know this is a wedding party?"

He turned around and said, "Is that why everyone's wearing white? Everybody's so friendly here. I've been asking about the jaguar pendant grandfather left me. I don't know what they're saying and I'm not sure they know what I'm asking. Can you help me out?"

Ana lowered herself beside him and muttered a hello at the group of people sitting with him, who displayed their bright teeth in a friendly response. Sanchia stood back and watched quietly.

"Is there a man named Balam here?" she asked.

A chorus replied. "Yes, he is over there."

Ana translated for Chance, who jumped to his feet, his expression growing instantly serious. He began to walk in the direction the locals had indicated and Ana scrambled to his side, grabbing his hand.

"Let's meet him together," she said.

Chance nodded absently in response, squinted and stared into a group of older men. They turned to face him and spoke words of greeting. A round, stout man stepped forward, stretching out his hand. Ana looked to Chance, who beamed at the older gentleman and introduced himself. Her heart raced in excitement as she watched them shake hands. Balam didn't look anything like what she expected. His short stature and plump form wasn't similar to Chance's or Niyol's. She stared at the man's tanned face and his dark coffee hued eyes. Then she knew.

Frowning, she checked Chance's face. He swallowed hard and nodded absently as he scratched his forehead. He forced another grin before shaking the man's hand again and waving goodbye. She knew him too well. His disappointment was clear. Ana slipped her fingers through his and let her chin settle on his shoulder as she said softly, "That wasn't *our* Balam."

Chance shook his head and sighed. Ana let her hands rest on his chest and felt him relax a bit.

"He'll find you, Chance. Remember what your grandfather wrote?" She uttered the word she hoped he wouldn't bristle at. "*Patience*."

After a few moments he said, "We're at a party, right? Let's have fun."

Afternoon rolled into evening and the fiesta continued without any sign of ending. Ana and Chance were offered a limitless supply of food, which neither turned down, although after her third helping, Ana had to sit back and rest.

The stray dog she saw earlier ventured close and stood beside them. It stared straight into her eyes and lifted its muzzle into the air, nostrils flared.

"Hi, sweetie. Do you have a home?" Ana held out her hand to the scruffy creature. Its gaze fixed on her face. The dog leaned forward and touched its cold, wet nose to her skin. She ran her fingers through its wiry fur and rubbed at its cheeks and neck.

"Found yourself a new friend?" Chance said. "It likes you. Guess you have a thing for dogs."

"They're just so loyal and sweet," she said while the animal closed its eyes.

Sanchia, who had been watching, said, "That is a new stray. It won't even come eat my special tamales." Resentment was etched on her lined face.

Chance muttered from behind, "I think I need to learn some Spanish. I barely know what everyone's saying." He planted a kiss on the top of Ana's head and jumped to his feet. As he brushed the dirt from his shorts Ana looked to her side and noticed the dog had disappeared. Her eyes combed past the broad-leafed bushes, seeking out its dark eyes, but found nothing.

"If you're feeling better, we should try to find a place to stay, or get a ride to a hotel or something. The sun's going down. I'm gonna go mime to some of the guys I was talking to, see if they can't help us out." He put his hands up to his cheek in a sleeping gesture. Then he added, with a roll of his eyes, "I guess you could ask, too."

Ana watched him saunter off into a crowd of laughing young men. He was the tallest one at the party and his blue shirt stuck out against everyone's white clothes. He looked like an indigo macaw surrounded by a sea of white cockatoos.

Sanchia watched him go too. Ana felt almost bad asking for more help, but she knew there was no way around it. They needed to find a place to stay.

Ana took a deep breath and said, "Grandmother Sanchia? My friend and I need a place to stay tonight. Is there a hotel nearby?"

Sanchia's eyes crinkled as she answered. "No."

Oh, no. What will we do? Ana imagined them lying on the jungle floor to sleep. She could almost feel the spiders and snakes crawling on her and she shuddered.

"You stay with me, child." Grandmother Sanchia brushed her arm.

Ana was touched by her kindness—by everyone's in the town. She couldn't imagine inviting someone she didn't know into her home—she would be too afraid— but the people here didn't seem to think twice about sharing, even though they didn't have a lot.

Ana's cheek quivered and she exhaled sharply. "Much thanks."

Loud voices broke the pleasant choral murmur of the townspeople. Women and children moved back, and most of the men jumped up and pushed forward toward the disturbance. Sanchia's face clouded over and she shooed Ana back into a group of young kids.

What was going on? And where had Chance gone?

She urgently searched the crowd for his towering head and blue shirt. He was nowhere to be found. After a sidelong glance at the worried elderly woman, Ana slipped away. She needed to find him. Where was he?

Ana ran back to the dusty road they'd walked in on, where a crowd of men had now gathered in a circle.

Another shout rang out. "Go. Leave here."

A throng of women eyed the disturbance from the side, pulling their children back. The light, cheerful mood of the party had quickly changed.

Ana continued to seek out Chance, her heart pounding in her chest. He would never leave her. So where was he?

"Leave these people alone," she heard a familiar voice say.

Fear tore through her body. She rushed forward and cut in front of the cluster of women and children, who glanced at her and made room.

Three darkly dressed men stood on the terra cotta road. Another man, clothed in white, lay with his back on the ground. A starburst of dirt stained the stark white shoulder of his dress shirt, and blood trickled from a cut on his brow. Chance had positioned himself between the outsiders and the man on the road.

"Chance," she whispered.

Ana saw his eyes flick to the side and she knew he had heard her.

"You have a funny looking gringo protecting you now?" one of the outsiders sneered and then snickered with his friends.

"Why weren't we invited? You invite strangers but not us?" another chimed in.

Ana knew Chance couldn't understand them, but you wouldn't have known it. His unyielding stance and narrowed eyes said everything. It was obvious these men were trouble.

Chance held his ground and a hardness crept into his eyes. She had seen that look before. It scared her then and it worried her now. It hadn't taken long for them to find danger.

"You need to leave. Go away and don't come back." Chance pointed and spat his words with such venom, Ana wouldn't have been surprised if they'd turned and left.

"Oh, does he think he's a Mayan? Well, then maybe he should just disappear." A broad-chested man with a gray baseball hat flexed his muscles and stepped toward Chance.

One of the other troublemakers leaned down and grabbed a rock. He pulled his arm back, poised to throw it at Chance. Just then, the stray appeared out of nowhere, its eyes on the intruders.

"You're all just Mayan dogs." The man with the stone turned and threw it instead, at the dog.

Ana could see the canine's muscles were pulled tight; it was poised to move away. She also saw the little girl who had so sweetly welcomed her to the party hours ago standing just behind the animal. As the dog dashed away, avoiding the launched attack, Ana rushed in front of the little girl and blocked her, her back facing the intruders. The stone whacked her mid-back, just missing her spine.

"Ah!" she exclaimed.

The pain wasn't too bad, though. The women rushed forward to absorb the little girl into the fold. Their muttered words of thanks were barely audible as they moved further back and away from the scene.

Ana turned around to face the men. Their eyes widened in surprise. Clearly, they'd been thrown off by the unexpected turn of events. The hairs on the back of her arms rose as she felt their lascivious stares trace over her exposed skin.

Chance stepped forward and said, "Leave. I won't ask again."

The man who lay in the dirt had been still the whole time, but now scrambled to his feet and stumbled back into the crowd. Ana watched anxiously as the confrontation escalated and she hoped for a peaceful end. She didn't want anyone to get hurt. Or for Chance to get agitated enough to shapeshift in front of the crowd.

***

The looks these guys were giving Ana made Chance's ears burn. *You can't shapeshift here. No matter what.* It took all his self-control not to try phasing into a bear and tearing them apart. Although, he did imagine doing it for a moment, which made him smirk wickedly.

The men pulled together and spoke in undertones, but Chance could guess what they were saying. And he didn't like it. Regret consumed his thoughts. He wished he had left Ana at home in Idaho. Maybe she would have been safe there. He closed his eyes and heard Niyol saying, *Chance, focus. You can do this.*

He glanced at the intruders. One had kept quiet and seemed to be along for the ride. Thin set and shorter than the rest, he watched everything that was transpiring from under thick brows. Chance decided to avoid wasting his efforts on him. He'd probably run away, given the opportunity.

The second man, the rock thrower, had attacked from a distance. He must not be good at hand-to-hand fighting, or he was afraid of getting his hands dirty. If it came to blows, Chance would start with him. He'd knock him down quickly so he could focus on the last man.

The instigator of it all, the Bull, Chance had named him, was trouble. He had broad shoulders, sledgehammers for fists and he seemed to be itching for a fight. The hunger in his eyes reminded Chance of Markus. He looked power hungry, full of ego, and it seemed the townspeople knew who he was.

Hopefully, it wouldn't come to blows but he had no intention of breaking his promise to keep Ana safe from harm.

Laughter erupted and The Bull spoke up but Chance couldn't understand a single word. Many of the onlookers' eyes widened and the women who were left snatched their children and scurried away. He glanced back at Ana, who had paled and stumbled backward.

The men advanced, their fiery gazes focused on her. It was time to act.

Chance leapt, striking the rock thrower square in the jaw and he fell back with a stunned expression on his face. Adrenaline pounded through Chance's veins and euphoria boosted his confidence.

Wind whistled in his ears and he ducked just in time. A balled fist arched past him. He exhaled sharply and cocked his head to the side just as something hard impacted his nose, thrusting him off his feet.

The sounds around him became obscured and ringing filled his ears. Disoriented and woozy, Chance attempted to shake it off, but a flurry of movement sent dirt directly into his eyes, blinding him.

C'mon, get up—get up! You're faster than them, you can do this.

Chance scrambled onto his belly and pushed himself upright. He shook his head, which only made him more dizzy, so he brushed the grit from his eyes and found the Bull poised in front of him, ready to strike again. He muttered something at Chance and sneered so that his mustache became a slanted line.

"Whatever. You can take your pencil mustache and go."

Something wet tickled Chance's lips and he spit the metallic taste from his mouth. Air passage slowed as his nose swelled shut. The pain brought tears to his eyes.

The Bull swung again at Chance but this time he saw it

coming and danced to the side. With effort, Chance slowed his movement, hooked his foot around the man's ankle and gave a sharp tug. It sent the Bull off balance and he fell onto the gravel with a grunt.

By this time, the rock thrower had drawn himself off the ground and joined his silent friend. Chance started toward them just as a stone whirled through the air and connected with his temple.

Damn it! Now the heat that radiated from his nose connected with the sting at the side of his head. His pain translated into anger. A storm raged inside him and he fought to remain human. The dark eyes and long claws of the grizzly bear toiled in his mind. It would be so much easier to let the animal within him settle this. So much easier if he could shift.

A growl rumbled deep in his chest as he propelled himself at his attacker. The rock thrower's eyes widened and he stumbled back a step just as Chance collided with him. They plummeted into the scrub at the side of the road.

Even in the twilight, a glint of fear shone in the man's face and Chance quelled his impulse to shapeshift. Movement from the road drew his attention. A few townsmen stepped forward, led by the man who'd been thrown into the dirt. They gave each other nervous glances as they approached and started speaking in low tones to the Bull and his friend. Their comments became more and more animated and they pointed down the road.

The rock thrower adjusted beneath Chance's weight

as he surveyed the agitated men. Chance took advantage of his distraction and pressed his forearm against the man's neck. "Go," Chance said through gritted teeth. Stray dirt in his mouth crunched under the pressure.

"*Sí.*"

Finally, a word he understood. The rock thrower nodded and extracted himself from under Chance. He turned without a second look and joined his compatriot, who was backing down the road.

The Bull watched his sidekicks disappear on the darkened street and gave a shout. "*Qué pasa?*" Then he grumbled a word Chance assumed was a curse. Rising slowly and standing tall, the disgruntled, dusty man grimaced at him. In one smooth movement, Chance jumped to his feet and pointed at the backs of the retreating men.

The Bull lifted his chin, blew a kiss to Ana, and strolled casually down the road as though he didn't have a care in the world. When he was about fifty feet away, some of the men walked up to Chance and slapped him on the shoulder.

"*Eso fue una estupidez, pero muchas gracias.*" The men laughed.

Stupid and thank you. That was about all he'd gleaned from what they said, and he figured stupid was about right. However he hadn't been able to just stand on the sidelines and watch these people being bullied. And when they'd threatened Ana's safety, all bets had been off.

A familiar voice cut through the crowd. Ana emerged with glistening eyes. With a strangled sob, she wrapped her arms around his neck. "You okay? I was so scared," she said in his ear. Moisture collected around the collar of his shirt, and wet eyelashes brushed against his neck.

He pulled away to look at her. The makeup around her eyes was smudged and her cheek was quivering.

"All it'll take is a quick shift to heal. Don't worry about me, Ana. How about you? How's your back?"

"It was nothing, but your face..." She shrugged off her backpack and rifled around until she found what she was looking for. Gently, she dabbed at his temple and nose with a handkerchief.

Chance winced at her touch and took the cloth from her. It was best he take care of his own injuries. He didn't like her seeing him in pain and he wanted to survey the damage for himself in a mirror. A huge swollen lump that no longer resembled a nose protruded from the middle of his face. If he had to guess, he would say it was broken. It burned, his vision was blurry and between his nose and temple, he had a splitting headache.

Momentarily disoriented from the pain, he hadn't noticed the elderly woman walk up to them. She stood beside Ana and, patting her arm, said something to her and walked away.

"Come on, let's go. We're staying with Sanchia tonight and I think she's got a remedy for your injuries. Grab your stuff. That's enough excitement for tonight."

Chance and Ana slipped their heavy packs on and followed after their host. As Chance walked along, his physical pain couldn't compare to his disappointment. *I just traveled hundreds of miles to get punched in the face and I didn't even find Balam. Awesome.*

Chapter 16

Pillows and cushions plopped onto the floor beside the yellow, flowery threadbare couch. Chance laid a sheet over them, and then Ana unfolded the well-worn fleece blanket Sanchia had given her and tucked it onto the sofa.

"Sure you'll be comfortable on the floor?" she asked.

"It's only for one night. No worries."

Sanchia came into the small room with two pillows tucked under her arms. She handed them to Ana and patted her hand.

"*Muchas gracias*," Ana said.

"*Sí, muchas gracias.*" Chance echoed after her.

Sanchia held up her index finger and scurried out of the room into the tiny kitchen. A metallic clang and scrape followed. A moment later, she reappeared with a dishcloth and a pot.

"*Siéntate!*" she barked at Chance and pushed him onto the couch. Gingerly, she dipped the cloth into the clear liquid in the pot and pressed the towel against the cut on his forehead. It stung at first and then the discomfort dissolved into numbness. After a minute, she repeated the procedure with his nose, although it took longer to gain any form of relief there.

Chance knew recovery was only one shapeshift away, but he considered it might be wise to stay under the radar and not draw attention to himself. If his broken nose healed overnight, it would be noticed. Plus, he didn't even know if he could shapeshift if he wanted to. His nose tingled under the pressure of the cloth and he took hold of it so Sanchia could let go.

The woman walked over to the only window in the room and pulled the curtains shut. Concrete walls once painted yellow showed a few cracks but the masonry kept the room cool, which was a relief after their long day in the humidity.

"*Buenas noches*," Sanchia said before disappearing into her upstairs bedroom.

Ana called after her, "*Muchas gracias!*"

Chance kept the cloth pressed against his nose and slipped onto the floor to his lumpy makeshift bed. A small lamp at the corner of the room cast angular shadows on walls, giving everything an unfriendly feel.

Ana dropped onto the couch with a groan. "What a long day. I'm exhausted. I think I could sleep on a bag of rocks."

He couldn't contain his anxiety any longer. Now that they were alone, he had to say something. He knew she wouldn't like it. Chance pulled the towel away so she could hear him, but didn't dare look at her. "Ana, I'm not sure this was such a good idea."

"What do you mean? Because of today?"

"Of course. I worry about you. Those guys, and the way they looked at you...I didn't like it. Things could have gone a lot worse."

Chance focused on one particularly long crack in the ceiling. His jaw clenched as the men's leering faces flashed in his mind. His nose throbbed as if he'd gotten punched all over again.

"Tough. You can just put that thought right out of your mind because I'm not leaving your side. The amount of trouble you get in, I'd never see you again!"

Ana's face hovered over his and her hair tickled his cheeks. From beneath her curtain of hair, her lips grazed his, and all previous thought about her going back home dissolved.

A thump upstairs sounded and Ana drew back and giggled silently. She jumped up, turned off the light and brushed past him as she slipped into her bed on the couch.

Her voice sounded through the darkness. "It's settled. You're staying out of trouble and I'm going nowhere."

Chance grabbed for her hand and gave it a squeeze. They were equally stubborn. He knew it wasn't worth the fight. But he would have to do what she said—stay out of trouble.

"I love you." Ana whispered.

"And I, you," Chance said.

Soon, her soft rhythmic breathing told him she was fast asleep. It took him over an hour to slow his mind and allow himself to join her in dreamland.

***

Chance woke suddenly.

He sat up, disoriented. His nose throbbed for a moment as the blood rushed from his head. The same dark room enveloped them. What time was it? He reached for his phone. Five-thirty.

His ears strained to determine what woke him. Ana's soft whistles and the gentle lullaby from a breeze rustling the trees and bushes outside wouldn't have alarmed him.

The hairs on the back of his neck rose. He wasn't alone. Using his sharp vision and half-functional nose, he combed the room in search of any living creature and searched in silence until he found a trail of ants marching across the wall toward the kitchen. Besides Ana, there were no other living things in the room. Although he couldn't shake the feeling he was being watched.

Ana would be safe in the house without him. He just wanted to take a quick look around. Chance gave her a gentle kiss on the forehead, slipped his shoes on and snuck out the door.

The town was empty and still. A bat flew over his head as it cut through the night in search of food. He turned to face the outlying wilderness beyond the sleepy community.

A twig snapped and he rushed toward an overgrown trail. Once in the jungle, he paused to listen for more movement. The veins in his neck throbbed with excitement. Chance didn't know if he was chasing after a parrot or a shapeshifter but it was exhilarating. He knew he was impatient to a fault. However, this was why he had come to Mexico—to find answers.

With a tilt of his head, he honed in on the sound of breathing, and, using the skills his grandfather taught him, he crept along the pathway silent as a doe. He moved like this for at least half an hour.

After he had let Markus go free in crow form, unsure if it really was him or not, he had promised himself not to dismiss his instincts again. He wasn't sure if he was being hypersensitive now or not. However, this time, he would see it through.

Daylight crept over the horizon, waking the forest inhabitants. Chatter from the birds quickly drowned out all the other noises. He stopped and stared up into the lofty tree canopy above. Small creatures darted from branch to branch. Movement was all around him now.

Frustrated, he swiped at a bushy vine that extended in front of him. All that effort just to lose all vestige of hope.

Then something deep, so deep Chance doubted average ears would be able to pick it up, rumbled nearby. The guttural sound gained power and rose in pitch. Now he wasn't the only one that heard it. The birds above went silent for a moment before resuming their chittering.

Through the dense jungle growth, a pair of brown eyes stared at him. Far away, nearly fifty feet from where he stood, a black form stood on a mound of mossy rocks. The abnormally large jaguar leapt down and disappeared down the trail.

Chance's breath caught in his throat. His mind raced. Digging his toes into the clay earth, he propelled himself on the path as fast as he could. When he reached the rock pile, he realized the trail he had been following was white unlike the orange clay earth surrounding it. Small, crushed pieces of stone and shell littered the path. Down a slope, another screech called and Chance scrambled on.

He continued running blindly after the jaguar until he reached a high overgrown hill. Trees crowned around it protectively as if they were hiding a secret. At closer glance, he noticed it wasn't a hill but a pile of hewn stone.

The wild cat's call had come from this direction. A high vantage point could give him perspective. He began to climb the rocky mound. Footholds were easy to find. He quickly scaled the stone mass. When he reached the top, he wiped the sweat from his brow and peered down into the dense forest below.

There was plenty of movement but from small creatures, not the jaguar. He sat there for ten minutes waiting for something—anything. Every time he swallowed, his dry throat pinched and begged for water. Why had he rushed off into the jungle unprepared? Now that he stopped to think about it, he wasn't even sure where he was. He had been gone for what felt like over an hour, and now that the sun was up, the air was warm and humid. His thirst and hunger were getting the better of him. If Ana was awake, she would be wondering where he was. He hadn't even left a note for her.

A veil of dirt and vines covered the upright stone he was leaning against. There was a design on the rock. A carving. Chance used both his hands to free it of its earthen mask.

Teeth bared in warning, a jaguar's face stared back at him. He took a step back and saw the head of a jaguar with a human body perched on a throne.

Balam.

As he traced the carving with his fingers, he had a thought. What if he had been led into the jungle for a reason? To get him alone, or worse, so Ana would be defenseless.

***

Ana woke to the sound of a horn outside. She stretched and sat up, rubbing the sleep from her eyes. Expecting to poke Chance with her toes, she pulled her feet back to discover his bed was empty.

"Chance?" she called softly.

When no answer returned, she stood and walked across the tiled floor to peek into the kitchen. Sanchia had her back to her and was busy at the counter chopping something, from the sound of it.

"Good morning," Ana said as a yawn slipped out.

Sanchia turned around, beamed at her and returned the greeting. Then she scurried over to the stove and spooned out something dark into a mug. "Hot chocolate?"

"Mmmm, yes, please."

The Maya know how to start the day out right. She blew into the steaming cup and the delicious smell curled up to her nose. Ana inhaled deeply before she took a sip. It was nothing like the instant hot chocolate her mother bought at the store. It wasn't nearly as sweet or creamy, and it had a spicy kick. She took another mouthful to decide if she liked it or not. When she reached the dregs, she asked for more. "What's in it?" she asked Sanchia.

"Cinnamon, chili, honey, vanilla, cacao and water. You like?" Sanchia asked as she returned Ana's filled mug to her.

"Yes. It's delicious." Ana blew on the dark, steaming liquid and said, "Have you seen Chance?"

Sanchia shook her head.

Maybe he went for a walk to look for signs of Balam. He could have left a note, though. Just to make certain, she slipped her phone out of her pocket to see if he'd sent her a message. He hadn't but she wasn't getting good reception there, anyway. She started to get annoyed. If Chance had left willingly, he should have thought about her feelings. Of course she'd be worried about him. Especially after last night. Did that mean he'd been abducted?

What was she supposed to do now? The person that was supposed to protect her was gone. She took a deep breath to calm her nerves. It was still early so she decided she'd give him another hour before she started freaking out.

She needed something else to focus on. "Grandma Sanchia, will you teach me more about your plants? Your remedies?"

"Yes, yes."

Sanchia led Ana out the kitchen door to her backyard garden. Plants grew all along the perimeter of her crumbling cinder block wall. Leaves padded the ground, layered in a thick carpet. The elderly woman led her around and pointed out the parts of the plants: the leaves, flowers, roots and stock. Each part was used for different things. They compensated for the language barrier the best they could, using gestures when words failed them.

Absorbed with her lesson, the hour slipped by quickly. She was engrossed, inspired by Sanchia's medicinal knowledge.

As she listened, she twisted the ring Niyol gave her between her fingers. Memories surfaced of the quiet talks they'd had together when Chance was off parading around in animal form. Of how he'd believed in her. She missed Niyol. Although he hadn't been a part of her life for very long, he had made a big impact.

A pair of eyes fixed on her through a crumbling hole in the cinder block wall. They were only a couple feet from the ground and surrounded with sandy fur. Ana walked to the border, lifted herself up onto her toes and peered down. The scruffy stray stared up at her. With a yip, it trotted to the road, stopped and looked back at her.

Ana called over to Sanchia. "One minute—I'll be right back."

She knew this was unwise especially with Chance gone, but for some reason she trusted the animal. Ana walked around the wall and followed the dog. An old memory surfaced of watching *Benji* on TV with her sister and grandmother on the couch. You always knew what the dog wanted when it barked.

Ana followed the dog with caution as it ran off the road and into the forest. She thought she detected an overgrown trail but stopped at the entrance.

She whistled. "Doggy?" She glanced over her shoulder at the town. She spotted hunched forms in the agricultural fields that ran alongside the road and kids playing soccer in the street. Sanchia was watching and waving her back.

Vines rustled and Ana expected to the stray to wander out but it didn't. Instead, something large collided into her.

Chapter 17

"Chance!"

His arms caught her before she tumbled over from the impact. Damp with sweat, his shirt clung to his body. Ana didn't care. She held onto him, relieved.

"You scared me. Where have you been?" she demanded as her anger bubbled to the surface.

His breath was ragged in her ear. "C'mon, grab your stuff. I want to head back—I think I saw Balam."

"Really? That's great!" she said, distracted. "But I'm still angry with you. You left without leaving a note or anything. What was I supposed to think? I didn't know if you'd been abducted or what." She crossed her arms and glared at him.

Chance rubbed the sweat from his temple and sighed. "I'm sorry Ana. I woke up early and just started following my instincts, which led me way into the jungle. I didn't even think about letting you know..."

"Well don't do it again, okay? You're supposed to be protecting me, remember? What would I do if you just disappeared and never came back?"

He placed his hands on her hips and looked her in the eye. "You're right. I'm sorry. I just wasn't thinking. I won't do it again, promise."

Chance leaned down and kissed her cheek.

"Well, c'mon, you look wiped out. Let's get you some water," Ana said.

They held hands and walked back to Sanchia, who had wandered out from her backyard to see the excitement.

"We need supplies—food and water, if we're going back," Chance said.

Sanchia's eyes were wide and she appeared concerned. "Did anything happen to you in the forest?" she asked in Spanish.

Ana translated for Chance and he answered, "No—just lots of animals."

His answer seemed to worry her even more, for some reason.

"If you look for trouble, you will find it," she said.

Ana distracted her with questions about where to purchase food. The woman didn't respond but led them back into her kitchen where she grabbed a bunch of bananas and tamales wrapped in corn husks. When Ana pulled out money, the woman shook her head and pushed it away.

Chance and Ana bustled into the living room to put it back the way they had found it the night before. As she tucked the last couch cushion in its place, Ana's thoughts fell on her mom. She hadn't sent her a message yet and knew her mother would be anxious to hear from her, so she slipped her phone out and sent a message: *Chance & I are safe with family. Don't worry. XOXO, Ana.* It wasn't exactly the truth, but she wasn't about to tell her that Chance had already gotten into a fight and they were about to disappear into the jungle. Not unless she wanted her mom to keep her on house arrest until she was sixty.

They finished packing their belongings and put the food Sanchia had given them into their backpacks. Chance went to fill their water bottles and their host pressed two folded sheets of paper into Ana's hand. She noticed leaves peering out.

"For your stomach, if it hurts again. You know which one it is. The other is for his nose, to reduce swelling and for pain."

Ana tucked them into her backpack and gave the stout woman a hug. "Thank you for your generosity, Sanchia."

Chance echoed her sentiment as Sanchia walked them to the road.

The old woman stopped to watch them step into the wilderness with a worried frown on her face.

***

Chance wanted to return to the path while the directions were fresh in his memory. The forest played tricks on his eyes and he had to backtrack a few times to find the trail. He refrained from running and slowed down so he wouldn't lose her.

Sweat dripped down his face. The humid heat at the peak of the day was too much and he stopped to peel off his shirt. A quick glance at Ana told him she wasn't in any better shape. Loose hairs were plastered to her forehead and her shirt clung to her arms and chest. The humidity made the air feel thick, almost palpable, and he was thankful to have water with him this time. Mosquitoes became a nuisance and they had to stop to rub bug repellant on.

He found the white gravel trail where he'd first spotted the jaguar. They were close now. Chance sped up and heard Ana's heavy footfalls behind him.

Just when he began to question if he had gone the wrong way, the dense jungle revealed the overgrown ruins. He slowed to a stop and Ana nearly ran into him. She leaned over, grabbed her knees and lifted the edge of her shirt to wipe away the moisture at her forehead as Chance stared at the rocky pyramid.

"This is where the jaguar disappeared," he said and slipped off his backpack.

"You think it was Balam? And that he'll be back?"

He repeated Ana's question in his mind. Had it only been an apparition? Or was it Balam? He worried he hadn't heard or seen anything on the way here this time.

"Maybe we should just wait."

Ana slipped her pack off and unzipped it, slipping out the wrapped tamales. She grinned and handed him one. "Let's eat lunch—I'm hungry."

At the mention of food, Chance's stomach growled. Ana arched her brow at the sound. "Here, take a banana, too."

They sat on a rock platform covered with tangled roots and plants. Chance was so hungry, he sat in silence while he ate. His nose was still swollen from being punched and it sent out shooting pains as he wolfed down his food.

Another rumble sounded and Ana smirked at him. "Still hungry?"

Chance couldn't respond. His attention was focused on the enormous black jaguar standing at the top of the ruins. He wondered if it really was a jaguar because of its unnatural size. The beast reeked of power like the regal thunderbird.

His breath caught in his throat as another deep guttural growl emanated from the feline. Its chestnut eyes penetrated Chance's stunned face...

Chapter 18

Ana shot up, gave a yelp and stumbled back beside Chance.

"Shhhh," he said. He wasn't sure who he was directing the order to, Ana or the cat, but he hoped both would quiet down.

"Chance," she said out of the corner of her mouth, her eyes wide.

He stood his ground and returned the huge feline's stare. The creature licked its lips and jumped down out of view on the backside of the ruins. Chance held his arm out in front of Ana, stepped back and pulled her with him.

Where had the animal gone? All he could hear were the monkeys in the trees, shaking branches and leaves. He couldn't detect any other sounds.

"Look," Ana said under her breath.

Her head pointed to the right, where a dark haired man stood. It appeared he had just wrapped his waist with a red cloth and was tucking in the end. He walked toward them. The man was tall and carried himself like royalty. Tattoos wrapped his neck, chest and arms, and Chance assumed more were on his back and hidden beneath the fabric that covered his legs. Long hair dropped past his shoulders and his chocolate eyes blinked back at Chance. They were so familiar. Like Grandmother's. She had her father's eyes. However, hers were softer, kinder. He had seen this man before in

Niyol's memories.

"Balam." Chance breathed the name in amazement.

The man stopped an arm's length from Chance and pointed at his neck.

"That is my jade jaguar," Balam said. His English was clearly enunciated, but he spoke as though he had just swallowed something bitter. It was clear he disliked speaking the language.

Chance lifted the talisman over his head, held it out and said, "My grandfather gave it to me."

Balam's stony gaze cut through him as he snatched it from his grasp. "Tell me, boy, who is your grandfather?"

"Niyol."

"We will see about that. And you are named Chance?"

"Yes, sir." Chance began to feel lightheaded but tried to shake it off. His skin tingled and the hair on his arms stood on end.

Balam's attention shifted to Ana. He squinted at her like an appraiser assessing a gem. What would happen if he found her lacking in some way? Chance didn't like this at all and wished he knew what was going through Balam's mind. On edge, he inched toward Ana.

"And you are named Ana," Balam stated rather than asked. He stretched out the vowels—ah-nah.

Ana seemed to sense danger but stayed strong. She lifted her chin and looked him square in the eyes. "Yes."

"I have been watching you—both of you. Do you know why?"

Am I being tested right now? Chance's palms were clammy. After his run-in with his unstable cousin, he now wondered if he could ever truly trust another shapeshifter.

"To see if we are trustworthy?"

"Yes. Honor, I think the word is."

His great-grandfather stood quiet, arms braced across his chest. Just when Chance didn't think he could take much more silence, Balam said, "You are infants. Young and inexperienced shifters make mistakes. Mistakes can end your life. Without a mentor, you are lost in a dangerous world."

Birds trilled from the jungle canopy. Their song rose in one voice, a perfect symphony. The buzz of activity pierced Chance's senses. Balam's remarks echoed his fears. *Am I alone in my fight to survive?*

His great-grandfather's serious manner worried him. Had he made a mistake seeking him out? Had he delivered himself straight to the enemy? They were in the middle of the jungle with nowhere to go. Entirely powerless in Balam's hands.

"You are a baby lost in the woods. Where is your mentor? Why are you alone? Did you kill him? These are natural questions I ask myself."

Chance swallowed the lump in his throat and ventured to answer. The truth was painful. But it was, after all, the truth. "My grandfather was my teacher...and he died to save my life."

"Did he give himself to you?"

Wisps of memories flooded Chance's mind. Niyol's steadfast nature, his patience and calm. Chance nodded.

"You do not look fragmented. Mostly whole," Balam

said matter-of-factly.

What does that mean? Chance wondered.

"You," Balam said to Ana, "are you a healer? How do you come to be here?"

Ana frowned, clearly unsure how to answer. Her hands twisted together into a knot but her voice came out clear. "I love Chance, I want to be here for him."

Balam stepped closer to her and rested his hands on her shoulders. Time slipped by as he stared at her. Ana, caught under the microscope, did nothing but stare back and tremble.

"Interesting… We will see." Balam withdrew his hands from Ana's shoulders and nodded as though he had made a decision. "Chance, I saw you stand up for my people. You did not use your powers to reveal yourself in the fight. Self-control—that is important. I did not know you were my kin, but felt it.

"And Ana, there is something about you. It is in your nature to protect and help. There are many reasons why you should not be here. But here you stand."

Chance put his arm around her. They had come together and they would leave together. He didn't know what he would do if Balam refused to allow her to stay; he would have to improvise.

Balam tilted his head very slightly and said, "I am curious. I will allow her to stay."

Without waiting for an answer, Balam turned and walked to the forest's edge and paused. Chance and Ana scurried to grab their things, flung on their packs and exchanged a guarded look.

The adventure had officially begun.

Chapter 19

Ana wondered when Balam had last spent time with an everyday human. Chance's deceptively youthful great-grandfather strode through the vegetation like an Olympian. She didn't want him to change his mind about allowing her to come along so even though they had just spent the last hour hiking through the jungle in tropical humidity, she dug in her toes and kept her eyes on Chance's feet ahead of her. She imagined an invisible tether linking them together to help pull her along.

The first time Balam stopped, Ana heaved a sigh of relief, all too ready to sit and catch her breath, but relief turned to disappointment when he continued only once she caught up. Chance stayed just ahead of her along their trek. His head would cock to the side and she could tell he was listening for her footfalls as he always did. When Ana became winded and slowed down, he fell back and walked behind her.

Blue skies were suddenly painted over with gray and white clouds as they rolled across the atmosphere. Like the lid sealed shut on a steaming bowl, the air got even heavier and it was even harder to breathe. Then she felt the first drop of rain slap against her already moist scalp. What next?

Balam, who had mostly stayed visible the whole way, dipped down out of sight. When Ana and Chance reached the point where he had disappeared, they discovered a trail leading into a dark, cavernous hole.

"I'll go first," Chance said and stepped lightly down the slope.

Ana waited a moment, then followed behind. To keep her balance, she let her fingers trail along the limestone wall on her left side. There was a suspended wooden walkway at the bottom of the earthen trail and it led into a vast cave. A pool of tranquil water gleamed below from daylight breaking through fissures in the corroded ceiling. Plants splashed with red and green dangled from the dark gray dome. Water droplets made their way through the cracks in the ceiling and splashed into the pool, echoing off the chamber. She had never seen anything quite so beautiful.

Chance's call beckoned her forward. "Ana, come on, it's okay."

She grasped the wooden rail for support and stepped onto the suspended walkway. She decided it was safe after the first two steps and moved more confidently in Chance's wake. They turned a corner and a series of steps carved into the limestone led them upward, above the forest floor, Ana guessed. It was dark yet she could see they were no longer in a cave, but in a structure. Large slabs of stone were woven together to create the solid walls and steps, which continued to carry them even higher.

Chance paused at an open archway and then passed through it, allowing her to see into the vast living space. A large room with broad window openings in the exterior walls exposed treetops and the cloudy sky. Ana first saw a long couch piled with hand-woven cushions before a hearth and just beyond, a rustic wooden dining set. A small kitchen was tucked into the corner. They walked inside, slipped their packs off and set them down.

Balam walked just past the dining area onto a deck that appeared to wrap the outside of the home. Chance and Ana joined him on the beautifully crafted overlook. From there, Ana saw they were a good fifteen feet from the ground.

To their left, a set of wooden stairs rose to another level and Ana assumed it led to the living quarters. Balam's voice broke through the soft whisper of the rain.

"I want to be left alone."

Ana edged backwards and exchanged a worried look with Chance. If he wanted to be alone, she would respect his wishes.

Unexpectedly, he continued, saying, "When I was your age, the world was a different place. There were more shifters and my people were stronger. This place—" he waved with distaste toward the hazy forest "—is different. So few of us remain now. It is dangerous. I want to be left alone."

Ana wondered if he meant there weren't many shapeshifters or Mayans. She knew more about the Mayas after their history lesson from Miguel the previous day. The Mayas had had a booming population that suddenly dropped to a fraction of its size. Scientists only had theories why. She stared at his profile and wondered. How old was Balam, really?

"I found Niyol when he was young. Before me, he had no mentor. But when he met my Itzel, he only wanted to grow old with her. That is why he turned his back on his powers. She was his mate but I believe he was afraid of what he was." Balam paused and stared at Chance. "Are you?"

Chance pulled back his shoulders and his eyes tightened. "No."

"He vowed to guide any children that followed in our ways and then let me mentor them. I am sorry his cycle ended but if what you say is true, his power lives in you. How many years are you?"

Chance said, "I'm eighteen."

Balam shifted his gaze focused to the bleary landscape as he spoke. "Did you turn at sixteen years?"

Chance blinked and said, "Yes. That's normal, right?"

In answer, Balam gave a brief nod. Ana was afraid to move or draw attention to herself. The conversation seemed fragile, as if at any time Balam could change his mind and disappear. But her legs were tired from the long trek through the jungle and begged for relief so she leaned against Chance.

"Did your grandfather keep his promise to guide you? It feels you have the power of a newborn, not a two year old. If what you say is true—if he gave himself to you— you should have more power."

Ana felt Chance's body tense. He shook his head and pinched his eyes shut. Balam had clearly upset him. She rested her hand on his chest and waited for him to respond.

"It's been different since grandfather died... I don't know why. I can't tap into my power like I used to. I just don't understand."

"What do you mean?" Ana couldn't hold her tongue. Why hadn't he said anything to her? She knew that when it came to protecting her, he was unpredictable but it stung that he hadn't shared this information with her.

Chance stepped back and combed his fingers through his hair. Balam's stoic gaze finally shifted and settled on his great-grandson. He seemed curious, like someone watching a worm coil and writhe on hot pavement. She didn't like how unemotional he was. It gave her the chills.

"You must hold the answer. Tell me, how did Niyol save you?"

"It was because of me—it all started with me." Ana found her voice and actually surprised herself. "My heart stopped, and..."

Chance stepped in to finish. "My cousin—a shifter— came looking for me. He kidnapped Ana and while we battled, her heart stopped. I couldn't let her die so I started a healing connection. Grandfather told me about it but I'd never tried before. It was too strong for me to control. I was able to save her and then Grandfather brought me back from death but he didn't survive."

Balam scrutinized Ana with renewed curiosity. "I see. That explains much. What about your cousin?"

Ana brushed off Balam's attention and waited for Chance to answer.

***

Chance didn't want to answer the question in front of

Ana. To have her worry he was still out there was just too much for him. She couldn't do anything to protect herself, anyway. She wasn't a shifter. She might as well live in ignorant bliss for now. He would have to tell Balam the story later.

"He's gone."

The lines around Balam's eyes tightened. "Mmm. You emptied your reservoir to save Ana and Niyol gave you his powers. I wonder. Did he truly give up shifting as he said he would?"

Still bitter about Niyol's omission regarding his powers, Chance said, "Yes. I never knew he was a shifter until the end. From his memories, I believe he thought he had lost his power."

"He emptied into you what power he had left. You will have the same animals, including his, but you do not have the same power as you once did. You will need to work to expand your energy again. Until then, you are weak and exposed."

"I am glad I found you, Balam," Chance said with a sigh.

"I let you find me. You said you are not afraid of your powers. To gain your energy back will take much work. Are you willing to work hard?"

Memories of practicing in the field with his grandfather flooded his thoughts. When he had a purpose, his focus was intense. His goal was saving Ana's life, and it would be again. He couldn't protect her if he couldn't even protect himself.

"Yes." He held Balam's gaze, staring him straight in the

eye.

Chapter 20

The upper level of Balam's home was the living quarters, just as Ana had guessed. Four sections segmented off into private chambers, with a bed in each. The interior limestone walls were painted bright colors, and each had an expansive opening to the verdant jungle. She was relieved to discover a washroom tucked into the hallway.

Balam stopped to ask, "Have you given Ana your name? You are mates?"

Chance frowned in confusion, but Ana thought she understood what he meant. "We aren't married, if that's what you mean."

Chance's almond skin flushed into a deep crimson as he said under his breath, "We just graduated high school."

Balam shrugged. "I have had many wives. I was first married at sixteen years. It was never the same after my true mate. No one compared. If you do not share a name, you do not share a room. All your energy must be focused on shifting now. No distractions."

Ana caught the trace of a smile on Balam's lips.

"Ana, this is your room. Come, Chance."

She wandered into her room, and dropped her travel pack on the bed. Chance's sad eyes relayed just how disappointed he was.

Balam led him away and presumably to his own room to settle in. Ana tucked her clothing into a small wooden dresser and flopped onto the bed once she was done. The rain had stopped and the birds were singing a chorus after their midday shower. The crisp fragrance of wet leaves and bark filled the room. Her favorite smell—fresh rain.

As she lay on the soft bed, her eyelids grew heavy. The last couple of days had been a whirlwind. Now that her body was at rest, exhaustion overcame her and she fell straight to sleep.

***

Chance dropped his backpack to the floor and stopped in the washroom to splash water on his face. He peered in Ana's room and found her resting so he darted downstairs to the main living space. Balam was busy placing wood in a hearth and Chance settled onto the couch to watch his great-grandfather. No longer covered only by a cloth, Balam wore a pair of thin cotton pants with a colorful red sash wrapped around his waist. After Chance reflected on Niyol's memories, he decided Balam couldn't have aged even ten years but his grandfather's memories had to be over eighty years old. If he had to guess, he would say Balam was in his sixties.

He was pretty confident that shifters weren't immortal. They could die. But he had never met an older shapeshifter before. Excluding Niyol. Although he believed his grandfather hadn't used his powers since he was a young man.

"Are you deciding if you can trust me?" Balam asked

with his back turned to him as a blossom of light grew into a crackling fire.

"Can you ever really trust another shifter?" Chance asked. "You said something about there not being many of us left. Is that true?"

"Yes. We take time to mature. Sixteen years to discover if a child has the birthright. When the seed takes root and the energy is awakened, it is a dangerous time. You have already met one who craves power, who has the sickness. Fresh shifters are easy to pluck, for they have little defense. The young are susceptible to misusing their gifts without guidance and can be tempted down a path, like your cousin."

The warmth from the fire radiated to the couch. A red glow illuminated Balam's face as he stoked the wood and cast shadows along the creases of his mouth. The last couple of months had been such a drain, but sitting here with Balam, Chance felt rejuvenated.

"Markus seemed insane. He said he'd killed his own grandfather. What happened? What would make him do that?" The memories of Niyol witnessing his brother murdering their father were unnerving. Were they just bad seeds or was it a shapeshifter sickness?

Balam seemed to understand the question. "Could this happen to you? That is what you want to know, yes? The true question is, what was Markus like before he sought his elder's power? I do not know what your grandfather taught you, so I will teach you everything as though you are an infant."

Chance hated that. Infant. It made him sound like a

baby—inexperienced, naïve. Balam pulled out a narrow stick from the fire and held it up for Chance to see. Its tip was aglow.

"When the power is awakened in a shifter, it is small like this flame. You must work very hard for a very long time to stretch your capacity to hold more power." He gestured to the belly of the hearth and its fiery contents. "When you absorb another's life force, it expands your own. It doesn't help that we are drawn to each other like moths to a flame. Youngsters are weak and most importantly, impulsive. If you have a strong character, you may not be tempted. At my age I have no use for more power and risking my mind is not worth it."

Balam reached into the fire and withdrew another stick engulfed in flame. "When you saved your Ana and died, you drained all of your power. And when Niyol saved you, he gave you all that he was. You did not lose your knowledge, but would have gained his as well. You feel him inside—his memories?"

Chance nodded.

"If you had been at full power when he gave himself to you—" Balam brought the sticks together and their flames grew as one "—your power would have grown. But you were empty and Niyol had very little power. Now you must work to refill your reservoir. It will be easier than growing from infancy again."

Well, that was a little bit encouraging.

Balam used the sticks to stoke the fire, and then thrust them back in, causing the pyre to spark and hiss. "You and your grandfather gave yourselves in a healing connection. This is very different from when you kill another shifter because you funneled all your energy. An impression of the soul is connected to your energy. This is why you have your grandfather's memories and know all the animals he ever shifted into. Normally, when a shifter dies or is killed, his power can no longer be contained and bursts out. If it is absorbed by another shifter, it is fragmented and incomplete. You must consider also whom you are absorbing. Was he kind or a murderer? Did *he* take on other's powers? Too many personalities. It is a sickness of the soul."

Chance shivered. He flashed to his sex education class in high school. The whole room had snickered when Mr. Daly informed them that when you have sex with someone, you're really having sex with everyone your partner's been with. Although this was altogether different, it was the same idea.

It wasn't all that bad having part of his grandfather inside of him. The memories had died down. They only really emerged when he called on Niyol for help and support. He considered what would be going on in Markus's head. He had killed his grandfather, who Chance knew had already killed before. Markus had a huge amount of power but was unstable. The memories and voices in his head would be murderous and nerve-rattling. The thought raised a serious question.

"What do you do if another shifter wants to kill you? Markus—I don't think he's dead. If he comes after me, what do I do? Is there another way to stop him outside of killing him?"

Natasha Brown

"Most shifters who grow and mature don't wish to kill others because they understand the cost—but sometimes it is unavoidable. We do not tend to stay around each other for very long, so the draw does not become tempting. Crazed shifters are dangerous. Distance yourself from them and avoid getting into a fight. If you can evade them, it is best. The only safe way to kill a sick shifter is from a distance so you don't absorb their power but that is not always possible."

Chance leaned forward and scratched his head. Without looking at Balam, he asked, "So how long can we be around each other before either of us gets tempted?"

"It feels good being around another shifter—rejuvenating. You will never become enough of a temptation to me. And you—I can protect myself from you if you ever become weak and cannot resist yourself." Balam smiled widely and his teeth gleamed white in the light of the fire. He seemed to relish the thought just a little too much for Chance's comfort.

"I don't understand. How could Markus have killed his grandfather? He must have been far more powerful."

"There are ways to weaken shifters. Shifters with the sickness live off their survival instincts. A sick shifter's strength and weakness is his fragile mental state."

"Can you identify other shifters? Can I?"

"At your age the best you can do is listen to your instincts. When you get to my age, you can feel the power inside of someone."

Chance was about to ask another question when Balam stopped him. "I can see you do not know much

166

about who you are. Niyol kept many things from you. It is a blessing you are alive. I will answer more questions later. Tomorrow we will rise with the sun and I will see what you do know. Now let us wake your Ana and feed your tired, empty bodies."

Chapter 21

Ana's body lay tangled in her sheets. Her sleep shirt twisted up, exposing her smooth skin and cotton underwear. Chance swallowed hard and tried to calm his desire.

He stepped forward in silence, not wanting to rouse her just yet. Long brown hair swept across her back and hung limply off the edge of the bed. The steady rise and fall of her chest mesmerized him. He fought the temptation to climb into bed with her. Balam was right—she was a distraction. A lovely one.

Chance knelt beside her and breathed in her familiar scent. He brushed her hair off her neck and placed a gentle kiss below her ear. She stirred and her eyes fluttered open. A soft groan escaped her lips as she stretched and rolled toward him. Her hands moved down to adjust the sheets and she covered herself.

"Good morning, beautiful," he said.

"Morning."

The clouds cleared overnight and the sun had just begun to illuminate the sky. Birds trilled loudly and their morning praise echoed in the bedroom. Ana's green eyes crinkled into a frown.

"Hmmm."

"What?" Chance asked with concern. Overall, he thought everything had gone pretty well yesterday.

"Aw, it's not a big deal. I just haven't gotten to

stargaze yet in Mexico. It was too cloudy last night."

"Oh, I'm sure you'll get your chance. Come to think of it, I bet Balam knows plenty of constellations. Weren't the Mayans astronomers?"

The thought seemed to brighten Ana's mood considerably and she sat up, her expression lighter.

"Good point. Well, if we want to get going for your first lesson with Balam, I need to get dressed."

Chance stood and waited. When it became clear he wasn't going anywhere, Ana laughed and pushed him away. "Go on. I won't be long."

He stopped teasing and leaned over to kiss her lips. Then he reluctantly left the room and headed downstairs. As soon as he saw Balam, the anxiety and excitement he felt upon waking returned.

A pile of bananas sat at the center of the dining table and a ceramic pitcher filled with dark steaming liquid. Something that looked like pancakes were stacked on a plate. Balam waved to the food and said, "Feed yourself. Is your Ana coming?"

"Yes, she's getting dressed."

He leaned in to smell the drink as he reached for a cup. Because it was so dark, he assumed it was coffee but after a sniff, he realized it was hot chocolate. He poured himself a cup and took a sip. A touch of spice bit at the tip of his tongue as he tried to identify the layered flavors. He was familiar with cinnamon, but the others were beyond him. Satisfied, he took another mouthful as he reached for a pancake.

"Did you make these yourself?"

Balam adjusted in his seat and said with a sour expression, "I do not take pleasure in cooking and cleaning. I miss my wives' meals. But I chose to be alone and not to bury another. It is the price for my solitude. I am Mayan. We made the calendar, invented the concept of zero and created an advanced writing system. I can learn how to cook."

"How many wives did you have?"

"Ten. Over time. I enjoy the quiet now but I would give anything to be with my true mate again—your great-grandmother and my last wife. I would have given myself for her like you did for your Ana but it was not possible." Balam shook his head and took a sip from his cup.

"Can you tell me—how old *are* you?"

"I saw the fall of the Yucatán to the Spanish conquistadors. I no longer count my years, but is somewhere between five and six hundred."

Chance coughed on his corn pancake, sending particles of his breakfast onto the table just as Ana emerged.

"Morning. You okay, Chance?" She leaned over the pitcher and said with a sigh, "Mmm, hot chocolate. It's my new favorite. Wish my grandma made it this way growing up. Instead, it was straight out of the packet."

Ana poured herself a cup and tilted her head at Chance. He cleared his throat and swallowed what food remained in his mouth.

"Balam was just telling me how many wives he had. And you won't believe his age."

"Do I look good?" Balam asked. He rose, struck out his

chest and held his head to the side. He looked like one of the hieroglyphs at the ruins, regal and proud.

Ana squinted and said, "Sixty?"

"Add a zero," Chance said as he put the last bite of pancake in his mouth.

Her jaw dropped. "Really?! That's amazing. Is that old for a shapeshifter? I mean, have you ever met anyone older than you?"

"The older shifters tend to stay hidden. If they do not want to be found, you will not find them. I am old but there *are* older shifters."

Chance's great-grandfather had actually seen the Spaniards invade and conquer the Yucatán. He had lived through an entirely different era. If Chance chose to live an extended life, he could see humanity change as Balam had. However, there was a problem with that scenario. Ana would age and die long before him. His grandfather's choice to turn his back on his powers made more sense now.

Ana sat down at the table and nibbled on a banana while she blew on her hot chocolate. Her brow furrowed and she remained quiet, clearly lost in thought. Chance reached across the table, grasped her hand in his and met her eyes.

"Ana and Chance, eat your fill and let us go. I wish to see what my great-grandson can do. If we look at the clouds, our work will not get done."

Ana finished eating and gulped down her hot chocolate. Balam turned to face the outdoor balcony and said, "If we were all shifters we could fly but it looks like we must walk out as we walked in."

Balam handed a square of folded fabric to Chance. "For you. Go put it on."

He ran upstairs, changed out of his clothing and struggled to wrap the cloth around his waist so it wouldn't fall off. When he was satisfied it was secure, he met Balam and Ana at the entry.

Single file, they descended the staircase into the dark cave and finally surfaced in the jungle. Balam guided them through the leafy wilderness. Animals stirred all around them and Chance's senses were overwhelmed.

They entered a clearing after a short walk. Palm trees lined the area and the uneven ground was punctuated with roots and rocks.

Balam stopped and said, "This is a good place. I want to see you shift into the largest animal you can."

Ana gave Chance's arm a squeeze and went to stand beside Balam. Chance took a shaky breath. He hadn't taken the thunderbird form since showing it to Ana just after Niyol's death. His power reservoir had been too depleted since then to re-try it or much else. The first time out with his great-grandfather he wanted to impress him but he wasn't confident. Each time he'd called on his energy recently, he'd had an underwhelming response.

Chance slipped off his sandals and as his grandfather had taught him, he lowered himself to the ground cross-legged and began to calm his thoughts. His energy was sluggish and did not crackle with excitement as it used to.

Minutes slipped by as he wrestled with his powers. With his eyes closed he envisioned the mapping of the thunderbird, its enormous wingspan and powerful talons, to no avail. It was like pushing a boulder up hill. He just couldn't take its form.

Filled with disappointment, he instead chose to focus on the grizzly bear. The black nose and massive furry body had quickly become one of his favorite embodiments. He couldn't remember the last time he'd taken its shape.

Again, his energy resisted the powerful animal's form. The tingle of his skin lasted but a moment before it released like a wave breaking against a beach. A branch snapped above, which reminded him he wasn't alone. He was glad he couldn't see his audience. *You're not going to impress Balam with your ability to sit still.*

Determined to take any shape at this point, Chance dug down and imagined the blue flame of energy at his core. Its heat penetrated down his arms and legs and the familiar prickle of his pores told him he was close. As he breathed out a sigh of relief, his world changed and he was standing on all fours. A cougar was better than nothing.

A spot low on his back still tingled and he arched his spine in an effort to relieve the itch. He turned to see Ana, who wore a bright smile of encouragement and Balam, whose arms were folded across his chest. His serious, watchful expression made Chance wary. He wasn't impressed, that much was clear. Chance wondered what *would* impress him.

"Now I want to see your smallest animal."

The smallest? What did that matter? After he'd

become a squirrel in his first shift, he'd never looked back. But if Balam wanted him to take on the smallest animal, he'd do just that.

He walked a tight circle, sat and wrapped his tail snugly around his feet. With his eyes closed, he collected his energy again. His skin contracted as he shrank in size. Trying to stuff his power into such a small form took effort. When he'd shifted down to smaller animals in the past, he had always gone down in size very slowly. This was different. It felt as though he'd put on a shirt that was three sizes too small. His lungs were instantly tight and he began to wheeze. A funny squeaky, chatter-y sound filled the air and he realized the sound was coming from him.

After a few minutes, he recovered and he scurried to Balam's feet. His tail twitched involuntarily and flopped over his head.

Ana sat and hugged her knees. He could tell she was suppressing a grin.

"Very good. Now I want you to switch between these two forms until you cannot any longer," Balam said.

He turned and attempted to walk with as much dignity as he could. Positioned on the piece of fabric he had wrapped around his waist earlier, he cleared his mind. The agitation rolled away and he set to work. The process exhausted him. Maybe it was supposed to. But he didn't give up.

Chance began to tire after the first couple of shifts, at which point it began to take a long while to generate enough strength to phase again. He paced around the clearing until his energy allowed him to change one last time into the cougar and he padded over to his great-grandfather with his head down.

"That is enough for now. Let us go eat lunch. Phase back to your human form if you can."

Chance skulked over to the rumpled piece of red fabric on the ground and tried to gather enough power to return to his own skin. His basin was empty. The last shift had completely drained him. Furry toes placed together, he lifted his chin to the forest and bellowed. The loud chatter from birds, monkeys and insects quieted for a second and then rose again.

"Come, Chance. Let us go home. You can shift back there when you have enough energy."

Ana grabbed his wrap and shoes, then Balam led the way through the jungle. Ana's fingers caressed his fur as she walked beside him. He leaned against her and purred.

When they got to the limestone stairs, Chance stared up the flight and waited for Ana and Balam to ascend to the top before he leapt up four stairs at a time. He entered the main living quarters and flicked his tail, proud of himself.

"Do you wish to eat as an animal or try once more to phase back to a human?" Balam asked as he entered the kitchen.

In response, Chance darted up to his bedroom and after a few minutes, returned in human form, wearing a pair of shorts. His energy had recharged enough during the walk back. He wandered into the kitchen and touched his healed nose, pleased it was no longer crooked and swollen. Ready to help prepare lunch, he threw a piece of fruit in his mouth.

Balam's deep voice echoed off the tiled walls as he asked, "Is the cougar your largest form?"

"I've taken much larger forms but I haven't been able to recently. Not enough energy."

"Have you been shifting every day?"

"No. I just didn't want to after Grandfather died—it only reminded me of him. Then once I realized something was off, I was afraid of losing my powers. Each time I've shifted it's been hard so I just haven't done it much. I didn't know if one of these times it wouldn't work at all."

Ana laid her hand on his bare shoulder. He could tell she was upset. She turned to the built-in grill and used a fork to flip the meat. He thought her cheek was quivering, but he couldn't be sure.

"After the loss of power you suffered, that was the worst choice. Shifting is like using a muscle—it needs to be exercised to grow. But you had no teacher to tell you this."

How stupid of me. Of course he had done the wrong thing. Sure, he hadn't known any better but he should have persisted and not hidden from his problem. 'Infant' did seem like a fitting label for him.

"We must work your shifting muscles. You do not want them to atrophy. The best way to do this is to use your largest and smallest forms. Have you seen divers prepare?" Balam's chest rose as he inhaled deeply and then he exhaled an equally long breath before repeating the process. "Was the exercise hard?"

"I'm exhausted. My body actually hurts."

Balam nodded and asked, "What is your form of choice?"

"Bear is my favorite."

"Other mammals are the easiest because their biology is closest to ours. Birds, reptiles, amphibians and fish all have their own challenges. I do not shift into invertebrates. You should not attempt it, either."

Ana said over her shoulder, "You mean, like, bugs? Why not?"

"The risk of losing yourself is too great. Some invertebrates have complex brains—others do not. Some flies have a lifespan of only thirty minutes. There are too many inconsistencies. I have seen shifters try and die."

Chance had never even considered turning into a bug. Although he supposed if he were trying to hide, something very small would be best. In his infant years with Niyol, he had never understood the need to hide. Now that he was unprotected and possibly being hunted, small forms began to make sense.

"Do you know any other forms that are not mammals?" Balam asked.

"I know the Horned Owl and I learned the thunderbird just before I lost my powers."

Balam shook his head and said, "You did not lose your powers but gave them away. Now, tell me of this thunderbird. I have heard whispers of a great bird of the Northern tribes."

"My Native American ancestors created the form. It is an eagle larger than a man."

Chance actually knew something Balam didn't. He tried not to let it go to his head.

"Hmm. Shifters have made their mark on history. People just refer to it as folklore today, but many cultures around the world have records of great mythological creatures. Only matured and powerful shifters have the experience and ability to create a creature that does not live and breathe in our world. It is much easier to learn a form that is already mapped. The mapping of these ancient great creatures are starting to die out. You are fortunate to hold the knowledge of the thunderbird. It is like my people's yaguar. It is believed the form was created by a powerful Olmec shifter and it became a revered creature to all the people of my land. It is like a jaguar, but much bigger, nearly as large as a horse. The jaw of the yaguar is great and very powerful. Like the jaguar it is modeled from, it was made for swimming, climbing and jumping. A true cat, it has stealth and power. It has been passed down through our line. I think I remember Niyol mention something of this thunderbird when I tried to mentor him. But he did not have this creature mapped. How did you learn it?"

"I tried it once with my grandfather's guidance, based off an eagle, but it went wrong. Then my grandfather gave me a talon passed down in our family. I was able to see its mapping and right when I needed it most, I got a boost from a lightning storm and was able to take the form."

Balam drove his paring knife into the cutting board and braced his hands against the counter, drawing Ana's and Chance's attention.

"Was I foolish to allow Niyol to train you? That could have ended your cycle trying it with so little experience. And he allowed you to begin a healing that killed you? Aiy!!"

"Listen," Chance said heatedly, "Grandfather may not have told me things he should have, and I don't understand all his reasons, but he was great man! He may not have known as much as you do, but he taught me how to be a man and to be the kind of person I want to be! It is my fault he's dead. I never asked his permission to heal Ana. It was my choice!"

Was this why Niyol had turned his back on shifting? Because of his teacher? He missed his grandfather so much it hurt. *Chance, calm yourself. He will always be with you.*

As he grasped the counter, Balam's gaze softened. He pursed his lips and looked Chance in the eye. "I see he taught you honor. I am sorry. I know what it is to lose someone you love. Your grandmother was a child made from love."

Chance's anger subsided. He tilted his chin down and cleared his throat. "Okay. I won't dwell on it. Let's eat. I could eat a horse."

Balam frowned, clearly confused by the reference.

Ana smiled weakly at Balam and carried a plate of grilled meat to the table. Chance and Balam followed her with tortillas and a platter covered with cheese, tomatoes and grilled onions.

They all stuffed food in their mouths as the midday

sun quieted the raucous bird sounds to a soft chatter.

"Balam, where do you get your food?" Ana asked. "I assume we're a long way from any town."

Balam finished his last bite and answered, "I hunt and townspeople leave items for me at the jungle's edge. I help protect them and look after them. There is also the town you stayed in. My granddaughter lives there, Sanchia. You stayed with her. She is the one who alerted me of your arrival. She leaves items for me at the edge of the jungle every week."

"Really? Sanchia is your granddaughter? That makes Dario your great-great-grandson. They're related to Chance?"

"Yes, she is the daughter of Itzel's younger sister."

"Any other cousins I should worry about?" Chance asked casually and noticed Ana's amused expression slip from her face.

Balam's dark features froze into a stony expression. "One must be cautious at all times."

Chapter 22

It was a lot to absorb in a few hours. Ana needed to unwind. Stargazing always helped her relieve stress.

Her thin white nightgown hung down to her knees. She sat on the wooden deck cross-legged, pulled the cotton down to her ankles and clutched her feet.

Secretly, she was happy to have a moment away from Chance. She needed time to herself to think.

Balam had made Chance run through more energy building exercises after a short nap following lunch. After dinner when his fork hit his plate, he barely made it to bed before falling asleep. His snores chased her downstairs to seek the stars. It had been too long since she had sought their comfort.

The stars flickered for her, or at least that was how she always felt—as if they were performing just for her. As she stared upward, she realized the unique dwelling offered a completely unobstructed view of the heavens.

She wondered how the stars could make her feel so small and yet so important. Her problems always seemed so silly compared to the size of the universe. She hoped her beloved stars would help her tonight, yet again.

Chance hadn't even thought of sharing the issues he'd had with his powers since Niyol died. After he saved her life, she thought they'd grown even closer. They were a team. It really hurt that he'd told his new teacher, someone he'd known for a day—mere hours—about his problem and hadn't revealed it to her, someone he'd been willing to sacrifice his life for.

Ana hated confrontation. When her dad left, she'd sworn to avoid relationships with that kind of conflict. It caused too much pain. She didn't want to start an argument by bringing it up to him. What if he got mad?

But what good would it do to swallow her feelings? Her voice deserved to be heard, right? *Yes.*

She sighed and rested her cheek to her knee. From her sideways view of the sky, she traced familiar constellations in her mind.

Ana sensed movement and jerked her head up. Balam's shadowy form glided toward her. She took a deep, controlled breath.

"May I join you?"

"Of course."

Unable to force small talk, she returned her attention to the sky above.

"Do you enjoy looking at the stars?"

Ana shrugged in response. Balam stared at her, and she realized she'd been rude so she said, "Yes. They are my friends."

"Do you like my location?"

"It's great."

"The Maya watch the stars. They are important to us. They tell us our future and remind us of where we came from. Would you like to hear a story?"

Ana nodded. A story before bed would do the trick. Keep her mind from her worries.

"This is from the Popul Vuh, the Mayan holy book.

Long ago, at the beginning of time, the cosmos were quiet, dormant. There was no rhythm or cycles because the sun did not rise. There was only the upper realm, the heavens; and the underworld, *Xibalba*. Supernatural beings lived in both planes and the primordial sea separated them. There was no earth yet. From the bottom of the deep sea, the great cosmic tree grew, its roots touching *Xibalba* and its branches reaching up to the heavens.

"Some divinities wanted to separate the planes with a level for earth, to create order and rhythm, to allow for sunrises and sunsets. There were also malevolent divinities who ruled *Xibalba*, who wished things to remain the same. To prevent the true sun's creation, they made a false one, the Seven Macaw. He did not move, but rested on top of the great central tree, preening itself. He was given gems for his eyes and teeth. You can see him there. I think you know it as the Big Dipper."

Balam pointed to the familiar constellation. Ana gazed up at the cluster of stars as Balam's resonant voice continued to narrate the fascinating story. "So the lords of the underworld were content. But the other divinities of the heavens were not. The first father and first mother, both ancient divine beings, manifested themselves as wild boar and mated. This union created twin brothers but because they were both males, they were unbalanced and unfocused. They made no effort to connect to their intuitive female, shamanic side. Nevertheless, they grew and tended the maize fields and in their exuberance, invented a ball game. They played often. Their footfalls and the tap, tap, tap of the ball created a rhythm. The ball arched up and down through the air like the sun's cycle. Seven Macaw saw this and knew the Lords of Negativity would be displeased so he told them of the brothers.

"The rulers of *Xibalba* summoned the twins to appear before them. Before they left, the brothers hid their ball and uniforms in the rafters of their home. When they arrived in the underworld, the evil lords tricked the twins and sacrificed them. Their bodies were buried below the ball field. The head of one of the brothers was set on top of the gourd tree and then the Lords of Negativity declared the place forbidden. One of the daughters of the Lords of Death was curious about the tree so she went and spoke to the head. He asked if she would help him to redeem himself and the evil that befell him by the hand of her father. She held out her hand and from the spit he placed on her palm, he impregnated her.

"Afraid of her father's wrath, she fled to the heavens and gave birth to a set twins, a boy and girl. When the twins grew older, a rat came and they captured it. To save its life, the rat told them of their father's hidden game equipment. They found his ball and costumes and began to teach themselves to play.

"The Lords of Death felt and heard the rhythmic patterns again and summoned the twins to *Xibalba*. Unlike their father, they were clever and used their magic through their many trials. Knowing their deaths awaited them and aware a sacrifice was required, the twins sought the help of two shamanic beings who could resurrect them after death. With their plan set, the twins walked hand-in-hand into a bonfire the Lords of Negativity had ordered them to jump over. Their bones were crushed and thrown into the river. Days later, the twins resurrected as fish and walked out of the river and onto land as humans.

"The hero twins disguised themselves as vagabonds and they traveled along, using their powers to create miracles. They danced and entertained so that word of their abilities reached the ears of the lords in *Xibalba*. Once again, they were summoned to the underworld to perform the miracle of resurrecting the dead. Convinced of the hero twin's powers, the gods killed themselves but the twins did not bring them back to life. The twins instead went to shoot down the Seven Macaw from his high perch. After the false sun died, the twins went to the ball court and resurrected their father and uncle.

"The twins climbed up and continued into the sky. One became the sun; the other, the moon. The great central tree was pulled down and a new one put in its place. It was the start of a new time. The chief creator god called all regal entities together and they created the earth. They attempted to make humans four times—all times unsuccessful. On the fifth attempt, they made the Maya from maize and they were pleased. And that is the end of our creation story." Balam paused to look at her and said, "It is thought that shifters and healers are the descendants of the mighty twins, and only together they have true power."

"Wow, it's just as dramatic as Greek mythology."

"Indeed."

"Except there were two heroes in your story."

"The Maya believe a journey or task is best accomplished as a team."

"Hmm. I'm not sure Chance feels that way. I don't know what I'm doing here. I came to be close with him and share this experience, but what can *I* do for *him*?"

After she said it, she heard the depression in her voice. Was she jealous, too? Ever since that day on the mountain, when her heart had healed, she'd been living in a dream. It was quickly dissolving into reality. She didn't have to dwell on her death any longer. Her future was open to her. Chance had found his great-grandfather. She was pleased he had found Balam, but now what was there for her to do?

"Are you lost?"

"I don't know."

"Everyone has power. Men were given the power to shapeshift, but the women in our lineage have the power to heal. Shapeshifters can alter their own energy pattern to resemble other animals and although we are able to connect our energy to others to heal, it is not natural to us and we don't have control. Women are able to push energy outside of themselves to heal, and in rare cases they have been known to shapeshift. My granddaughter, Sanchia is a healer, but she has no mentor to learn from and her knowledge is limited. Without the help of a healer when I was young, I would not have been able to cure the sickness."

"What do you mean? You were sick?"

"We were at war with the Spaniards. Killing another shapeshifter has its consequences. It poisons your soul."

A chill ran down her back. She was sitting next to a murderer. Maybe that was commonplace for a shifter, but not her.

"I would have gone mad if a shaman had not saved me. There are not as many healers as there once were. Their power is more subtle and easy to overlook, so if it is not taught by an elder, they can go throughout life unawakened. When I met you, I sensed dormant power in you. You may have the gift of healing."

Healing? She had never thought of herself as a healer. Just as she was trying to wrap her mind around what he just said, he continued. "Life with a shapeshifter is dangerous and can be hard. It is a risk—you already know this. I must be honest with you, Ana. You must know what you are up against if you choose to bind your life with Chance's."

She appreciated Balam's frankness. Flashbacks of Markus revisited her thoughts and she rubbed her arms to soothe herself.

"It is important for a shapeshifter to remain balanced. Being part of a team, a partnership, can be beneficial. Not any one person can hold all the answers. It is good Chance has you but he is still young and I sense he can be quick to react. You are watchful. You can be a good counterbalance."

Maybe she was a good counterbalance but she wanted to be more than just that. She loved Chance. He had become the most important person in her life and imagining herself without him was painful. One life-threatening danger had been removed and now it seemed her life was just as at risk as before her heart had healed.

Ana said goodnight to Balam and headed up to bed. Tired and ready for rest, she quickly fell into a deep slumber. A noise in the night roused her to an in-between state of sleep. She was in that familiar place again, at the lake. A beautiful voice hummed a sorrowful song that mixed with the echo of a bird's cry. It was something she had heard before. She wasn't alone or afraid, but with a friend.

I am here, when you're ready.

Chapter 23

"Chance, it is time to wake. Come downstairs and we will leave."

Chance woke with a start. Wildlife chattered and sang as daylight broke above the horizon. Balam left his room and with a groan, Chance flipped out of his bed onto the floor to do pushups. His muscles were sore but quick to react. The previous day was exhausting but had gone well. He now understood why his energy reserve had drained and he was no longer afraid of losing his powers. The figurative weight on his shoulders had finally lifted. He could breathe.

Last night was a blur. He could barely remember going to bed. Had he even seen Ana before going to sleep?

Chance rummaged through his belongings, turning them into a heap on the floor, and pulled out a pair of shorts. He padded downstairs and found Balam in the kitchen, heating water on the hearth.

"Ready for more?" Balam asked.

"Yes. I'm ready to go." Chance walked to the dining table, snatched up a banana and peeled it in one swift movement. He swallowed it down in three bites and plopped himself onto the couch, watching Balam prepare the morning hot chocolate.

"I am glad to see how eager you are. We will leave after we have a drink."

"What about Ana?"

Natasha Brown

"She is still sleeping. She was up late last night. That is okay. We will be back soon."

"She could probably use the sleep. I'll leave her a note."

Balam poured the boiling water into a pot of cacao and other seasonings. Then he carefully stirred the mixture. He poured the molten liquid into a ceramic pitcher and two mugs. While he sipped his, he held the other cup out to Chance, who readily accepted it.

Chance blew at the hot chocolate and inhaled too large a mouthful, nearly choking on it as his nerves registered the boiling temperature. No big deal. He'd feel fine after shifting. He winced as he gulped down the rest and darted to the kitchen to drop off his mug. Then he ran up to his room, scribbled out a note and placed it at the door of Ana's room. By the time he got back down to the main level of the home, Balam had drained his breakfast drink, placed his cup on the table and was walking out to the deck.

"You said you know owl form?" he called back to Chance as he walked.

Chance jogged up to him and said, "Yes. It shouldn't be a problem. I'll give it a try."

Without Ana there he didn't feel the need to cover up. Balam waited as Chance dropped his shorts on the wooden planks and closed his eyes. His energy was more alert than the day before and ready for instruction. Blue threads appeared in his thoughts, outlining the shape of the Horned Owl. A prickling sensation traveled down his arms and legs as feathers rippled in waves across his body while he shrank and contorted into a bird. He flapped his wings, collecting big scoops of air as he lifted off the ground and rested on a narrow rail hewn from a tree trunk.

Balam draped two long cloths on the rail beside Chance. He dropped his thin white cotton pants and leapt from the ledge, almost immediately becoming a blue-winged, black-hooded bird.

Chance scrambled, eager to keep Balam in his sights. Air currents lifted him upward and he tucked his wings to pick up speed. From above the treetops, the jungle seemed to be covered in thick green carpeting. Hidden beneath were ancient ruins, underground caverns and camouflaged wildlife.

Balam arched in a wide spiral above a clearing and began to descend. He perched on a crumbled pile of rocks and preened his feathers. Chance landed nearby and panted. He opened his beak wide to collect as much oxygen as he could.

His great-grandfather's voice startled him and he realized Balam had already shifted back to human form. "You can stay as a bird if you would like but I have some things I need to say. Just listen."

Chance readjusted himself, clutching at the crumbling rock with his talons.

"I admit I do not know the place of a shapeshifter in this modern world. I do not know how to advise you. I sense there are more dangers today than there were when I was in my youth. And I saw the conquistadors conquer my home. There are dangers for those you love.

Niyol made his decision. He loved my Itzel more than he loved being a shifter.

"You have already had beginner training from your grandfather. It is time to be forthright so you know the struggle ahead. Ana already died once. You saved her. The price you paid was losing your teacher and mentor. I think it should be clear to you now just how dangerous this life can be. You have told me you believe your cousin is alive. If that is so, than you can never rest easy. He has the sickness—it is likely he will never stop."

Chance momentarily forgot he was in owl form and started to speak but it came out in hoots and coos.

Balam's face was tight and he nodded as if he understood what Chance was trying to say.

"A healing connection delivers your power and essence intact, but when a shifter is killed and you are near enough to take in that energy, that essence is fragmented and absorbed incomplete. Having a murdered soul soak into you is dangerous. It is as though you have many personalities. If you kill one who is more powerful than you, than it is likely that essence will become the dominant power and voice within you.

"You have the loving imprint of your grandfather. It is very different when you have powers within you that are evil and angry. I tell you this because you need to know the weight of being a shapeshifter and the responsibility of bringing someone into this life. You think hard about this, Chance, because it is more than your own life you will affect. I lost more than half my wives to other shifters, and I know the pain of absorbing another's power as well. I had many dark times I would rather not remember but with much effort and help from a healer, I overcame the voices and unwelcome memories.

"If you choose to stay with Ana, it is not fair to keep information from her. A team requires two people making choices together. She should know about any threats—and how to protect herself. This is why I will be training her as well. You think about all I have told you. Use your senses and find your way back home. That is all for this lesson."

Balam shrank into a red, yellow and black striped snake, slithered down the moss-covered rocks and disappeared into the jungle.

A wave of nausea coursed through Chance and he nearly fell backward from his dizziness. He had gone from one teacher who barely told him anything to another who divulged everything, no holds barred. But he appreciated knowing the reality of his circumstances.

Chance had kept Ana uninformed, thinking he was protecting her. Now he realized he was only being a hypocrite. How could be expect others to be candid and truthful with him if he wasn't doing the same?

He had to come clean with her. It was the only way. Markus was alive and he was probably searching for them now. Chance had to build his powers and prepare for the time his cousin revealed himself. Ana needed to understand the reality of the situation. He had no idea what chance she had against a shapeshifter and he hoped Balam had answers.

All he wanted just then was to be near Ana, to

apologize and lay it all out for her. Would she forgive him?

The sun's rays penetrated his feathered armor. He twitched his head and extended his feathers. Chance jumped into the air and let his wings do all the work, lifting him up above the treetops. Now, where was home?

Chapter 24

The flight home took longer than Chance hoped. From above the forest canopy, everything looked the same. He wished he had noted some landmarks to help guide him back. Just as he wondered if he would ever return home, his grandfather's soothing voice echoed in his mind. *Chance, focus.* Words he had heard so many times before.

Chance blinked and let his cluttered thoughts fall away. *Remember, you're not a human right now, you're a bird.* Slowly, the air augmented and warped. Or at least, it appeared to. He sensed ripples fanning out from the earth. In the past, he had always used landmarks to fly from his house to Ana's. This was an entirely new experience. Unsure what he was looking at, he continued forward and followed his instincts.

A bubble-like field bulged above a section of the forest. Chance flew ahead, curious to see what was at its core. As he approached, he discerned a tall, vertical shape hidden under the trees.

Finally, he was home. He swept in and landed on the deck. His nails tapped on the wood as he inched himself forward to peer into the main level of the house. From his perch a foot off the ground, he couldn't see anyone so he turned around and waddled over to a cloth hanging on the rail. After a little effort, he returned to his own skin and wrapped the fabric around his abdomen. It was too close to a skirt for his liking. The shorts he had worn before he shifted were gone. As he turned to race upstairs, he nearly collided into Ana.

"Oh, hey. I was about to go look for you," Chance said. He seized the wrap as it slid down his waist and his cheeks flushed with warmth.

"Got your note. Thanks for keeping your promise. How'd training go?" She offered him a weak grin, but it seemed forced. Something was brewing below the surface and he suspected it was the reason he needed to talk to her.

"Can we talk in private?"

"Balam said he'd be back later—we're all alone."

Chance clutched her soft hand in his and led her into the living room. They settled onto the cushions and she waited with a strained expression.

He leaned forward, resting his elbows on his knees and began. "I'm so sorry, Ana. I haven't been honest with you. I didn't tell you I was having issues with my powers. I should have just told you what was up. I trust you, it's not that. I didn't want to admit that there could be something wrong. I thought I was protecting you but I understand now how wrong I was. And there's something else I haven't told you…" Ana eyed him uneasily and he pushed on. "I have reason to believe Markus is still alive. It's likely he'll come back for me."

He dropped his head, unable to look at her.

"It hurts finding out you've been keeping things from me." Her words came out choked and a wave of guilt forced his eyes shut.

"I'm so sorry. I never meant to hurt you. After Balam's talk with me, I realized that I wasn't doing you any favors by keeping it from you. I won't keep anything from you from now on, I promise. Just please forgive me?"

"Swear not to keep anything from me again?"

"I swear," Chance answered.

"So, you really believe Markus is still alive?" Ana said.

Chance held his palm out to her and she hesitated before placing her delicate fingers in his grasp. He kissed each fingertip and gave her hand a squeeze.

"I do. In Grandfather's memories, Markus just disappeared and I don't think that's how things work. Plus, he would have absorbed Markus's power if he'd died and I know for a fact that didn't happen."

He could hear her raspy breath catch in her throat. The fear and pain on her face was the reason he hadn't wanted to tell her to begin with. But as frightened as she was, she needed to know and be prepared.

She braced her fingers against her forehead and said in a strained voice, "After Markus, I knew there would be others out there that could hurt us. I knew it was dangerous. It just felt safer knowing he was dead. I can still see him when I close my eyes." Her body shivered beside him and she closed her eyes.

"Listen, you know I'll do anything I can to keep you safe. Balam thinks it's a good idea you start training as well, and I do, too. If you choose to stay beside me in this crazy shifter world, you should know how to take care of yourself, too."

Ana lifted an eyebrow at him and he shrugged in

response. "I don't know. It was Balam's idea."

"You promise to never keep anything from me again?"

"I swear it, my love. You are everything to me. Everything."

A tear dropped from her cheek and she giggled as she wiped it away. She pulled her hair back and twisted it up into a ponytail. "I'm going to have a second cup of hot chocolate and I hope Balam's back soon because I have some questions for him." Ana moved to the hearth and picked up the pitcher.

"And I need to get a pair of shorts on. This is too drafty." Chance picked at the edge of the cloth wrapped around his waist and grimaced.

Ana's laughter bounced off the walls and chased him off the couch. He wrapped her up in his arms and bit her neck gently. The need to change clothing was forgotten as he bathed himself in her scent, nestling his nose against her neck.

"Chance," she said in a low tone.

"Mmmm?"

"Balam."

A noise from the deck drew his attention. The regal silhouette of his great-grandfather moved past the open windows. Chance left a quick kiss on Ana's neck, released her and bounded to greet Balam.

"You found your way home."

"Wasn't easy but yeah. I'm here. Saw something I never did before. Have you ever seen the air warp, in ripples? It looked like there was a big bubble above your house."

"Birds are able to see magnetic fields. This helps to navigate if you neglect to remember landmarks. I chose this location for my home because of the magnetic field—it's strong here. It helps reenergize. Have you felt it?"

"I think so."

Now that he mentioned it, Chance was already beginning to feel recharged after his long morning.

"Excellent. Then you are ready for your next training session."

***

Ana's heart raced in excitement. They stood in the same clearing as yesterday but this time she wasn't an observer.

"Ana, I will teach you some traps. Chance, pay attention as this is valuable to you as well."

Balam sank a long flexible branch into the ground and tied a piece of twine at its end. Then he drove two short twigs into the earth about two yards away. Ana squatted down to see how he tied the end of the branch to one of the small twigs. He arranged the remaining rope into a lasso and sat back.

"Chance, take the form of one of your small animals. No bigger than so." Balam held his arms out over the ground, indicating the size of a large house cat.

Chance pinched his lips, scratched his bicep and said, "I might know something that would work…"

He shifted his footing and glanced down at the maroon fabric that encased his thighs and abdomen. Ana refrained from smiling. It was obvious how uncomfortable he was in his new shifting gear. She, however, didn't share his view of it. It provided plenty of what her Aunt Tera referred to as 'eye candy'. Plus, his discomfort was appealing; it made him vulnerable.

After another minute, his muscular body shuddered and condensed into a burnished wooly mammal. Folded within the fabric, the wolverine appeared innocent, harmless. Chance swayed and nearly toppled but spread his legs out and braced himself.

"Is this a new form, Chance? I do not recognize this creature."

"I think it's a wolverine, but I haven't seen him do it before," Ana said.

"Take your time adjusting. Then I want you to go explore the area and Ana and I will prepare some surprises for you."

A groan rumbled from Chance's chest and he shook his head, appearing dazed. He dragged himself from his wrappings and took a few cautious steps. With a backward glance, he wandered toward the wilderness, his elliptic stripes disappearing into the foliage.

"Let us try to catch a shapeshifter," Balam said and his stony face cracked a slight smile.

Over the next half hour he showed Ana how to dig holes and camouflage them to disguise the trap. Ana got the hang of it almost immediately. Thin vines and branches were strung across the pits and then leaves, rocks and dirt were strewn over top to conceal the hidden cavities.

"Very good, Ana. These traps are useful when you believe you are being followed and have time to prepare them. They are meant to subdue your attacker so you can keep your distance. Another day I will show you other, more dangerous traps."

Balam sniffed the air, stepped to the center of the clearing and said, "Come. Stand with me. Let us see if we can fool Chance."

Ana brushed off the dirt from her hands, scurried over to him and waited. She glanced over her shoulder and squinted at a patch of thick, tall blades from a succulent plant. Mottled green and gray, its stalks swayed ever so slightly. A pair of eyes blinked at her, and the dark wolverine emerged from the jungle and sneezed.

Chance blinked lazily at her and scurried forward. He stopped suddenly, his nose quivering. His snout lifted and then dropped to the ground before he started forward again. As he stepped onto a cluster of stones, the earth below him buckled and he plummeted out of sight. Angry screeches burst from the hole while dirt flew out in a spray.

"Calm down, Chance. I think your Ana has taken to trapping. Once you settle down, climb out and try to find the other traps."

The noises settled until only a low grumble reverberated from the pit. Privately, Ana was proud of herself but she didn't want to gloat. She kept her expression serious as Chance's wet, black nose materialized from the trap.

His body flattened as he pulled himself over the lip of

the hole. Woody debris littered his shaggy fur and there was a scowl on his face.

She knew she may have caught him this once but knowing Chance, he would be hard to trick again. When he focused on something, there was no shaking his determination.

The wolverine's eyes narrowed into slits as it edged out cautiously and settled onto the clay soil.

"Very good, Chance. Are there any others?"

He got back up and perched on a rock. His front paws lifted as his eyes scanned the clearing. After time spent in study, he trotted over to a spot near the edge of the alcove, reached his paw out and pressed down. The ground collapsed and Chance stared at both Balam and Ana. If wolverines could look smug, he was doing it.

"Good. Shift back so we can talk," Balam said with his fists on his hips.

Chance trotted over to his maroon cover-up and looked at Ana over his scruffy shoulder.

"Oh, right. Sorry," Ana said, and turned away, her cheeks flushed.

Chirping echoed around them; the jungle was alive with activity. As Ana waited, she observed a large iguana sunning itself on a broad stone. It blinked at her lazily, clearly unconcerned with her presence.

"Okay, you can turn around now," Chance's familiar voice said from behind her.

Ana pivoted on her heel just in time to see him adjusting the fabric around his waist. Chance added with a smirk, "Nice job on the traps."

"Thanks for testing it out."

"Chance, what other smaller animals do you know?"

Chance folded his arms in front of his chest and said, "Well, the smallest is the squirrel. Then I've got the red fox, bobcat, owl and eagle. Grandfather shifted into a wolverine before he died and I figured I'd give it a try. When I thought about the animal I felt its mapping, gave it a shot and it worked."

"Yes. It is common to get the mapping as well as the power and memories, especially since you were given his essence in a healing connection."

Chance combed his fingers through his black hair and loose strands fell across his hazel eyes. Then he clapped his hands together and said, "So, I feel like trying bear again. I bet I could do it today."

Balam blinked and shook his head. "No. You have a youthful perspective. It is true that large animals are strong but smaller animals can stay hidden and help conserve your energy. I will teach you a new animal today. Study my mapping and join me.

"Ana, I want you to sit and be still, to listen to your surroundings. You have watched Chance sit and focus before shifting. I want you to do the same. You have instincts, too—listen to them. Let us see if we can surprise you."

No sooner had he stopped talking than he shrank into a black, knee-high monkey. It showed its teeth and shook free from the orange cloth that, seconds earlier, had been wrapped around Balam's waist.

"Hmm, okay," Chance said under his breath.

Ana watched him stare at the small primate while its tail curled and flicked as though it had a mind of its own. She had asked Chance once before what it was like mapping an animal. It must be exhilarating. She could almost imagine the glowing threads lacing the monkey's body.

Chance remained still for nearly ten minutes, entirely focused on his great-grandfather, who had begun to pick through his fur while he waited.

"Here goes…"

He sat down cross-legged and closed his eyes. Wrinkles formed at his temple and he dropped his chin to his chest. Black fur began to sprout from his skin. He shook as his body shrank down and contorted. Finally, a long tail extended out and coiled over his head. Chance braced against the ground, his small beady eyes pinned on her.

The other black monkey jumped in place and then somersaulted toward Chance. Balam's mouth opened and a loud screech cut through the clearing. Ana and Chance both covered their ears as the sound reverberated loudly.

Balam pulled at Chance's arm and led him, stumbling, toward the jungle. At the first tree, Balam leapt up four feet and grabbed hold of it with his hands, feet and tail. Quick as a shot, he bounded up the trunk and surged from tree to tree like a ball bearing in a pinball machine. Ana giggled as she watched, thoroughly entertained.

The woozy monkey on the ground clutched at the trunk as though it offered support and not a means of travel. It stared up into the canopy and after another screech, it lumbered up the tree.

"Have fun!" Ana called out, a little bit jealous.

She tried to keep her eyes on the monkeys but after a short time, they disappeared into the leafy cover. With a deep sigh, she walked over to Chance's maroon sarong, folded it, and laid it out in a neat square on the ground. She sat down, crossed her legs and felt the position strain her tendons. *Guess I'm not as flexible as I thought.*

Not entirely sure what to do, she took a deep breath, closed her eyes and dropped her shoulders. She thought about Balam's instructions and was tempted to open her eyes, worried they would try to scare her. She didn't like surprises, at least not that kind.

Time to focus. Listen to the rhythm of your breath. Let it guide you to your center. All her anxieties and inner noise quieted as she fixated on the rise and fall of her chest. *Now, let in the noises around you. Identify the rhythmic sounds the earth makes. Wind, trees, leaves. Let those noises fall away and listen to what is left.*

It almost felt as if Niyol was there with her, guiding her. Ana reached out with her senses and imagined the earth breathing. The trees moved, leaves rattled and air murmured like the rhythm of a song. She needed to identify the harmony, the unique, irregular static. Birds all around her called out their heart songs, announcing their presence. Distant screeches and taps rang out, and leaves shuffled on the ground. Something that reminded her of a gear whirred from nearby. It was probably just a bug.

A series of soft noises from the forest drew her

attention. She cocked her ear to hear better. Her eyes opened and she zeroed in on a pair of black shiny eyes peering at her from behind a tree trunk.

"Gotcha," she said.

She couldn't tell who it was, Chance or Balam. As she was trying to decide, something warm touched her shoulder and she gave a start. A monkey sporting a toothy grin was resting its tiny fingers on her.

Ana snorted and held her hand out to the small, hairy primate. It placed its hand in hers and launched onto her shoulders.

"Oh!"

The other ebony monkey waddled over to them, walking on its hind legs like Charlie Chaplin. It stepped into her lap, sat down and then wrapped its arms around her neck.

"Chance?"

His warm breath touched her cheek in a kiss and she gave him a scratch. The muscles on his back twitched and he guided her hand to his back again.

"Haha, sorry. Are you itchy?"

The other monkey slid off her back and went over to the orange cloth. He lifted it up and in one fluid motion, shifted back into Balam. He did it so smoothly he wasn't exposed. Once the transformation was complete, he wrapped the sarong around his abdomen and walked over to them.

"Very good. Both of you. Ana, you sensed Chance before he could get to you. Chance, you are getting used to this new form. Monkeys are flexible and fast. Power is not everything. You must be quick to react and problem solve. This comes with experience and knowledge. I imagine you are tired and hungry. Let us return home."

After Chance shifted back, he said in her ear, "You did good. You really must have been paying attention when Grandfather trained me. But you always seem to know when I'm near."

"Ditto."

The voice in her head hadn't led her astray. She learned that she could trust her instincts. Hopefully, those instincts would be enough to keep her safe if Markus found them again.

Chapter 25

Silence enveloped them as they ate a late lunch following the long training session. Ana and Chance had two helpings of tamales, beans and rice as Balam sat back and watched them, his lips curled upward. He was clearly pleased.

As usual, Chance had plenty of questions but his appetite won out and he focused on satiating his hunger. After a long week of similar lessons, Chance was learning new smaller animals: dove, rabbit, mouse and shrew. He had begun to feel stronger and now that his power was, for the most part, back, he was more confident he could protect them from a threat.

He watched Ana across the table as she ate in silence. "You did great today," he said in between bites.

She beamed at him in response. Even though she was frightened of Markus, she was handling the news of his non-demise well. She poured herself into learning the skills Balam taught her. A part of their new routine involved Ana attempting to trap Chance while he endeavored to surprise and capture her. He was proud of her efforts, but found it frustrating that he couldn't seem to catch her unguarded. No matter what form he took, she always knew he was near.

He was very good at sniffing out most of her traps, however not all. She was getting better at hiding them, but she just couldn't hide her scent, which was always the tip-off.

While he thought about their most recent challenge, Balam said, "I have something new to teach you both this afternoon. It is a well kept secret that has the power to harm shifters. Ana, I will give you this knowledge because you and Chance are one but you must never speak of it or share this information with anyone. Do you understand?"

Something with the power to destroy a shifter? Chance washed down a mouthful of tamale with some water, pushed his plate away and leaned forward. Ana swallowed a large bite and said with a gravely voice, "Yes, I do. I will tell no one. I swear."

They trailed behind Balam through the cave and out into the jungle. Balam walked off the trail, cut between the tall, narrow trees and stopped in an area filled with what looked like weeds. Ana reached out to pull some tiny, white upside down blooms clustered into an umbrella shape.

Balam caught her hand. "Do not touch, Ana. I keep this plant nearby in case I need it. It is poison. For mortals and shapeshifters alike but it affects us both very differently."

Chance took a second look at the plant. It was similar to anise. He sniffed the air and recoiled after identifying a sickeningly sweet aroma that warned him of danger.

"That is right, Chance. Smell it so you remember. This is hemlock. It is dangerous to touch and can kill humans that eat it or consume animals that have eaten it. It paralyzes the body until your organs cease to function and you are dead. For a shifter, it paralyzes the part of the nervous system that controls shifting and blocks us from using our powers. It freezes a shifter in whatever form they are in when it enters their bloodstream. It makes us very sick and an easy target to kill. If we can not shift to heal ourselves or escape—"

Ana stepped back and grabbed Chance's hand. He cleared his throat and said, "How do you use it?"

"Every part of the plant is poisonous. I handle it with gloves and boil it down into a tincture but I do this outside. I make a fire but even the fumes make me ill. You can dip a spear, arrow or knife tip into the poison. If you are in animal form, a weapon will do you no good. So wherever I go, I take with me a small amount of protection."

Balam removed a small blade, a few inches in length, from a sheath hidden under his waistband. He handled it carefully, touching only the handle, and slipped it back. Then, he lifted an arrowhead-like stone that hung around his neck.

"What's that do?" Ana asked.

Balam said through thin lips, "It is a weapon."

He held it out so they could see it closely. From a distance, it looked like a simple tool but upon closer inspection, Chance saw a dark tarry substance at the blunt end. It looked like a seal. Was the weapon hollow? The smoky edges gleamed like glass. Its point was narrow and sharp. No doubt it could cause serious harm.

"Let me show you how this can be used." Balam lifted it over his head and before Chance realized what had happened, the weapon was a breath away from his chest.

"Once it has pierced your attacker, break the tip off and let the hollow chamber dispense the poison."

"Don't leave home without it," Ana whispered with a slight grimace.

With a nod, Balam answered, "Yes. In my time, mortals hunted us as well. It was thought if you killed a shifter, you could steal their power. Life begins with a seed, and because killing a shifter only releases part of their energy, it does not provide the seed one needs to awaken that power. Many died. Out of the few people who know of our kind now, some still wish to kill shifters simply to rid the earth of us. However most are not that foolish..."

What happened to those shapeshifter hunters? Chance could only guess. Judging from Balam's downturned lips and sour expression, it must not have ended well for them.

"I have a pendant for you both. Keep them safely around your necks." Balam handed each of them one of the decorative weapons strung on long leather cords. Chance slipped his around his neck and grasped it between his fingers. Ana stared at hers as though it could kill her at any moment. Then, with clear hesitation, she hung it around her neck.

"What if it breaks?" she said, frowning.

"It would be foolish to be so careless with such a dangerous weapon."

"Right."

Chapter 26

"But I don't want to hurt Chance or you," Ana said as she ran her knife along a branch, sharpening its tip into a deadly point and considered lopping the end off.

"It is good practice for us all." Balam answered. "We can heal as long as you do not kill us on impact. You are aiming for the legs and not the head."

That wasn't very comforting. She thought she had been holding up fairly well, considering she was being trained to trap and kill. In her past life, Ana never would have imagined herself going native in the jungle. Just yesterday, one of her snares supplied them a delicious dinner of rabbit, something she had never eaten before. Now Balam was encouraging her to rig even more dangerous traps.

Ana bit the inside of her lip and shrugged. "Well, I guess."

"Ana. This is what it is to be with a shifter. It is important to know how to survive. This Markus has the sickness. I am almost certain he will come for you. I teach you in this way so you live. I would take it slow if I knew we had time."

He was right. She knew he was but it just wasn't natural for her to think like a predator. The sky overhead had darkened considerably since their trek from the house and Ana squinted at the threatening clouds. "Okay but be careful! Looks like it might rain."

Chance stretched his arms over his head and said, "Awfully confident. Don't think I can evade your traps?"

Ana tested the tip of her spear with her finger. She knew he was just trying to lighten her mood but she didn't like the idea of impaling him with her trap. She couldn't bring herself to smile.

"Chance, while Ana is busy with her traps, I have something new for you to work on."

Chance leaned in and kissed her neck.

"Be careful," she warned again as he disappeared into the wilderness. His spicy scent lingered in his wake.

***

"I like your tattoos, Balam. Mind telling me where you got them?" Chance stared at Balam's back and arms as he walked behind him. An inky face glared at him. It had every appearance of a Mayan glyph. He had a hard time imagining Balam striding into a tattoo parlor.

"I earned them in my youth. My teachers gave them to me. They are my *naguals*—my animal spirits. The animals that I am one with. Your test will come soon and you may earn your first."

"Really? I can't wait. Is that a jaguar on your back?"

"Yes, Balam, the jaguar. It was my first tattoo. The jaguar keeps the forest balanced. When it hunts, it does not make its prey suffer. It is beginning to disappear in these jungles, just like my...our kind."

"When did you learn the yaguar form and can you teach it to me?" Chance asked while he eyed the sizeable teeth on the creature tattooed onto Balam's browned skin.

"Ah, you have seen me take yaguar form. I was taught the revered yaguar form after I passed my first test. As your thunderbird is not truly an eagle, the yaguar is not just a jaguar, it is mighty—a display of power. After you earn your tattoo I will teach it to you."

Excitement bubbled up as he thought about learning such a powerful and unique form. Having a mentor certainly had its benefits.

"Can you do anything special as the yaguar? When I'm in thunderbird form, I can direct lightning."

Balam stopped and turned to face him. His brow arched as he said, "Really? I have heard of shifters who could do this as large birds. Maybe you could show me your thunderbird when you are strong enough?"

"Yes, of course."

"The yaguar embodies stealth but I will tell you more of that later. All right, you can use the skills of the animal you shift into, but you must be discreet. You have an elevated sense of smell, taste and have superior strength, but have you ever borrowed abilities from an animal while you are in human form?"

"No, but I think I remember Ana mentioning Markus shifting only his head into some kind of beastly form. It really scared her. She doesn't like talking about it much."

"I do not do that. There were some of my ancestors who did. But I find it is unsafe to meld different animals together like that. I have heard of peoples who favored that kind of shifting—desert people with dog and crocodile heads."

Chance recalled the time he tried shifting into the thunderbird form and his painful failure. He wasn't excited to feel that kind of discomfort again.

He could taste the rain before it began, a fine mist touched the air around them. Within minutes, it turned into pronounced droplets tapping against the leaves and ground.

Balam scanned the area before he said, "I will leave you now. I want you to track me back to Ana but remember her traps. Tracking is a very important skill. When I leave, sit in silence. Focus on the smells around you and pay attention to your own body. Other animals with a great sense of smell have more receptors—little folds hidden inside." He stroked his nose and high cheekbones. "Like bears and dogs."

"Do you have bears here?" Chance asked in excitement as a raindrop slapped against his forehead.

"No longer. One of the many things the Spaniards defiled and destroyed. They had no respect for life." Balam's expression darkened. "The rain washes away scents so you will need to work hard. Remember, he who walks without looking will fall into trouble. While you track, watch around you."

With agility, Balam uncoiled his sarong and fastened it loosely around his neck. As he stared at Chance, his body grew into an ebony jaguar the size of a horse. A rumble emanated from his chest as he turned and disappeared into the noisy jungle.

He was alone. Balam had led him into a new area they

had never visited. They hiked for half an hour through the wilderness, up hills and down rocky ravines. He knew his great-grandfather would make his way back to Ana quickly. Would he travel the whole way as a jaguar or would he try to throw Chance off and shift into different animals? If he got lost, Balam would find him. He hoped.

Time to focus. Chance settled on the ground and faced the direction the jaguar had gone in. His eyes snapped shut and he cleared his thoughts.

Smells specific to the Yucatán filtered into his nose. The terra cotta soil smelled like clay baking in the sun. A floral aroma suggested sweet blooms were nearby. He let the scents steep in his senses while he thought about his favorite form, the grizzly bear. He visualized its wet, black nose and his power buzzed with electricity. After nearly a month's training, his energy reacted more quickly. He was so much closer to having his powers back to where they were before he gave it all away. To save Ana.

His nose tingled and the skin on his face grew tight. Shooting pain stabbed at his sinuses. It felt as if he'd been punched, and he almost expected to taste blood as he lifted his hand to inspect the damage.

A wet, porous snout extended under his fingers. But his great-grandfather wouldn't be happy if Chance cruised into the clearing sporting a bear's snout. He cupped his muzzle and called on his powers once more. This was very different from letting go and allowing a full change to take effect. It was pinpointed, and took all of his control. Energy hummed below his palms and he felt his nose shrink back to normal. He flared his nostrils and dropped his hands back to his side.

Did he still have the extra sensors he needed? After a deep inhalation, he knew he did. The things he'd smelled before the transformation were just a few of the many he detected now.

Chance leapt to his feet, ready to move. He sniffed the air and attempted to identify the various scents. Finally, he caught a familiar aroma that had to be a mammal.

The trail zigzagged through the jungle for nearly an hour and he knew he was close when his heart began to race from Ana's distinct floral and pine fragrance.

He raced down a ravine, crossed a small creek and flew up the opposite bank. A cluster of rocks densely overgrown with vines was at the top and he hurdled over them. Something cracked nearby but he thought nothing of it and continued on, propelling off a pile of leaves. A projectile launched toward his legs. He moved fast to avoid it but Ana's sharpened spear moved faster and tore through the muscles in his calf.

"Argh!"

Damn it! Why hadn't he paid attention? Ana would lose it if she saw him hurt by her own hand. Blood flowed down and pooled in his shoe. The spear hadn't implanted into his flesh but he felt queasy, nonetheless. Raindrops trickled down his body and he wiped the water from his brow.

No one had to know about it. Just as he was about to shift and heal, Balam and Ana emerged from behind some trees. He turned sideways to obscure her view of his leg and planted his foot on the ground. It took all his effort not to wince.

Balam spoke first, "Good job, Chance. You followed my trail very well. I made it easy for you this time—even in the rain—but you did well."

"How do you know I followed your trail? Were you watching me?" Chance asked as he tried to ignore his painful wound.

"Yes. I doubled back as a bird and monitored you until you came close enough. Then I joined Ana to check and see how she did. I see the trap surprised you."

Why couldn't Balam hold his tongue? Chance sighed and stared at the ground rather than risking a glare at his great-grandfather.

Ana frowned, shuffled around Balam and arched her neck. She cringed and shouted, "Chance! Are you okay?" She turned a furious gaze on Balam. "I told you I didn't want anyone getting hurt!"

"He will be fine after he shifts. It is good experience. Better this way than at the tip of an enemy's spear, do not you agree?" Balam crossed his arms on his chest.

"No, I don't! I just speared my boyfriend's leg! There is something just wrong with that. If my or my loved one's life and health are threatened, I will do whatever it takes to keep us safe. But Chance was not threatening me. It's just not right!"

Before she turned and ran off toward home, Chance noticed her cheek quiver and her eyes well with tears. Great. Just great. Now he'd upset her. If he had paid more attention, he could have easily evaded her trap.

"She is headstrong." Balam stated.

"Yes."

"I suggest you heal before we go home and clean up. When your mate is unhappy, no one is happy. Woman are natural healers. They get conflicted about causing harm." Chance couldn't decide if the expression on Balam's face represented sadness or remorse...

***

"See? I'm fine. Just took a quick shift and I'm all better."

Ana was sitting on the bed with her back to him. He settled behind her and rubbed her shoulder. As soon as he touched her, she spun around and wrapped her arms around him. Nothing compared to having her against his skin. He tucked her head under his chin and embraced her.

"Chance, I'm so sorry. I won't do it again. I can't." Her whispers caught in her throat.

"Shh, don't worry about it, my love. You don't have to do anything you don't want to." He lifted her face to look into her watery green eyes. His heart thrummed. "God, I love you," he said before kissing her on the lips.

All the attention spent on training had certainly drained the passion from their relationship. He only had enough energy at the end of each day to collapse in bed before the sun met the horizon. Chance had felt a distance grow between them and he didn't like it. Ana was by his side every day and they were in a beautiful land steeped in history. Life surrounded them, but the precious moments were lost under the ever-present weight of survival.

He clung to her, not wanting the moment to end. She seemed to be of like mind and lowered herself back onto the bed. Chance slid his hands up to cup her face and nuzzled into her neck. Short gasps escaped her lips, which nearly drove him into a frenzy.

"Oh, Chance, I love you."

He laid a trail of tender kisses from her jaw line back to her mouth, silencing her. Her hands dug into his back and Chance growled. The sound brought him back to the present and he raised himself off of her. She appeared confused so he said, "Believe me, I'd like to do this every minute of every day, but I'm not sure it's smart to keep going." He brushed a stray lock of hair from her face before he sat up.

Ana sighed, readjusted her tank top and got up. They were silent for a minute before Chance changed the subject. "Balam's a trip. He's so hard to read. One minute he's all serious and the next, he appears to have a heart."

"I'm not sure. But he's not so scary to me anymore. I think he's just lived through so much, he's lost...I dunno. His hope? Something." Ana sighed, pulled her hair back into a ponytail and said, "Should we go downstairs?"

"Sure. Balam was getting some food together. I'm hungry."

Ana clutched her belly and said, "Boy, I am, too. My appetite has been out of control since you healed my heart. I'm just glad I'm all muscle now."

They chased each other downstairs and found Balam at the table. A platter of meat, beans and potatoes waited for them.

"Help yourselves to food. You must be hungry after your hard work."

Chance and Ana sat down and began to serve themselves.

Balam took a sip from his cup and said, "You both have worked very hard. I think you have earned some fun. Our work is done for the day. Let us drink to your accomplishments." He snatched up a narrow bottle filled with a clear liquid and poured some into three small glasses.

Balam handed one to Ana, who eyed it cautiously and said, "What is it?"

"It is made from fermented corn. I made it myself. It is for those who seek answers."

Chance held his glass up and grinned at Ana, who sniffed at hers before she clinked it against his.

"Thanks, Balam, for mentoring us and welcoming us into your home," Chance said.

He was the first to lift the drink to his lips. The liquid ran down his throat and burned the entire way to his stomach. "Hooh!"

Ana's glass paused at her lips as she stared wide-eyed at Chance while he sputtered and winced. He gave her the thumbs up sign and she sipped at Balam's concoction.

"Oh, my," she said and added, "I think I could take it with some hot chocolate. Do you mind if I make some, Balam?"

Ana had already learned the recipe and taken over the morning preparations. Balam nodded so she went to the hearth and stoked the fire. As she got to work making hot chocolate, Balam stood with the bottle in hand and sat on the couch. Chance followed him over and stared at the fire, fascinated with its movement.

"I have been alone a long time. I waited for you to come, Chance. I had begun to wonder if Niyol had kept his promise or if the bloodline had run dry. The end of my cycle is drawing near. I have no place in this world any longer. When I lost my true mate, there was nothing left for me but to find one I could pass my knowledge to. I had hoped Niyol would be the one but it is you. Both."

Ana turned around to look at him and asked, "Are you dying?"

"I am nearly six-hundred years old. My shifting has kept me alive for this long, but it is time to pass my power back to the earth. I am ready. I am tired."

Chance tried to see it from that perspective. He couldn't imagine a world without Ana and couldn't imagine what it would be like to live that long.

"How did she die?" he asked.

Balam's face darkened. "I do not like talking of it." He appeared to consider answering, and spoke slowly, "Another shifter with the sickness. Looking for others to feed off of. He sought power and chose my mate—Itzel's mother. Your great-grandmother, Chance. She had healing power, like many of the woman of our line. He sensed her energy and killed her. I came to protect her too late. Her body had run cold. There was nothing for me to do but bury her."

Balam poured more of the corn alcohol into their

glasses and Chance said quietly, "Did you kill him?"

"The one time I killed a shifter was from necessity. But no, I never found him and he never came back. My little Itzel saw it all, hidden and safe."

"I'm sorry," Chance said, staring into the fire.

"Oh, me, too. That is such an awful story, and your daughter saw it all...terrible," Ana said and Balam tilted his head and nodded.

After expelling a sigh, Ana stirred the hot chocolate once more, poured it into a mug and then mixed in the alcohol that remained in her glass. After she blew on it, she gave a quick sip and muttered, "Yummy."

Chance lifted his glass to Balam, shot back his drink and swallowed quickly, trying to avoid the fiery bite. His stomach was warm, along with his cheeks and ears. His muscles, which had been sore from the long day's work, no longer ached. The padded cushions beneath him felt like clouds as he slouched lower and Ana curled up beside him.

"Tell us about the Mayans. What happened? Weren't your people powerful?" Chance asked. His voice sounded funny and he chuckled.

"I was born after the shifter war but my father survived it and told me of our downfall. Yes, my people were brilliant. We watched the stars and they guided us. They taught us how to measure time so we created the calendar. We had scientists and mathematicians. The Maya grew to great power. It was believed shifters were given power to help encourage balance and order within the earthly plane. Our natural powers gave us status.

Many became rulers, shamans, or elite warriors.

"As cities grew large and prosperous, resources were strained when rains did not come to our great land and the maize turned yellow and died. People were suffering and kings were desperate to heal the land so they led attacks on neighboring kingdoms in search of people to sacrifice for the Gods' favor. It was not widespread knowledge that a shifter could absorb another's energy. It began when a young shaman desired more power. He told his king the Gods wished more sacrifices to bring rain and misled their people into war just so he could locate and kill more people with our gifts. It only takes one person, Chance. One with the sickness and the power to destroy everything.

"City after city was devastated as his quest for power continued. He only told his king the Gods were not happy yet and needed more. Whispers spread amongst shapeshifters about what was truly happening, and alliances were made. That was the beginning of the Great Shapeshifter War and nearly the end of the Maya and our kind. No city was left undamaged. Some thought the only way to stop him was to build their own strength off others and soon, there were many struck with the sickness, leading the innocent to their deaths. It was over nearly as fast as it started. A healer discovered the power of hemlock, which led to the downfall of the evil ones. But the damage had been done. Within a year, the Maya went from being the most powerful in Mesoamerica to just trying to survive.

"For many hundred years, my people fought amongst

ourselves and other groups. The poisonous thought of stealing power had begun. I was a fledgling, just learning our ways, when the Spaniards came. It was a dark time. They sought riches—gold. Many more deaths and destruction followed. They called us heathens, barbarians. It was all we could do to save our lives and bury our precious monuments. For an age I led my people, until the times changed. No one believed in shifters any more and it became unsafe for me to remain in the city. I have never stopped looking after my people."

Balam swirled the transparent liquid around his glass before slinging it back and swallowing it. It all made so much more sense now, Chance thought. He couldn't even imagine what his great-grandfather had lived through. Chance's head hurt trying to do so. Then again, maybe it was the alcohol.

Ana's voice whispered beside him. "Wow, Balam. What a sad story. I can't imagine what it was like."

Balam's eyes remained on the fire as he said, "It is hard to forget. But you are my new hope. You will carry my people's history and my lessons with you. I believe a new cycle will begin and I have hopes our kind will not disappear but become strong once more and do as we were intended to do—keep balance in the world."

He tipped the bottle to Chance's glass and said, "This is enough talk like this. Let us see if you are ready to discover your *nagual*. Shifters can have many but we all have one animal that represents us."

Chance gulped down the liquor and closed his eyes as

its warmth spread through his body. His mind was fuzzy and playing tricks on him. Dark shadows curled through the air above the hearth. Was he seeing things? He shook his head, which only made him dizzy.

"Look into the fire," Balam ordered him. "What do you see?"

Ana leaned forward and stared at Chance.

Chance did as Balam said and focused on the glowing embers under the logs in the hearth. Shapes flickered and danced before him. His blood pounded in his ears and he dropped his head forward despite the vertigo. A pattern began to form in the tangerine glow. Dark orbs blinked and Chance nearly choked in surprise at seeing a beast in the inferno.

Ana's warm fingers curled around his arm. "What is it?"

He was afraid to blink; he didn't want to lose the face in the fire. Below the coal eyes, a black nose formed and then a mouth opened in a silent roar and he couldn't help but laugh.

He should have known. He'd always had a special connection with the grizzly.

"Do you see your *nagual*?" Balam asked.

"Yes. It's the grizzly bear."

"I see. Good work, Chance. Let us sleep off the drink so that you may be prepared for tomorrow."

Chance groaned, "Ugh, more work."

"This I think you'll be happy about." Balam stood and delivered the dirty glasses and the nearly empty bottle of corn alcohol to the kitchen. "I will see you both in the morning."

***

Ana helped Chance to his feet. Her strength had grown immensely over the last couple of months, especially now that she was so active. Chance's weight would have been a burden mere weeks earlier. She found good footing and lifted him up. The way he was lolling around, she was glad she'd had only one shot of Balam's liquor.

"Mmm," he mumbled and added, "I'm so tired."

"Well, let's get you to bed then. Sounds like Balam has more planned for you. No rest for the weary."

Now that Chance was standing, he was steady enough on his own and started for the stairs.

"I'm just gonna take care of the fire. Be right up," Ana said. Chance waved over his shoulder and continued up.

Ana used a stick to spread out the remaining logs in the hearth. It made her nervous to leave the fire, which was still going strong. Sparks flew like tiny geysers as she rolled the wood over, and heat radiated into a warped halo around the sooty embers. Then, as though life were breathed into the flames, they arched in slow motion, fanning out into feathery wings.

I'm staying away from alcohol from now on. She blinked, rubbed her eyes and the apparition was gone. *Must be time for bed*, she laughed to herself.

Chapter 27

A strange noise woke Chance the next morning. He opened his eyes reluctantly and groaned. A gecko stared at him from his side table and repeated its high-pitched sound.

The light was too bright and made his temples throb so he covered his face with his arms. When had he gone to bed last night? The end of the evening was somewhat of a blur. He sat up slowly and held his head in his hands, hoping doing so would stop the world from spinning. He glanced back over in search of the lizard but it was gone.

He skipped his normal pushup regimen and padded through the hallway and into the washroom. After returning to his room, he looked for some fresh clothes. Fresh being a relative term. Without a washing machine, they had been rinsing their clothing in the subterranean river below the house. After a quick sniff at his shirt, he realized it was wash time again. The sheets on his bed spilled onto the floor, half covering the lumpy pile of shirts, shorts and underwear. If his mom could see his room, she'd give him 'the look', for sure. He thought of his parents and sent a quick message to them from his phone. He didn't want them to be concerned.

He peeked into Ana's room and saw her bed was made and her belongings sat tidily in place as though a housekeeper had stopped by. It was already late morning and he wondered why Balam hadn't awakened him earlier. He was glad he had allowed him to sleep in, though. He had needed to. His headache had dulled, leaving a pulsing in his temples. It probably would have been a good idea to pace himself when partying with a five-hundred-year-old.

Down in the dining area, half the table was spread with the remnants of breakfast. On the other half, a long carved stone box lay on a cloth and Balam sat beside it with his hands resting on either side. Ana was stretched out on the couch, unmoving. He assumed she was napping.

"Good morning, Chance."

"Morning, Balam. Not so sure it's good. Bad headache."

"Drink some of this," Balam said as he held out a cup filled with something that smelled of lemon.

Chance eyed it warily and hesitated. "I think I've had enough."

"No, please. It will help you."

He accepted the cup from his great-grandfather and took a tentative sip. It definitely had lemon in it but there was another flavor he wasn't familiar with. If it would help his headache, though, he was game. He plopped down into a chair and began to eat some fruit and corncakes.

"Thanks for letting me sleep in. I needed it."

Balam nodded and neglected to cover up the grin on his face. "Did you enjoy yourself last night?"

"Yeah. Good times. Not sure I remember everything."

"Do you remember your *nagual*?"

Chance remembered the dark eyes that stared out at him from the fire and said, "Yes, the bear."

He took another sip of the lemon drink and noticed his headache was dissolving. "This stuff works great. My headache is gone."

"Very good. Then we can start when you are ready."

"What are we doing today?" Chance said as he eyed the strange box now in Balam's hands.

"You are ready for your *nagual* tattoo."

"Really? Excellent!"

Ana stirred on the couch and sat up, stretching. "You're up, Chance. Been waiting for you. What's going on?"

Balam opened the carved box and pulled out something wrapped in aged cotton. He unwrapped it, revealing a long stick with a metal piece that looked like a nail at its end. Ana wandered to the table and said, "Is that a weapon?"

"This is a tattoo tool, Ana."

Chance wondered how many other people it had been used on. It looked very old. The wood was dark and the metal no longer shone but had a hazy black sheen to it. He was glad he was up to date with his tetanus shots. Ana exchanged a concerned look with him.

"You gonna sterilize it?" she asked, and Chance was relieved she'd saved him from asking the question.

"I will rest the tip in the hot coals. Let us go to the couch. Now, Chance, lay on your stomach."

He knew he had said he wanted a tattoo but as he stared at the tool, he began to feel anxious. Ana held his hand and they walked to the living room. The hearth was smoldering with hot coals from the morning fire and Balam rested the tip in the glowing embers for a few minutes and then set it aside. He produced a stone pestle filled with a tarry black substance and another stick etched with designs that had a thick, hammer-like end.

Chance pulled off his shirt and lay down as Balam had instructed. He rested his chin on a cushion and watched as his great-grandfather settled beside him. Balam dipped a brush into the black ink and touched it to Chance's back. The cool, wet bristles trailed across his skin. It was almost relaxing. "I use the brush to make the design," he explained.

"How's it look?" he asked Ana, who was hanging over the back of the couch, observing everything. She gave a low whistle and said, "Looks great, Balam. You're an artist."

"And now this instrument will draw your blood and leave ink in the wound. As you know, when you are injured and shift back into human form, you return to health. Tomorrow we will see if you can shift and hopefully return to your shape *with* your tattoo. It is not easy and it requires much focus but I believe you are ready."

The mental image of Balam driving a piece of ink-tipped metal into his skin for hours on end turned his stomach. And it would all be for nothing if he wasn't strong enough to retain the tattoo. He wanted to prove to Balam and to himself that he was truly strong enough.

"Your *nagual* will look out for you if it is meant to be.

Are you ready, Chance?"

After a deep breath, Chance rested his chin onto his clenched fists and said, "Yes."

Balam withdrew the tool from the edge of the hearth, dipped a cloth into a clear liquid and cleaned the metal tip with it. Then, he immersed it in the ink and rested his arm across Chance's shoulders. One hand held the metal-tipped tool; the other, the hammer-like stick.

The first jab at his skin was like a bee sting, and the repetitive poking made his nerves jump. Balam kept tapping one stick against the other and soon a rhythm formed that echoed off the limestone walls. Chance closed his eyes and lost himself in the sound. After a few minutes, a cool cloth was being dragged across the newly tattooed section of his back. Like a storm bringing rain to an inferno, it soothed the fiery pain but only for a moment until it began again.

Chance wondered if conventional tattoos were this painful. He didn't want to show signs of discomfort so he tried to meditate. Niyol's voice echoed in his thoughts, a welcome diversion. *Let yourself relax, Chance. Take a deep breath. Feel it go down to your feet and up to your head. Then breathe out all your pain and tension. Keep nothing. Only focus on your energy center.*

His jaw was clenched tight as well as his abdominal and back muscles. With his eyes shut, he began to take long, slow breaths. He allowed his body to relax and visualized his energy core. Its blue electricity was ready and awake, so different from over a month ago when he'd had to strain to get it to react.

He remained in his meditative state until Balam's voice broke his concentration. "I have done my part. How are you, Chance?"

He cleared his throat and said, "I'm okay. What time is it?"

Chance opened his eyes and discovered Ana was no longer hanging over the back of the couch. She walked over from the kitchen. A delicious smell filled the house.

"Chance, it looks amazing," she said enthusiastically.

"It is evening, nearly meal time. How do you feel?"

He envisioned an open wound on his back and answered, "Well, getting a tattoo isn't like getting a massage. It burns like a son of a gun, but I should be okay."

"Ana, it's time for the leaves."

"Oh, right."

She disappeared from sight and came back with a stack of dripping leaves. As she held them out to Balam, he rose to his feet and said, "Would you like to do it? I need to take a moment before dinner to rest."

"Sure."

Ana watched him move away, walked around the couch and knelt beside Chance. Her hands trailed along his neck and shoulder. His back radiated with heat, but the cool touch of her fingers on his skin instantly tamed the pain. She laid wet leaves on him, which quelled the heat.

"Does that feel better?"

"Yes."

She kissed his shoulder and helped him up. As he sat

up, he braced his hands on the cushions to avoid passing out.

"Whoa." He shook off the dizziness and said, "So what have you been up to?"

"I started dinner. Oh, Balam let me look through a very old book that was compiled by some Mayan healers, like an encyclopedia of plants and their uses. I can't understand most of the glyphs but some of it is written in Spanish and that I can work my way around. But mostly I'm looking at the sketches. I recognize some of the plants from Sanchia's garden."

"Cool. Sounds like you've been busy. Say, you willing to help me to the bathroom mirror so I can take a look at the tat?"

"Of course."

Ana held her hands out to him and he rose tenderly to his feet. The leaves clung to his back like bandages even as they walked upstairs. The washroom was small and there was barely enough room for them to maneuver. She peeled off all the leaves and palmed them in her hand. Chance turned his back to the mirror and looked over his shoulder.

He sucked in his breath as he took in the giant tattooed glyph. It spread across his upper back, touching both shoulders, and went down to his mid-back. The bear's body stretched over his skin and its face glared at him with its claws extended. His skin was red and swollen and blood beaded along the black lines of the body art.

"Wow. Mom's gonna freak."

Ana snickered and began covering up the artwork with

the wet leaves again. When she finished, Chance turned and pressed her against the gray stone wall. His fingers played with the edge of her shirt, and he experienced an almost electric charge from brushing against her skin. Her cheek came in contact with his and they stood breathing in unison for a while until his stomach rumbled.

"Hungry?" Ana asked breathlessly.

"Oh, yeah. Always," he said with a smirk.

"C'mon, you can get a snack, but we should wait for Balam to have dinner."

They left the tight confines of the bathroom but Chance didn't want to let go of her so he kept his hand on her shoulder as they walked downstairs. Just being in her presence made him feel centered, calm. He truly couldn't imagine life without her...

***

"You have rested, but now it is time to see if you have the strength to keep your *nagual's* mark. Your power has been restoring and expanding. If you can pass this test, than it is time to teach you the Yaguar. But the first form you take must be the animal you are tattooed with."

Chance fidgeted with the fabric around his waist and stared at the ground as his great-grandfather addressed him.

"Spend time as your *nagual*. Discover its secrets. When it is time to return to your human form, keep your mark in your thoughts and reject the restorative power that takes over. You only have one chance."

Ana walked up to him and gave him a hug, careful not to touch his back. She whispered in his ear, "Good luck, Chance. I believe in you."

Where her hands trailed along his shoulders, his skin tingled in response. He gave her a squeeze and kissed her lips. "Thank you, my love."

He wanted to get this over with. Although he was a bit anxious about giving it a try, he knew he was ready. His eye was on the prize—learning Balam's mighty Yaguar form. Chance had every intention to learn every skill he could.

He didn't need to sit and meditate to collect his focus now but stood with his eyes shut and thought about his favorite form. Blue iridescent lines created the silhouette of a grizzly bear in his thoughts. His energy core ignited, surging power throughout every cell in his body. The familiar sensation of fur erupting over his skin tingled and the aches from his tattoo dissolved away.

A deep rumble resonated in his chest. The world appeared the same through a bear's eyes, but his sense of smell had been significantly heightened. Ana's intoxicating aroma had so many layers to it he would know it anywhere. Balam had his own musky odor that Chance had begun to memorize. And then there was the scent of the local fauna and flora.

Any concern about returning to his human form and retaining his tattoo were gone. He wanted to do nothing but relish in the embodiment of his *nagual*. Ana ran her fingers through his fluffy brown pelt and said, "Go on. Introduce the grizzly to Mexico."

Chance lowered his muzzle to touch his nose to hers and a throaty purr escaped his lips. Then, as quickly as his hulky body could move, he turned and thundered into the jungle.

His cumbersome form made it hard to navigate through the lanky tree shoots and dense growth but he forced a path anyway. Delicious and nauseating smells stirred around his feet and to the far corners of the jungle.

He pushed through a grove of trees and vines and something sweet-smelling caught his attention. Just above him, a cluster of red fruit the size of a fist hid behind some leaves. He lifted his paw up and hooked a claw behind the bough, sending the fruit down to the ground.

Even though he didn't have use of his hands and thumbs, he did his best. Soon, juice and tiny seeds covered his fur as he pressed the fruits flesh into his maw. He could have purred in contentment.

Without warning, his nose picked up the smell of sweat and chocolate. A human.

It wasn't Ana or Balam. He knew their scents and this one was unfamiliar to him. He was curious. It could just be a local, but what if it wasn't?

He righted himself to his feet and lifted his snout as he honed onto the stranger's location and propelled himself forward with purpose. Power and strength didn't fail him as he surged through the jungle. He lost all track of time but felt the weight of the setting sun on him as though it were lowering onto his shoulders.

The scent led him to a ravine. He paused at the tree line, cautious as he remembered Ana's trap catching him by surprise. The stinging bite of the spear had made a lasting impression.

Chance scanned the area and inhaled, searching for answers. The amulet Balam had given him for protection swayed from his neck as he teetered on the edge of the ridge, ready to explore. It appeared to be safe, so he stumbled down the hill, his burdensome load pushing him off balance. His snout led him to a large stone and the trail stopped there. So many animals had passed through the area. Too many to count.

The lively sounds of the jungle told him that whomever had been here earlier was gone. But how did he or she leave and in what form?

It was a long run back home, but now that he was an experienced tracker, it wasn't much trouble. He simply followed his own scent until Ana's and Balam's got stronger. Meanwhile, day became night and as dusk set in, Chance's vision sharpened.

They were nearby now. Their aroma got stronger the closer he got to home. He moved carefully through the prickly shrubbery and wandered into the clearing.

Ana sat on a stone with a pile of various leaves on her lap. Balam stood beside her and pointed at a flower she was holding. Without looking up, Balam said, "Welcome, Chance. How was bear form?"

Chance made an effort to answer, but the growls that came out sounded like a Wookie's. He rose on his hind legs and towered above them.

"Are you ready for your final test?"

Right. All feelings of anxiety where thrust aside. He knew the grizzly was his *nagual*. He perched on the fabric of his sarong and recalled Balam's instructions. The memory of his tattoo became his focus. He would have to try and keep his body from automatically healing and removing it. When he shifted into an animal it was almost like squeezing into someone else's clothing, but returning back to his human form was akin to going home. It was safe, normal and most importantly, it fit.

Slowly, he began to change. His flesh ached as the transformation slowed. He kept his mark in his mind and a raw spasm rippled across his back.

Had he done it?

Cool air brushed over his naked body and goose bumps skimmed his arms and legs.

"Oh," Ana's voice said from behind.

Quickly, he snatched up the fabric at his feet and wrapped it around his waist. When he turned around, her cheeks were flushed red and she avoided his gaze.

"Did I do it?" he asked, searching Ana's and Balam's faces for the answer.

The stoic expression often worn by Balam dissolved into a grin. "Congratulations, Chance. You did well."

Pride and relief washed over him. He was one step closer to learning the mighty yaguar form and hopefully, growing strong enough to protect them from Markus.

Ana set the plants on the rock, sidled up to him and placed a kiss on his cheek. "I just couldn't look away. I wanted to see if the tattoo was there."

Chance wrapped his arms around her and growled in her ear. "S'okay. Any time you feel like evening things up—I'm there."

They took a few steps toward home when Chance remembered the smell of the stranger who'd disappeared. "Hey, when I was in the jungle, in bear form, I smelled a human and followed the scent. Just where it was strongest, it cut out."

"Did you recognize the scent?" Balam asked.

"Smelled like sweat and chocolate, but I didn't recognize the scent. Do you think it could have been a shifter?"

"It is possible. The last time I went to town to pick up supplies from Sanchia, I smelled something new. Most shifters are curious about each other. It may be nothing to worry about but a shifter must always be on guard."

Chance felt Ana tense up beside him and he squeezed her hand. "We're okay. It wasn't Markus, I'd know his stench anywhere. Next time we see him it won't be an uneven match."

He wasn't as confident as he made himself sound. He wanted to believe it, but deep down he was very much afraid of another run-in with his cousin. *Was* he prepared?

Chapter 28

"So, what are we doing today?" Chance asked Balam but Ana could tell what he really wanted to ask. If it had been Niyol, he would have just said it. *Will you teach me the yaguar today?*

Their relationship with Balam had changed over the past month and a half. At first, neither had known where they'd stood with him but now Ana knew that beneath his harsh exterior was a man of sensitivity and depth. It was in the little things. Like in the morning, when he left a small chunk of chocolate on the counter for her because he knew she liked sucking on a piece as she made the morning batch of hot chocolate. Or when she caught a glimmer of pride flash across his face when Chance picked up a new ability.

"Today I will teach you the yaguar form. And Ana, I have some new techniques to teach you as well. If you will allow me."

She bit the inside of her cheek. Since she had injured Chance with one of her traps, Balam had taken her lead and backed off. She was good at trapping. Really good. A natural. When she wandered through the jungle, it was easy for her to spot the best locations for traps and figure out how to camouflage them. She could discern the most likely path an animal would take just by looking at the curvature of the ground and the growth pattern of the plants.

Balam had pulled out the plant guidebook. She particularly enjoyed learning about the pharmaceutical properties of local flora and was fascinated with the hand drawn pictures and tidy notes. Most of them had Mayan glyphs, which she couldn't read, but with Balam's help she had begun to familiarize herself with important words like, 'poisonous' or 'healing'. The last few times they trained, he'd pointed out some of the plants in her book. She would have loved to talk with Sanchia again. Balam knew various facts but he wasn't a healer and couldn't elaborate on the information in the book.

Chance followed Balam down the stairs and Ana trailed just behind. His eyes were bright with excitement and she was happy for him. After nearly two months of training, he was stronger than he used to be and now he was reaping the rewards. No matter how many small creatures he learned to map, he was still more excited about large, powerful animals. Ana had to admit, the yaguar form was pretty amazing.

Balam led them off to a new location and stopped. "Chance, you have earned the right and privilege to learn the yaguar. Remember that it is a revered creature to all the people of my land. You must understand this. It is to be used with respect."

Without taking his gaze from Balam, Chance nodded and said, "Of course. I understand."

Balam paused to look at Chance, who appeared beside himself with excitement. Ana thought she saw a tiny smirk touch Balam's lips. He placed his fists to his hips and said, "Are you ready, Chance?"

"Yes," Chance said quietly.

The rate of transformation was so fast, she could hardly discern it. One moment Balam stood proud beside them, and the next, a huge black jaguar blinked back at her.

Chance lifted his brows, blew out a breath and mumbled, "Here goes."

He stared at the enormous feline and remained quiet for a while. Soon, his muscles relaxed and then his eyes closed.

Unlike Balam, Chance did not instantly shift. His body warped and enlarged, black fur rippled across his tan flesh until he was unrecognizable. The piece of maroon fabric tied around his waist pulled open and fell onto the ground. A mirror image of Balam now, Chance's face was mere inches from her own. Familiar hazel eyes stood out against his ebony guise.

"What a pretty kitty." She breathed out, eyes wide. Ana touched the bridge of his nose and then scratched him under his chin. A purr drummed in his chest and poured from his lips.

Movement came from her right. She glanced to the side and saw Balam back in his human form just finishing covering himself with his sarong. He cleared his throat and said, "Chance. Stay in the jungle and keep away from the towns. The yaguar must remain a legend. And be cautious."

Chance blinked back at his great-grandfather, turned and disappeared into the wilderness.

They were alone.

What did Balam have in store for her? She hoped he wouldn't make her try to trap Chance again. She just didn't have it in her. Maybe it was good practice but he simply wasn't the enemy.

"Ana. You have proven yourself with impressive trapping skills. I do not feel I have any more to teach you."

Well, that was a relief. She let out a sigh but remained nervous. Would he teach her how to throw a spear or wield a knife? Without thinking, she held onto the protective pendant Balam had given her. Its sharp point bit at her skin and she loosened her grip.

"I understand it is not natural for you to do harm. You are a healer at heart. I do not know all there is about plants and their properties. I do not have more to give you. The next trip to town for supplies, you should visit Sanchia."

"That would be great. I've wanted to see her again."

"Today I will teach you how to quiet your mind and we will see if you will be able to connect with your own power."

"What do you mean? Why would I need to know how to do that—and can I?"

"Everyone has power. Humankind leaves it untapped, unused. I can sense you have power. I can see your hunger for knowledge of the healing arts. It speaks to you."

He was right about that. "Ever since Chance healed me, I've had this...I don't know. This calling. I've felt empty almost. Like I'm not doing what I'm supposed to be doing. But I don't even know what it is I'm supposed to be doing. Does that make sense?"

Balam's gaze remained pensive, almost unreadable. "I cannot tell you your purpose or future. The answer is in you. I think when you are ready to know, it will be revealed to you. Learning to quiet your mind may help you find these answers."

Ana followed Balam to a fallen tree and sat down beside him.

"Close your eyes and take long, deep breaths."

Ana did as instructed. She had seen Chance do this numerous times before shapeshifting but she was a little unsure of herself and embarrassed. Warmth spread across her cheeks.

"Now, try to clear your mind. Do not think of what you must do or what you may be worried about. Be free and allow yourself to become open like the sky."

How did one become open like the sky? She had no idea but figured she would give it a try. All her concerns about protecting herself from unknown jungle visitors and finding her place in the world fell away. Instead, she thought about the night sky and kindled the feeling she had when she stargazed. A calm settled in her chest and her pulse slowed.

"Now you must focus inward. It may take a while for you to recognize your power but once you do, it will be easier next time to access it. I think there is a saying about a bike?"

Ana smiled. She hoped it was like riding a bike.

She imagined herself searching around in a darkened

closet for something tiny. It seemed futile. What did it look like and where was it hidden? Was her power shrouded in the rafters of her mind or the hollows of her stomach?

Just chill out, Ana. Clear your mind. Chance can do it. So can you. She thought of her time spent with Niyol. He'd had faith in her. Like Balam, he had said something about her having power as well. She had trusted him and grown to love him like her own grandfather. The first time Chance took bear form during the thunderstorm, Niyol had sat with her while she cried. The memory was fresh in her mind. He had held his hand over her chest, where her heart was.

As the memories filtered through her mind, something clicked. Warmth spread out from her heart and flowed through her body. Butter yellow sunlight poured out from her life source. Happiness radiated from her and she started laughing. Something wet dropped on her hand and she realized she was crying. Her arms shook as she wiped away the tears.

"You found your power?"

"Yes."

"Good. It will help guide you. If you quiet your mind and seek inner strength, you will find it. And if healing is the path you take, you will need a teacher."

Was he serious? Could she really be a healer?

"But I don't understand how this happened? Was I born this way?"

She looked to Balam for an answer, but he remained silent. When she thought of a healer, she imagined a woman draped in beaded necklaces, wearing a flowing dress and chanting while waving a rattle. She must have made a funny expression because Balam asked, "What, Ana?"

"No. It's just, I've never thought of myself as a healer. I don't know anything about it."

"Sanchia is a healer but she had no teacher. Knowledge was passed on through the generations but her abilities are limited. She uses herbs and some of her natural instincts to diagnose illnesses. But she is nothing like the shamans in my time that could heal shifters of the sickness and many other ailments just with their powers."

Well, that sounded pretty good. If she could help people as Chance had helped her, it would give her life new meaning. However she wasn't so sure she had the power and most importantly, she had no teacher.

"Remember, Ana. Like the hero twins, it is easier to overcome a quest when you are a team. You must work together and use your strengths."

"Of course. I will always stand beside Chance. There's nowhere I'd rather be."

Balam nodded and stood up. He held out his hand out to her and she eyed it before accepting the gesture. His skin was soft and warm and practically buzzed with electricity. Ana slipped off the fallen tree trunk and although it had been months since she suffered from a dizzy spell, she teetered precariously on her feet. Thankful Balam had offered her his hand, she closed her eyes and waited for it to pass. When the flurry of blood subsided, she freed her fingers from his grasp.

"Are you ready to go back home? Chance will find his way when he is done."

"Sure. I could use a snack. Getting in touch with your energy core really takes it out of you," she said, grinning.

Balam cut through the wilderness with deft agility and every bit of his five hundred years of experience showed. Ana leapt to meet his footfalls, reminding her of when she was a child, trying to step in the deep pits left in the snow from her father's footsteps. It was possibly one of the only happy memories she had of him.

They made it back to Balam's stony fortress in record time. As they walked through the underground cave, Ana thought she saw something glimmer in the water below the walkway.

"Balam, what's that in the water? Do you see it? Looks like gold."

As he continued along the wooden suspension path, he said over his shoulder, "That is because it *is* gold."

"Really?" She squinted in the dusky light trying to make out the treasure that lay beneath but wandered on when she couldn't.

When she reached the top step and entered the living space, she temporarily forgot about her hunger and asked, "Where'd it come from?"

Balam's white teeth showed against his dark almond skin. "I could not allow the Spaniards to be rewarded for destroying so much. Gold is what they came for but I couldn't let them leave with it. Some of it is Mayan gold and some, Spanish."

"Serves them right. So what's it like having lived so

Prodigy

long?" She could hardly imagine what it would be like watching your children age and die while you remained youthful, almost ageless. Balam had survived so many wives and children. It seemed more like a curse. Unless your loved ones were shifters too, it would be a solitary life. This was something she didn't like thinking about. If Chance continued on his path, he would remain ageless while she grew old. She would never ask him to turn his back on who he was, but it was a concern of hers.

"I am a book of history. I have seen all. I am a witness to the world. I have been blessed and cursed. I am not all good. I have hurt my share but I have hope for you and Chance. Your future is ahead of you and you are untarnished."

It almost sounded as if he was saying goodbye and it made her uneasy. He wasn't done training them, was he? She was unsure how to respond, so she didn't.

In the absence of her answer, Balam said, "I have something for you, Ana. Please wait a moment."

He disappeared upstairs and minutes later returned with his hands behind his back. His lips turned up as he placed in her hands a shiny, weighted object. A golden snake stared up into her eyes. Its body was curled into a knot and mounted on a crosspiece with a hole at either end. A wooden stick that looked like a chopstick braced through the holes.

"It's beautiful. What is it?"

Balam took it back and said, "Turn around, please."

Ana did as she was asked and was surprised when his hands combed through her hair and twisted her locks into

249

a knot. The wooden stick grazed her scalp as he secured the hair ornament. She touched the top of her head when he was done and felt the snake's form.

"Thank you, Balam. Are you sure? It looks valuable—"

"It was my mother's and now it is yours. The snake represents healing and rebirth. You wear it well. You look like the young goddess Ixchel."

Ana tried to say the name. "Ee-shell?"

"Ixchel, a woman of many names. The jaguar goddess, goddess of the moon, the medicine or fertility goddess. Ixchel was beautiful, with skin like pearls. All the gods were captivated by her, but she was the Chief God's consort. She gave him thirteen sons. Two of their children created heaven and earth and the four jaguar gods, who were named after the four directions and held up each corner of the sky. Her followers, the medicine women and shamans, sought her guidance."

"You said a healer saved you from the sickness?"

"Yes. It was a dark time. I was protecting my people from all sides. The Spaniards were destroying everything. They had already decimated the Aztec and other Mayan kingdoms were just trying to survive. A nearby city sent a war party to my door and I did what I had to protect myself and my people. The shifter I killed was young and had never killed another so I was not weighed down by many angry voices. But without the help of a healer, I would have gone mad."

Balam stopped and smelled the air. "Chance is coming."

Ana walked out to the deck and looked at the billowy

forest canopy. Clouds had blown in from the coast and were now covering the blue sky like a woolen shield. Moisture hung in the air, threatening rain. She spotted a dark shape flying toward them. A yellow bird with brown wings and a black mask swooped in and landed on the railing. Balam walked out and held up Chance's worn piece of maroon fabric. The creature chattered and hopped down to the ground. A moment later, Chance rose.

"Welcome back. How was it?" Ana could tell from the cheerful expression on his face that he had had a memorable day.

"That was fantastic! Came back and found you guys had left so I thought I'd fly home. Hungry and all." He patted his muscular abdomen and Ana thought she detected his stomach rumbling.

"Say, what's that in your hair?"

"Balam just gave it to me. Isn't it amazing?" Her fingers traced over it once more.

"It's beautiful on you," Chance said.

"Ana accessed her own power while you were gone. I thought it was a good time to give her a healing totem."

Chance frowned, clearly confused. He stared at Ana and she wasn't entirely sure what he was thinking. Uncomfortable in the spotlight, she explained quickly, "Balam thinks I may have the ability to heal. Strange, right?"

Chance took a moment and then he beamed with pride. "Fantastic!"

"Chance, your grandfather left this for you and I gave

it to him. It is part of your heritage. I would like to return it to you."

Balam pressed something into Chance's hands. He responded by shaking his great-grandfather's hand and said, "Thanks, Balam. I appreciate it. I promise to keep it safe."

The jade jaguar pendant gleamed in his fingers.

"You're both hungry from your day of accomplishment. Let's celebrate!"

Ana remembered Balam's idea of celebration and was wary. Maybe she would skip the corn alcohol and brew some hot chocolate instead. Chance seemed to read what she was thinking and snickered before lifting her in the air unexpectedly. She squealed in surprise and exclaimed, "Oh!"

Balam wandered into the kitchen, pulled out a tall, clear bottle, and then started a fire in the kitchen grill. She had a feeling it would be yet another memorable night.

Chapter 29

The darkness made it feel like night, but it was morning, Chance was sure of it. Raindrops replaced the sound of pleasant birds chirping and created a white noise that pulled him deeper into bed. The moisture in the air filled his lungs. It was a nice change from the dry weather they'd experienced over the last few weeks.

Unsure of the time, he glanced at his watch. It was after seven already. Why hadn't Balam come to wake him? He figured he was probably letting him have a well-deserved rest. His feet slipped out from under the sheets and touched the cold stone floor. The previous night he had eaten and drunk way too much; his stomach and head were paying the price today. Some hot chocolate would probably soothe his aching stomach and Ana would likely have herbs for the splitting headache. His hands rested on his temples and he decided to skip pushups today.

He picked through his pile of clothes and pulled on a wrinkled t-shirt and cargo shorts. A strand of hair tumbled into his eyes and he scratched his scalp. It had been too long since his last haircut. Maybe if they could find a pair of scissors, Ana could give him a trim.

A draft from the open windows followed him into the hallway as he stopped to see if Ana was awake. Her sleeping form wasn't under the sheets and most importantly, they lay in a twisted heap on the floor. She was meticulous when it came to her room and belongings. He liked to tease her about it. He felt instinctively that something was wrong and sped downstairs.

The living space was empty. No sign of Balam or Ana. Chance's heartbeat pounded in his ears as he raced back upstairs to make sure they weren't in Balam's room for some reason. Not finding them there, he darted to the kitchen. Had they eaten and left for an early training session without him? Balam had once taken Chance out alone and left Ana behind. He tried convincing himself it was just like that time. But it just didn't feel right.

A carafe of hot chocolate that had cooled to room temperature sat at the center of the hand-hewn dining table. Beside it, a mug lay on its side, its contents spilled across the surface and onto the stone floor.

"Ana!" he yelled half-heartedly, not expecting to hear a response.

Chance flew down the darkened stairwell into the underground cavern. Water dropped from the cave ceiling and slapped against the pool below. The irregular cadence unnerved him even more. He shook the suspended walkway while he ran and eventually emerged from the mouth of the grotto into the gloomy jungle.

Leaves wet from the storm gleamed and the air smelled of clay and wood. Rain was his favorite smell. But not today. Not now. He would give anything to catch Ana's scent but he couldn't. The earth had been washed clean.

Chapter 30

Ana was glad she had slipped on her hiking shoes. Balam was almost too fast for her but the thick rubber soles gripped at the slick ground and propelled her forward so she could keep up. Her hair was pulled into a ponytail and the end dripped water down her back. It didn't matter because she was already soaked.

Her eyes bore into the back of Balam's head as she grumbled to herself. She hadn't exactly been pleased to learn he wanted to start at six o'clock and insisted she participate in one more test. Her displeasure changed to anger when she realized he wanted to leave without telling Chance. Her lip quivered as she thought about Chance's distress when he woke to find her missing. No doubt he would flash back to Markus kidnapping her. She hoped he would forgive her, especially after the hard time she gave him for leaving without telling her only weeks ago.

Balam glanced back and nodded grimly. She stared at the ground and pressed on. She understood that Chance's confidence had crumbled after his run-in with his cousin and that he would never try as hard as he would if nothing was at stake. Balam wanted him to have faith in himself and his abilities. He said they needed supplies, anyway, and she would get the opportunity to see Sanchia again. It was strange thinking about her being Balam's granddaughter since he appeared to be around the same age.

Even if the sun were up, it wouldn't be able to break through the heavy clouds and leafy canopy. The trail was hard for her to make out and she hoped she wasn't being led to any sleeping predators.

"I know you are tiring but we must press ahead. If Chance chooses to take animal form to track us, he will move faster than us."

Ana panted and replied with as much venom as she could muster, "Well, after the amount of alcohol you gave him last night, I'm sure he won't be up any time soon."

Balam stopped beside a large Ceiba tree, its spiky trunk a warning to anyone who thought about touching it. The amazing boughs reached up into the slate sky.

He surprised her when he said, "I am proud of Chance. He is a good student. He works hard and he does it all for you. It is easy to see you are his true mate and he is yours."

She regretted her spiteful response after his kindhearted praise. He cared very much for their well-being. She just wished there was another way to test Chance.

"Are you ready to continue?"

She pulled out her water bottle, took a sip and shrugged. She was glad the bottle had a carabineer and clipped it back to her belt loop so she could keep her hands free as they hiked.

"We are almost there. A little further," Balam said and walked on.

He wasn't wearing a shirt, and his back appeared slick

even in the murky light. The black lines of his tattoos wrapped over his exposed skin like vines overtaking the crumbled ruins. They had only gone a short distance before Balam stopped and lifted his nose in the air.

"What's up?"

He turned but his expression made her nervous. Eyes wide, he continued to sniff and said, "Let's hurry. I will leave you with Sanchia. You should be safe in town with her."

Before she could ask again, he dashed ahead and she scrambled to keep up. The trees thinned and without much vegetation, it got muddy fast, but at least she could see better. She thought she caught sight of a planted field and knew Balam was right. They were close.

According to her watch, it was nearing seven o'clock. She wondered if Chance was up yet and hoped he was because being away from him like this made her uneasy. Her mother had always warned her never to go anywhere without letting someone know. It was a safety thing. Balam knew where she was, of course, but Chance didn't. At least this was the last hurdle to get past. Soon enough, they would be sitting around the fire back at home and eating dinner. *Think positive.*

After ten minutes they arrived at the opening of the trail, revealing the town Sanchia lived in. Balam turned and said, "Wait here. I will make sure everything is safe. I will get my granddaughter."

He phased into a tortoise shell housecat and scampered out onto the street, carefully avoiding rivulets of water collecting into a stream. His ears pressed down as his head and body got soaked.

"But—" She thought about snatching him up on his return so she could get some answers. Ana had the distinct feeling things weren't going according to plan.

She stayed under the protection of the forest canopy. In time, a hunched form emerged from the corner house, Sanchia's home. It was the kind, elderly woman, and in her arms, she held the cat, whose fur was matted and spiky. Ana muttered words of greeting as they joined her.

Balam struggled from Sanchia's grasp and leapt to his wet sarong. The women respectfully turned away and then Balam's voice broke the silence.

"Ana, you must go with Sanchia. I need to go check on a new scent I just picked up."

"Wait a minute. Is everything okay? What about Chance?"

"I am sure he will be okay. Chance said he smelled a new scent recently. I just need to check and make sure we are safe. Stay here, Ana. I will come back soon or if we are lucky, Chance will be here soon."

Then Balam spoke in an undertone to his granddaughter but it must have been in Mayan, because Ana couldn't understand what he said. Sanchia pursed her lips and nodded quickly. Balam squeezed Ana's shoulder briefly and turned into the jungle.

"Come," Sanchia said, gesturing to her. When Ana got close enough, the woman hooked her arm through Ana's and they set off to the modest home.

When they were safe inside, Sanchia scurried off and returned with a towel and a welcome smile.

"Thank you."

"Do not worry. Balam will be back soon. Come and have some hot chocolate."

Sanchia led her into the small kitchen. The aroma of her favorite drink triggered a deep rumble from her belly. Ana had only had time for a few sips earlier before Balam whisked her into the jungle. She was starved.

Her host gave her a wizened grin and filled a cup with the dark steaming liquid. Then she piled up a plate of corn pancakes and fruit.

"You are a good eater. Take your mind off your worries and fill your stomach, child."

Well, the woman made sense. She was beyond hungry after hours of hiking; she wouldn't be of any use if she couldn't think straight from hunger. As she wolfed down the breakfast, she hoped Chance and Balam would get there soon because it was doubtful she would be able to keep terrible thoughts from racing through her head for much longer.

***

Chance ran into his room and dove for his phone. He hoped he it had enough battery as he switched it on. It chimed and he breathed a sigh of relief as he tried calling Ana but it went straight to voicemail. He had a message from his mother, but nothing from Ana. Discouraged, he tossed his phone aside. He was wasting precious time. If he couldn't smell her scent in human form, he knew what he needed to do. Chance stripped down, grabbed the maroon fabric from his bed and looped it around his neck, covering up the long cord of the protective talisman Balam had given him as he flew downstairs.

As soon as his feet touched the clay earth of the forest floor he shifted mid-step. Bear was the best tracker he could think of and hoped his *nagual* wouldn't let him down. What with the rain, it was harder to pick up Ana's scent but it was not beyond the capabilities of the best nose on earth. Monkeys squawked above him, sending shouts of warning out to hidden family members. It was probably a surprise to see such a large, unfamiliar beast crashing through their jungle home.

Stay calm, Chance. It's probably just a test. There's only Balam's and Ana's scents. It was the sort of thing he could see his great-grandfather doing. He hoped he was right.

Ana's emerald eyes flashed through his thoughts and he snorted. Ever since he met her, he knew she was the one. They fit. He couldn't imagine living his life without her. He would have made the same choice as his grandfather if he felt he had the option. If Markus weren't still alive, he'd consider settling down and giving up his powers to grow old with Ana.

He stampeded through a waterfall of vines that fell onto the trail and felt leaves tumble off his back and shoulders. Deep snorts escaped his lips as he panted with exertion. His muscles burned but instead of focusing on his own discomfort, he thought of Ana.

Life just seemed to keep coming at them. Would they ever get a break from the excitement? He hoped so, but if they didn't... Chance made up his mind.

He wanted to be with Ana for the rest of his life. Amongst all of the belongings left to him from his grandfather was his grandmother's wedding ring. It was perfect and it belonged on Ana's finger.

In that moment, he made a promise to himself that if and when he found her, he would propose.

Chapter 31

Chance tromped over vines and half-submerged rocks that burst roughly from the earth. Then he smelled it. A new, sickening scent. It was familiar. It brought back all of the painful memories of their deaths: Ana's, Niyol's and his own on the mountaintop in Idaho.

Markus.

He froze. The scent mixed and overlapped with Ana's and Balam's. Had they been joined by Markus? Were they following him? Or worse, was he following them?

His heartbeat thundered in his ears like an echo off a canyon wall as he searched the gloom for another set of eyes. Panic stricken, he envisioned Ana laying in the mud, her heart still and Markus's twisted sneer looming over her. Rivulets of water poured from the top of his broad head onto his face. He shook off the rain, to no avail.

The storm wasn't letting up and it only caused more issues for him as he tried to hone in on the various scents left from recent travelers. He was having a hard time deciding if Ana and Balam or Markus had walked through the area first.

It didn't matter now. He needed to catch up with them. Chance sank his paws into the wet clay and propelled himself forward, sending a spray of mud into the air.

Finally, the scent trails split. The fragrance of car exhaust and pavement told him he was near a town. To his left, he could smell Ana and Balam heading toward the community and straight ahead, he detected Balam and Markus going further into the wilderness. He hoped this meant Balam had stowed Ana away in safety before confronting Markus.

Torn, he wanted to ensure Ana was safe but he also wanted to track down Balam and Markus. If he could help subdue his cousin, they wouldn't have to look over their shoulders for the rest of their lives. If he couldn't find a peaceful resolution, Markus's death would do.

Ana, I love you. Stay safe. With a grunt, he charged resolutely ahead. Chance had been training heavily for an encounter with Markus. He hoped it was enough.

***

Ana helped clean the dishes in Sanchia's kitchen after she finished breakfast. She stared out the little window above the kitchen sink into the storm. She supposed there was nothing to do but wait. Maybe Balam would come back soon, or even better, Chance would arrive.

After drying the plates and mugs with a cloth, she joined Sanchia in the living room. Her concern must have been clearly written on her face when Sanchia offered her sympathy.

"Come sit with me, Ana. Tell me about your stay with Balam. You are lucky he took you into his home. He has not had any visitors in a very long time."

Ana slid back on the sofa and wrapped her arms around herself. "Well, it's been interesting," she said carefully in Spanish, "Balam let me look at a book filled with information about plants and herbs. I recognized many plants you had growing in your garden." Ana waved toward the back of the house in the direction of the backyard and added, "He also showed me how to set traps, but I didn't enjoy that as much." She winced as she recalled the bloody results of her efforts.

Ana wasn't sure just how much to divulge. She figured as a rule of thumb, it was best not to talk about shapeshifting too much. Obviously, Sanchia was aware of her grandfather's abilities, so Ana decided it was safe to speak freely.

"You must have much power," Sanchia said and patted Ana's knee.

"Why do you say that?"

"For Balam to take time with you."

"He said I might be a healer," Ana said.

Sanchia's eyes widened and she raised her brows. Ana felt like the last of an endangered species walking on earth. "I sensed it, too."

"You never had a teacher?" Ana asked.

"Aiy, no. There are not many left. They stay hidden and do not reveal themselves." She spoke so low, Ana barely heard her.

"But, I thought you were a healer, too? That's what Balam told me. Did he ever try to help you?"

Sanchia pressed her palms against the top of her legs and said, "He cannot teach what he does not know. He is not a healer. He did try to help me when I was young but he could not. It was my mother who taught me the wisdom of medicinal healing that has been passed down by the women of my family. But she was not a true healer, so she could not help guide me with my power."

"Well, what am I supposed to do now? Balam said that maybe you could help me."

"I can teach you what I know, but it is little. I know much about plants, but I cannot help you with your power. It can be dangerous and unsafe if you do not have practice, and I have never had guidance. A teacher must find and choose you."

"What do you mean?" Ana asked, confused.

"You must be chosen because finding a true healer would be almost impossible. But maybe Chance will be able to help you."

"Did you know who we were when we first met you?"

"No. But I know to signal Balam when anyone comes looking for him. When you came asking for him I left my sash at the trail. And a couple weeks ago when Grandfather came for supplies he told me that Chance was our family. I would like to see him again and give my distant cousin a hug."

Ana gave a weak smile. "Maybe soon."

Sanchia was being a good host, keeping her engaged in conversation, but her skin crawled with anxiety. How long was Balam going to take?

Ana hoped someone would come soon because she didn't know how much longer she was capable of waiting.

***

He tried to keep up with the pace his heartbeat had set but couldn't. The thought of tearing Markus away from this world pleased him and it was all he could do to steady himself, focus on his surroundings and track both the scents of Balam and his cousin. Adrenaline pulsed through his veins and heightened his senses.

He pressed on until Balam's trail split off from Markus's. It veered away, down a slope dense with vines and creeping growth. Chance stopped, panting. Time to make a quick choice.

With his eyes closed, he centered himself before shifting into his human form. The hemlock pendant hung low on his neck, and brushed against his abdomen. He searched the wilderness for any sign of movement. When he was satisfied, he tugged his maroon sarong from his neck and secured it around his waist. He was drenched and his hair hung limply in his eyes.

In the rain, all his senses were deadened. He couldn't see, hear or smell as well as he would have liked. It took but a moment to adapt the internal structure of his nose like Balam had taught him. His great-grandfather's scent was faint but traceable. Down the hill he went, toes trying to grip the slick clay as best they could.

At the bottom, water collected into a swift moving stream that looked like a brown flood of hot chocolate. He searched the air for a sign of his great-grandfather. However his earthy fragrance faded at the foot of the bank.

"Balam?" Chance said as softly as he could.

A pair of brown eyes blinked out at him from behind a

wall of vegetation located on the opposite ridge and he immediately recognized Balam's human silhouette. He scrambled up the hill as deftly as he could but got caught in the quagmire along the way. When he pulled himself out from behind the cover of some limestone ruins overgrown with vines, his great-grandfather's regal form confronted him, nose to nose.

Balam didn't have to say a word for Chance to understand he was upset with him. He also didn't have to stretch his imagination to figure out why. He hadn't exactly approached in silence. Maybe they should have had more lessons on stealth. Chance hunched down and winced in apology. Balam turned, lifted his nose into the air and appeared to try to pick up a scent.

"Is Ana safe?" Chance whispered.

His great-grandfather nodded.

"Where's Markus?"

Balam's eyes narrowed and he pointed behind Chance, who spun around in time to see a shadowy figure materialize.

Chapter 32

Out of nowhere, fear penetrated every pore of Ana's body. Danger. Someone was in danger. Her head swam and she grew dizzy. Something was wrong.

What's going on? Was this what it was like being drunk? She tried to focus on Sanchia but the sweet, elderly woman had split into two blurry shapes. Ana rubbed her eyes.

"What is wrong, child?"

"I don't know. I don't know what's happening!"

"Calm yourself. Close your eyes." Sanchia touched her shoulder and as soon as she did, Ana felt a jolt, like an electric shock. In her mind, she saw the jungle. A deluge of rain pelted the leaves and ground. Noises and fetid smells were all around her. She wasn't alone. Balam was there, but so was the one person she hoped she'd never see again.

Markus.

Ana scrambled off the couch, her heart drumming dangerously in her chest. Sanchia's eyes were wide and filled with concern.

"Is something the matter, child?"

Ana's voice was trapped. Her throat clamped up. She let out a slow, shaky breath as tears pierced her eyes. "They are in trouble...I need to leave."

She stumbled toward the door but Sanchia moved like her shadow and placed her hand on the door. "No, child.

Balam wants you to stay safe. He does not wish you to leave here."

Sanchia's words had no effect on her. She had no plan but she couldn't sit still. The vision made no sense but she wasn't going to question it either.

"Sanchia, I am leaving here. I will not stand by and let anything happen to Chance or Balam." She spoke with such vehemence and conviction, Sanchia withdrew her hand, clearly surprised.

"Ana, you must stay..."

"I'm sorry," Ana said. As she flung open the door, a wave of wind and rain lashed her in the face. She raced outside and sped to the trail opening and the dank jungle.

***

A pair of eyes stared at Chance from the shadows of an overgrown mound of limestone rock. His muscles tightened as he glimpsed the tall outline of his cousin.

"Hello, Markus," he said, and felt the veins in his neck throb.

He heard Balam move near him. At least he wouldn't have to face Markus alone.

Markus took a step forward and Chance's stomach turned. His cousin was recognizable, but he wasn't in the same condition as the last time he saw him. Long wet black hair lay tangled over his shoulders and a foul odor signaled his lack of hygiene. He was naked and dirty and Chance wondered if he had been more animal than human over the last many months. There was a wild, frightening quality to Markus's expression. He appeared completely unhinged.

He smirked at Chance in a way that made him revisit those terrible moments on the mountaintop in Idaho, when he'd heard Ana's irregular heartbeat stop and when he discovered his grandfather's lifeless body beside him. How he wanted to witness Markus's own last breath. He wasn't a violent person but the anger rooted in him had been planted by his cousin.

"Hello, cousin," he said lazily. "You spoiled my surprise. I was about to jump the old man but I can finish you off for dessert. Or if you want, you can be the appetizer."

"What, I can't be the main course?" Chance looked to Balam. He wasn't so sure that Markus's presence had gone unnoticed. If he could keep Markus occupied for a bit, maybe he could figure out what to do. He wished he'd had a moment with Balam to talk and discuss strategy. Knowing his great-grandfather, he probably already had a plan. He edged back, closer to Balam, who stepped forward.

"Ha, ha, ha. Not even close." Markus snorted.

"So, how'd you find me, anyway?"

"Well, I was doing fine hanging out in the van with you on your road trip until you ditched me in Denver. I knew you were heading to the Yucatán. I've been combing the area forever. I wasn't even sure you were still here. But as luck would have it, I fell into a trap covered in your girlfriend's scent. I think I'll have to find her when I'm done with you both. She may serve me better alive than dead." Markus pulled his lips up into a suggestive smirk.

Chance strained to remain still. He couldn't let his anger get the better of him so he asked another question to distract them both. "Why didn't you just attack me back in Idaho when I was weak?"

"I had to heal up after our fight. And once I found out about your great-grandfather, I decided to let you lead me to him. What's better than one shapeshifter?" Markus laughed and answered his own question. "Two shapeshifters."

Balam's deep voice said, "Son, are you sure you want to make this choice? You don't have to do this. Killing us will only poison your soul and cause more unbalance."

"Who do you think you are? Your hippie talk means nothing to me." He paused for a moment, then frowned and mumbled, "Shhh, no! Stop talking, I can't think! It's my turn!"

Chance frowned in confusion. Then he realized Markus wasn't speaking to either of them. Was he completely mad?

Chance felt Balam tug on the leather strap of his necklace. He turned and met his steady stare. *What, Balam? What are you trying to tell me?*

Chance glanced down and suddenly knew what he was hinting at. The pendant filled with hemlock. Of course. If he could get close enough to stab Markus with it, they wouldn't have to worry about him using his powers. It would be an easy fight.

He didn't want to draw attention to his weapon, even if it didn't look like much of one. The cool, sharp stone rested against his stomach. Under the guise of stretching, in one slow, fluid movement, he grabbed it in his palm and lifted it over his head, along with the cord. He subtly repositioned the spear-like stone, preparing to sink it into his opponent.

Just then, Markus stopped muttering to himself and clapped his hands together. "Who wants to go first?"

Not entirely sure if he was directing the question to him or not, Chance answered, "What makes you think it will be that easy?" He edged forward, confident it would be easier to stab Markus as a human. In the form of an animal, he would be too dangerous to approach and able to evade his attack more easily. Knowing Markus, he would probably want to show off in animal form sooner than later.

"Do you know how many shifters my grandfather killed before he died?"

Chance glided closer to his cousin and said, "You were weaker than your grandfather when you killed him. What makes you think I can't do the same to you?"

Confusion muddled Markus's frown. "I caught him by surprise. I wasn't going to be his livestock any longer. He was just waiting for me to grow strong before doing the same to me. I did it to save myself but got so much more."

Unexpectedly, Chance felt pity for his young cousin. Markus had obviously grown up in an entirely different environment than he had. Surrounded with love and support from his parents and grandfather, Chance may have struggled but he knew his family would always be there for him.

Focus, Chance. Remember what you're doing. If he could just sink the chiseled stone into Markus and release the hemlock into his system, they would have time to think about what to do next. Although he had daydreamed about ending Markus's life, he wasn't sure, now that the time had come, that he would be able to do it. He was glad Balam was there with him because he didn't know the right thing to do.

Chance threw himself at his cousin and aimed the pendant toward his stomach. Surprised by the attack, Markus let out a grunt and spun away but the sharp obsidian cut his arm, despite his effort. The pendant remained intact, to Chance's disappointment.

Desperate to keep him from shifting, Chance goaded him. "Why don't you fight me like a man?"

Markus sneered and answered, "But I'm not a man, I'm a shifter." The dripping wet teenager shuddered and expanded as though he was being inflated until a muscular black gorilla stood leering at them.

"Balam!" Chance called over his shoulder.

"Move!"

Chance scrambled to move away from the huge beast as it thrust its fists into the clay and propelled forward, its lips pulled back into a frightening grimace. Chance tumbled over as he scrambled behind two thin tree trunks just as the great ape sped past.

Balam shouted at the immense primate. "I am who you want, boy."

He locked eyes with Chance for a moment and gave a

brief nod before phasing into the yaguar. The gorilla turned on the huge feline and paused a moment before charging. Balam leapt aside just before impact, and Markus hit the overgrown stone wall where Chance's great-grandfather had just been standing. As his cousin shook his head, the yaguar swiped at it and sent him into the wall yet again.

Chance almost laughed. A wave of relief flooded over him. Balam would be able to take care of the problem. He was nearly six-hundred years old and had lived through the Spanish invasion. He wasn't short on fighting experience.

The magnificent and legendary yaguar leapt up the hillside. Chance slipped the pendant back around his neck. With his eyes on the silverback, who had just righted himself again and heaved up the slope after Balam, Chance edged along, sinking his feet into the wet soil, scrambling to keep up.

The trees and growth above him shook violently. A deep, angry scream erupted and he was sure it was Markus. If he was going to keep up, he'd need to shift. He didn't want to use up too much energy but he needed to take a form that wasn't entirely powerless to maintain their pace.

He untied his sarong, flipped it around his neck, blew out a quick breath and let his power surge through every cell, transforming him into a sleek, tawny cougar. Chance raced ahead and followed the noises and scent trail laid by his cousin and great-grandfather.

It took him a couple minutes to catch up but he was

careful not to get too close. He didn't want the wrath of the gorilla focused on him. As Balam forged ahead, Chance wondered what he was up to. Was he trying to lead Markus somewhere? He wasn't moving as fast as the yaguar could go, that much was clear to him.

The storm began to let up as they moved through the jungle. Gray clouds washed the sky in an ominous cover and the heavy rains slowed to a soft mist. Nearly twelve hours of showers had made the ground extremely slick and in certain areas, swampy.

It wasn't till he caught a familiar scent and landmark that he realized they were nearing an area they had trained in. Balam was leading them back toward home. But why? He couldn't help but worry. He didn't want Markus anywhere near the house. It went against his survival instincts. Chance hoped Balam knew what he was doing.

The sounds of crashing brush and trees fell silent. He slowed down and stopped. Chance lifted his snout into the air. What now?

Noises echoed around him. Now that the storm had abated, the treetop inhabitants chattered noisy warnings as the predators rushed through the jungle. Monkeys screeched and birdcalls pierced through the canopy, which didn't help Chance's concentration.

Then through the brush came the yaguar on top of the silverback. Their teeth and the whites of their eyes pierced the gloom. If this was where Balam wanted to fight, it was time for Chance to shift back and wait for his opportunity to paralyze Markus with his poisoned talisman. The two brawling animals did not appear to notice him as he crouched behind some vines.

Quick as he could, he returned to his human form and ripped off his only opportunity at stopping Markus: the pendant filled with hemlock. He wrapped the piece of ratty maroon fabric around his waist and proceeded to study the clearing with his weapon grasped in his hand.

***

Ana stood in the spot where Balam had left her, having second thoughts. It wasn't too late to turn around and run back to Sanchia's warm, dry house. But, she couldn't.

She was confident that somewhere in the jungle, Chance and Balam needed her help. *I can't stand by and let something happen to them. I can't.*

Unsure what to do, she closed her eyes and tried to clear her mind, which was hard to do while rain slapped against her body.

A strange sensation came over Ana and made her woozy. She saw something in her thoughts she had never seen before. It seemed like a memory, but it wasn't hers. As in so many dreams she'd had before, she was flying. But, it wasn't enjoyable because she was so upset and scared.

I have to get to her in time. Your life isn't worth a thing if you can't save her.

What was happening? She didn't understand. Was this something to do with being a healer?

Then as fast as it came, the vision faded and another

surfaced. She was in a field. A familiar field. Niyol was there with her. Her joy at seeing him again turned to concern as she saw the look on his face. What was wrong? He seemed scared and upset.

Ana practically tipped over when she saw her own limp body laying on the ground.

"Grandfather! What should I do?! Her heart!" The voice that came from her mouth was the voice that filled her days with joy. Chance's. Was this Chance's memory?

"You can save her but you must hurry," Niyol said to her urgently.

"But I haven't been able to take that form yet!"

"Chance, you must hurry! She needs you! Believe in yourself."

The thoughts in her head weren't her own.

Focus, Chance! You can do this. You know the mapping for the mustang. It can carry her home quickly. You can't let her die.

Fear coursed through her. Then another image emerged. The butter yellow energy she had recognized inside her just a day earlier was pulsing through her pores, raising the hairs over her arms and legs, despite the cold, abrasive rain.

Oh, my God!

Chapter 33

Chance lingered in the cover of an overgrown, flowering bush as he watched Balam push Markus around the clearing. The yaguar clubbed the hefty gorilla repeatedly until it couldn't get back up.

For a five-hundred-year-old, Balam was holding up well but Chance could tell he was beginning to get winded; his ears were no longer erect and his pink tongue showed between his teeth. If his great-grandfather was winded, then Markus must be exhausted but clearly his cousin wasn't ready to throw in the towel yet.

Markus's knuckles pressed into the ground and he stood once more. His eyes caught Chances and narrowed for a moment before he continued on with the yaguar. The horse-sized cat raised its hindquarters, ready in wait.

The ground thundered as the silverback charged forward and its loud screeches filled the air. Chance's great-grandfather leapt aside, avoiding the collision once again. Chance was ready; the cool blade projected from his fist like a talon. As the primate stormed past his hiding place and ground to a stop, Chance propelled himself forward, the weapon poised for its shot.

Maybe it was the unavoidable noise he made as he moved, but Markus seemed to predict his approach. He tucked himself into a ball and rolled away just as Chance landed in the mud. He was stunned. All that waiting for nothing.

Powerful fingers closed around his wrist and bashed his hand onto a nearby stone. Pain receptors screamed out in agony and he heard an ominous crack. He let go of the pendant, unable to hold on any longer.

Oh, no!

In a flash, the primate morphed into the sadistic guise of his cousin. He snatched up the weapon and inspected it as he said, "What do you have here? What's so special about this little thing that you won't even shift to attack me in animal form? Maybe I should just use it on you if it's so powerful."

Markus lifted the glistening obsidian point into the air. A noise, barely detectable, rose from behind them. As the pendant came down, it arched around and to the side.

Chance flinched, half-expecting to be impaled. Instead, Balam, back in his human shape, tumbled over him and landed with a groan.

"Balam?" His great-grandfather met his gaze, and fear was etched in his eyes.

The sound of Markus's laughter faded in his ears as Chance watched Balam remove the shiny point from under his ribs. Only it wasn't a point any longer. The end had broken off.

"Oh, my God!" Chance's breath caught in his throat.

"Big whoop. So I stabbed him. It's not like he can't heal himself," said Markus, chuckling.

Chance ignored him. He searched Balam's face for a sign of what to do next. Instead, what he found there was agony. His jaw was clamped and his eyes pinched shut. The blood flowed from the wound in his abdomen down to the coppery earth, a red plume fanned out, carried away by the rainwater.

Not only would his great-grandfather not be able to take another shape, he wouldn't be able to heal himself. The only thing he could do for Balam was deliver him to Sanchia to care for him until he could heal himself.

By this time, his cousin had quieted down and was watching Balam suffer with an almost hungry expression. He stood and started to pace. It appeared a debate was being waged in his noisy mind. Finally, he mumbled. "Why isn't he shifting? It must be the weapon. It's time to act."

Markus phased back into the gigantic silverback. But before he could step forward, Chance reacted. Without putting much thought into it, he shifted into bear form, the form that most represented him and the one he hoped wouldn't let him down. He leaned forward and swiped Markus with his paw, raking his claws across the gorilla's surprised face.

Markus let out an angry screech that echoed through the canopy and sent camouflaged birds into flight. Chance shoved the gorilla away from his wounded great-grandfather. Equal to the fight, Markus reacted to his touch, flung his furry black arms around Chance and started beating his head. Teeth sank into his shoulder, sending a shower of spasms through his muscles. Chance gave a final shove before using his claws to pry the primate off him.

The confidence he experienced while Balam had been there to protect him was gone. Memories of his fight with

Markus in Idaho were fresh in his mind as his cousin's spiteful eyes seared into him. It was all he could do to keep the paralyzing fear at bay. Doubt crept in like a disease without a cure. How would he beat Markus this time? Niyol wasn't there to save him. He would have to save himself.

Markus rose onto his hind feet and Chance did the same. Then the other beast showed its teeth, gave a wicked sneer and the assault began. The primate clubbed him with its fists so quickly Chance didn't have time to react. Stunned from a knock to the head, he grunted and held out his front legs in an effort to protect himself. His heart raced and echoed in his ears. This wasn't working very well. Markus had the advantage over him. With more energy and power, plus opposable thumbs and hands, he would tear him apart in no time. Maybe going big hadn't been the best approach.

Chance recalled the days and weeks of practice spent with Balam and what he had said about smaller animals helping win a fight. He had an idea and acted on it. When Markus lifted his arms over his head to go another round of punches, Chance shifted into a squirrel. He shrank down until the form of the gorilla towered overhead. As quickly as his small body could move, he scurried up Markus's back legs and clutched the silvery fur on his back as he pulled himself onto his shoulders. Markus howled in surprise and tried to grab him with his arms. His fluffy tail was nearly snatched, so he flipped it behind his lanky body.

Ready for his next move, he phased again. The squirrel

expanded and distorted into a cougar. His weight was clearly unexpected and too much for the gorilla, who stumbled forward onto its fists. Before his cousin could react, he sank his claws into flesh and his canine teeth penetrated muscle as blood washed into his mouth. His instinct was to let go and retch, however he resisted the impulse and held on. Markus started flinging his fists back, impacting Chance's head so he let go and used the skills Balam taught him to shift again into a finch.

Chance flapped around in front of the gorilla's face and saw the confusion etched there. He darted through the air and hid in the branches of a nearby tree as he watched Markus stumble around in the clearing. While his opponent was disoriented, he noiselessly swooped down behind him and shifted back into cougar form. Chance surged forward and sunk his claws into the silverback's flesh as he clamped his jaw around his cousin's neck and shoulder once more.

Markus howled in pain and started to shake, but not from anger. His coarse black fur changed color and augmented into that of a golden cat with an abundant mane. Chance tumbled onto the ground as the lion whipped around and its eyes narrowed. Markus radiated anger.

Oh, no.

Without hesitation, the king of the jungle leapt through the air as if he had springs strapped to his feet, landed on Chance's chest, sending him skidding a couple feet. For a moment, he was unable to take a fresh breath. His lungs felt like they had been cast in clay and were unwilling to absorb any oxygen.

Markus swatted his claws across Chance's muzzle. Blood began to drip down his face. A series of blows pounded his ears and temple, making him lightheaded.

Stay awake, Chance. Keep it together. You need to protect Balam.

His head lolled to the side and he sought out his great-grandfather. He spotted Balam thirty feet away, sitting and clutching his side. His hand was stained dark red. It appeared he had lost a lot of blood, but it wasn't over yet. Balam met his gaze, rose to his feet in silence and walked a few steps and reached down.

Distracted by his great-grandfather's actions, he didn't see Markus lean in with his mouth open but he felt the pain when his jaws clamped on his shoulder. Chance howled in surprise.

Just then, the bearded cat released its hold and Markus's head knocked forward unnaturally. He growled when it happened again. The lion stumbled to the side and off Chance, revealing Balam holding a large rock in one hand and a branch in the other.

Chance was too surprised to do anything but watch his cousin round on the descendent of Mayan royalty. Although clearly hurt, Balam held himself tall and strong. Crimson blood streaked down his abdomen and leg from his wound yet Balam still seemed ready for a fight.

As the lion edged forward, Balam struck him on the snout with his branch. Markus shook his head, bared his teeth at his opponent and advanced again. This time, he was smacked by the rock and roared so loudly a spray of spittle dropped from his jaw. Balam danced to the side, light on his feet, but Chance knew it had to be costing him a lot to move like this. The grimace on his face was evidence enough.

Chance realized suddenly he should be helping and stumbled to his feet. As he stepped forward, Balam swung his branch at the African cat, who grabbed at it, clamped it firmly in its jaws and ripped it from his great-grandfather's grasp. The branch unexpectedly whipped back and cracked Chance upside the head. A small limb punctured his forehead and he dropped to the ground. Shapes swirled in his vision and a wave of nausea made him grab the earth for support.

Balam skirted back and away from the lion, swooped down and located another branch. The stick in Markus's mouth fell to the ground and splashed in a puddle. He gave Chance a glance before skulking toward Balam, ready to hunt.

Chance watched, entranced, as his great-grandfather leapt through the air, swinging his weapon at the oncoming cat. When the wood connected with Markus's head, a loud crack echoed through the jungle. As Balam descended, the lion's paw flew out and hooked him in its claws and threw him to the ground.

Chance tried righting himself on his feet but another wave of vertigo hit him and it was all he could do to stay upright. A strange noise rumbled from his chest as he watched in horror as the lion stood on his great-grandfather like a doormat. He took a step but tipped over, helpless.

Balam suddenly spoke, but it was directed to the opposite corner of the clearing. Balam gave a sudden shout as green light radiated from the lion's paws. Blood flowed from new wounds on his great-grandfather's chest just as Chance heard an eerie crack.

Chapter 34

What was going on? Ana didn't understand.

She was now standing on four brown furry legs. She gathered from the image that had seared into her thoughts a moment earlier and from her hooves that she was now a horse. How on earth had that happened?

It didn't matter. Not now. She needed to get to Chance and Balam. She knew something was wrong and she needed to help them.

Her skin quivered and erupted in waves all over her new body. The long muzzle that stretched from her face was a strange new addition, and it took a few snorts for her to get comfortable with it. Ana stepped forward tentatively. Her round hooves supported her as she trotted on the trail. Drops of water from the wet canopy above slapped her back and forehead and she blinked at the world through a fresh set of eyes. Although it was all strange and new, it was almost...normal.

Her need to find and save her love had triggered this, she was almost certain. She hoped it would help deliver her to him. Her snout lifted in the air and she breathed in deeply. So many scents were all around her. So many more than she had ever experienced. In the tangle of aromas, she identified two she was familiar with.

As she propelled herself forward, her hooves caught in the mud, almost sending her to the ground but she caught herself and slowed down for a few strides until she was more confident. Speeding up again, she trotted into the wilderness after the scents that she hoped would lead her to Chance and Balam.

Eventually, the scent trail grew stronger and so did something else. Intuition. Instincts. One of them or maybe both.

Ana recognized the area. They had come out this way to train a few times. It was near Balam's home. The sound of movement distracted her and she stopped. Her new and much more sensitive ears lifted of their own accord. Sounds of wet footsteps and shuffling urged Ana forward. Then she saw them.

A tawny cougar stumbled to its feet as a huge African cat rounded on something she couldn't see. As it moved aside, Balam, in human form, came into view. He leapt through the air, a large branch in his grasp, and smacked the lion with it. Then, to her surprise, Balam was caught and pressed into the clay by the powerful claws of the feline.

No!

Everything moved so fast she felt powerless. If she could have screamed, she would have. Instead, a snort escaped her muzzle. Balam looked up and they locked gazes. His lips moved and he spoke in a trace of a whisper but her erect ears caught his words perfectly. "Ana." He said her name in the way she always thought was so pretty: 'Ah-nah'. "It has happened. I knew you were special. Protect each other…"

The lion's bloodied paws glowed green as the vicious beast sneered from its perch on top of its prey, its head hovering inches over Balam's. Why wasn't Balam shifting? She didn't understand. He was strong enough to take Markus, right?

Balam shouted in pain. Everything moved in slow motion as she tried to understand the nightmare playing out before her.

A burst of bright blue light coursed out of Balam like a supernova. The yellow cat seemed to glow green as it arched its head back into a yowl. The cougar, which had staggered and collapsed on the ground, dragged itself toward the two. In the blink of an eye, the puma shifted into Chance and he dove to his great-grandfather's side calling out. "Balam!!"

The lion focused on its next target and roared. Even from where Ana was, she could see the fear in Chance's eyes. She may have been too late to save Balam but she wouldn't allow Markus to take anything else from her.

Ana raced into the clearing, reared up on her hind legs and let her front hooves drop down on Balam's murderer.

***

Chance stared into his cousin's eyes. They were glowing amber from the power he had just absorbed and filled with madness. Markus hunched down and reared on his haunches.

Chance's mind was racing. He had no time to dwell on the fact his mentor and great-grandfather had just been murdered before his eyes. He would be dead himself soon if he didn't think of something quickly. It was then he noticed Balam's pendant. Just as he reached for it, a blur of movement behind Markus made him stop short.

The lion tumbled violently off Balam and into the mucky clay, where a chestnut mare stomped on it. The yellow cat lay still in the mud as Chance gawked at the animal that had saved him. Its head bobbed up and down and whinnied excitedly. It was then he noticed something about the horse. He had never seen a horse with eyes that color in his life. They were mesmerizing. Familiar.

"Ana?" he whispered in disbelief.

The response was immediate. The horse nodded its head furiously at him as its feet shifted in a funny dance.

Distracted, he hardly noticed the lion stir until it was nearly too late. The beast grew and changed its shade from sun-kissed wheat to coal black. The yaguar began to stretch.

He had to move fast. His hands fumbled to slip off Balam's pendant just as Markus leapt to his feet and whipped around. The horse reared nervously. The sight of his cousin taking the form of Balam's and his ancestors made him furious. How dare he steal it from Balam! He hadn't earned it like he had.

Markus stared back at him as he held the pendant and then tilted his head at the mare, who turned and ran into the wilderness. The yaguar bolted after the horse as it disappeared through the hazy jungle.

Chance dropped the obsidian weapon around his neck and closed his eyes. The reservoir of energy inside him had been half depleted already but there was enough to shift into his homage to Balam. If anyone had the right to use the regal yaguar form, it was him. A screech ripped from his chest as he launched after Markus at full tilt.

Chapter 35

Ana felt him come after her. His footfalls, although soft, echoed in her ears. Her back twitched as she imagined his hot breath on her.

It was only a little farther. Her hooves slipped in a muddy section of earth and she scrambled to find better footing. Vines caught around her neck but she pushed through. Her legs contained more power than she had ever experienced. Her strength was exhilarating.

Ana's ears tilted back and she thought she detected two sets of footfalls. Good. That meant Chance was on their tail but she wasn't about to turn her head and check. She was new to navigating the world in this foreign body and with an unbalanced shifter right behind her, she wasn't about to slow down.

Many aspects of her eyesight were improved, but it was strange not being able to see the greenery around her; everything was various shades of gray. And while she ran through the jungle, she had to keep lifting and lowering her head to adjust her depth perception. She thought she caught sight of what she was looking for and raced ahead. When she got close enough, she leapt, clearing the obstacle, then slowed and waited. All she had to do was incline her head slightly to see what happened next.

The yaguar raced toward her and then, as if snagged by an invisible rope, it tumbled forward over its head and sprawled out on the ground. Deep snarls erupted from Markus as he thrashed in the growth Ana had used to cover the line of her trap. It had been a few weeks since she'd set the snag and she gave a silent prayer of thanks that it hadn't been touched since.

Ana heard movement from behind her on the trail and then another black yaguar burst from between two Ceiba trees. Markus scrambled onto his feet, drew the thin line between his teeth, and began to gnaw at the cord that ensnared him. The other yaguar slowed and then phased into Chance. She didn't want to stare at his naked body but she couldn't look away as she watched him lift the pendant from his neck.

Markus's ears were flat on his head in a menacing posture. Ana immediately backed up and did the best thing she could think of—she kicked Markus in the head with her hoof and he crashed into the scrub.

Chance didn't hesitate. He thrust the hemlock-laced weapon into the growling yaguar's shoulder and kept twisting, grinning in satisfaction. The growls almost doubled in volume as the poison released into Markus's blood stream. Ana moved nervously ahead on the trail.

When the angry beast lashed out at him, Chance let go of the pendant. The brown cord still dangled from the wound. Mad as ever, Markus jumped to his feet, teetered for a moment and yanked with all of his weight, snapping the weakened line to the trap. With a snarl, he leapt toward Ana, who sprang ahead on the trail.

As fast as she could, she raced away from the yaguar. Her heart thrummed in her chest, sending adrenaline coursing through her veins. Wet leaves slapped against her body as she shot through undergrowth. A resonant sound made her ears prick up and she tried to locate its source.

A familiar ravine came into view. What was once a tranquil stream had now engorged into a violent river. It was too wide for her to jump and she was confident she would break her neck or drown trying to swim across. Ana slowed at the edge and spotted a downed tree that made a perfect bridge. She placed one foot down to test it and it slipped off.

I can't do this. What do I do?

If she were back in human form, she would be able to scale it, no problem. She needed better balance and toes that could grip.

That was when the tingling started. The strange sensation washed through her like a gentle wave. No longer weighed down, she felt light, almost weightless. She had the warm sensation of being home. Ana lifted her hands up to touch her face. She was human again— she had shifted back.

Her moment of relief was cut short. An onyx yaguar stood thirty feet away and licked its lips. Ana scurried onto the fallen log and began inching herself toward the other bank. The slippery wood prevented her from running across it. As she moved sideways, careful to keep her balance, Ana remained aware of the cat skulking toward her. The way it stared made her conscious of how naked and vulnerable she was out in the middle of the log, without any means of protection.

Was this it? The moment of her death?

Chapter 36

Chance raced behind Markus, not letting him out of his sight. He didn't want to shift needlessly just yet. He wanted to save all the energy he had left and make it count. Chance's energy was low. He just couldn't compete with Markus. His only consolation was the fact he had poisoned him with hemlock. No more shifting or healing for his cousin. At least for now.

The yaguar had stopped just ahead and started to purr. The sound frightened Chance and he wasn't sure why. As he moved closer, he saw the ravine engorged with rainwater, rushing past a fallen tree that braced each bank. There, teetering on the trunk was Ana, her eyes wide with fright.

God, no. Not again. How dare that freak even think about touching her. Never again.

It was then he recognized their location. This was where Ana's trap had caught him unawares and stabbed his leg. He searched for what he was looking for and saw it. The remains of the trap were near Markus's feet.

He had to move fast. Markus wouldn't wait long. The yaguar could leap across the log and kill her in mere seconds. Chance phased quickly into a small finch.

Wings spread, he flew the short distance, allowing wind that cut through the canopy to carry him. Markus stepped forward, his foot inches from the fallen tree, and growled again. Ana backed away and slipped. She squatted down and saved herself from falling into the sweeping current of brown water below her.

Chance landed on the leaf-strewn ground, folded his wings back and shifted back to his human form. In one motion, he snatched up the stake that had his dried, blackened blood on it, leapt on top of the unworthy yaguar and drove it into the base of its skull. The screams that filled the air morphed and changed into that of a man's as the mighty beast fell forward with its head on the trunk. The large black jaguar stopped writhing just as Chance remembered an important detail.

I've got to get away from him.

"Ana, back away!" he shouted as he scrambled back.

But it was too late. A wave of light arched out of his cousin and soaked into Chance, knocking him over.

For a brief moment, everything was still.

"Chance, are you okay?!" Ana's voice barely permeated his mind.

Energy coursed through his body, touching everything, leaving nothing unmolested. Strength like he had never known was awakened.

Then, the voices and the memories started.

Tears poured down his cheeks as vivid images of pain and death pressed on his mind. He couldn't get away from it. There was no stopping it.

Take her. She may not be worth much, but she has energy.

The voice in his head was not his; in fact he had never heard it before. But its power of suggestion was too great to fight. Hunger possessed him. Ana clung to the tree trunk on her hands and knees—so helpless. It would be nothing for him to pluck her life away like a grape off the vine. He sat up, his focus entirely on her.

Stop, Chance. Protect her from yourself. Protect your love.

He shook his head. Too many thoughts and emotions were swirling around for him to focus on anything clearly. All except one. *Protect Ana.*

Chance stood, gave one last glance to the beautiful girl on the log and closed his eyes. Power surged through him as he took to the ashen skies as an eagle. He arched up and above the dark canopy of trees and away from the one he loved.

Chapter 37

"Chance! Where are you going?" Ana said with a shout, "Come back!"

She watched his silhouette cut through the clouds and disappear. Ana was in shock. She tried to wrap her mind around what had just happened but there was too much.

A cool wind brushed over her body, raising goose bumps. At the very least, she needed to get off the tree trunk and find herself some clothes. Ana crawled forward and found Markus's animal remains ahead of her. She was forced to stand to step over him.

When back on solid ground, she turned and looked at him. The yaguar's eyes were open but empty of life. Her skin crawled. Although it made her stomach turn doing it, she tried pushing the animal into the rushing water but it was futile. The creature was too large and heavy to move.

Ana gave up and stared up at the skies again. Where had Chance gone? He wouldn't leave her. She waited for a while until the chill of the storm cut through her exposed skin and then decided to head back to Balam's house.

She ran as quickly as she could. The grotto below his home was cold as she darted along the suspended walk above the cenote. Water flowed down from openings in the ceiling and showered down on her. She leapt two stairs at a time up the staircase until she emerged into the main level of the limestone tower.

It felt different somehow. Empty. Balam wouldn't be coming back. Not ever. She tumbled onto the couch and started crying. Salty tears stained the cushions as she clutched them to her face. Her emotions twisted and churned inside and erupted into sobs and moans.

After she pulled herself together again, she stumbled upstairs to her room and got dressed. With her brush in hand, she wandered into the hallway and peeked into Chance's room. She was stunned. Although some clothing still remained strewn across his floor, his backpack was gone, along with most of his things. Ana ran inside and began searching for his wallet and phone. She couldn't find them anywhere. On the side table lay his jade jaguar pendant and bear heartline necklace. She picked them up in her hand and stared at them.

He couldn't have left her. It was impossible.

Ana slipped his necklaces around her neck. She would keep them safe and give them to him when he came back. Her stomach rumbled and she took a deep breath. Whatever was going on, she needed to take care of herself.

Numbly, she wandered downstairs and found some leftovers. Everything was tasteless. The normally cheerful jungle inhabitants were silent, tucked inside their homes after the rains. Ana felt even more alone.

When she was done, she cleaned up after herself and walked out to the deck. The view was muted and hazy. As she stared into the mist, she decided what she needed to do. Balam deserved a proper burial and the only person she could trust was Sanchia. She would know how to honor him.

Ana pushed away from the balcony, sped through the house, down the stairs and out into the aqueous jungle. Her muscles were ready for what she asked of them and kept her moving at a jog along the trail to the town. Finally, when she reached the split in the path, she found a pile of fabric. Her clothes.

She hadn't spent much time thinking about her strange and unexpected new ability. It made no sense to her. It was hard enough for her to wrap her mind around the fact that Balam thought she could be a healer, and now what was she? A shapeshifter, too? How did that happen?

Ana bent down, grabbed her things and set off to Sanchia's house. She must have been waiting for her, because as soon as she stepped off the path and into the street, the elderly woman opened her door and waved. Ana allowed herself to be led inside the small, warm home that smelled of cinnamon and chocolate.

"I am happy to see you. You worried me, child," Sanchia said and squeezed Ana's hand.

She wasn't sure how to reply. *How do you give news like this?*

"Is there something wrong?"

Ana nodded and pinched her lips to stop them from quivering.

Sanchia seemed to understand she couldn't speak and pressed on. "Is it Balam or your mate?"

Again, Ana nodded in response and was unable to hold back the tears. Balam's granddaughter, albeit shorter than her, pulled her into a warm embrace. When she couldn't cry any more, she stood up straight and looked at Sanchia and noticed that she, too, had reddened eyes

"Balam's dead. I need your help—I don't know what to do."

This time, it was Sanchia's turn to nod wordlessly. She left Ana in her cramped living room and disappeared into the kitchen. With a large sack over her shoulder, she returned and opened the door.

It took a while for Ana to lead her into the jungle and to Balam. Sanchia was far more resilient than she appeared, refusing any assistance with her sack. As they approached his still body, Ana was unable to look at him. This wasn't Balam. His soul was gone. It was only the shell of the man she had grown to love.

"Tell me, how did he die?"

"He was fighting to protect Chance from another shifter when he was killed."

Sanchia frowned and said in a whisper, "That is honorable. Did his powers go back to the earth or were they absorbed?"

Ana's lip quivered as she answered. "They were stolen."

"Ay, no. His spirit will not be at rest."

The elderly woman removed some folded white cotton from her bag and laid it on the ground. She diligently moved the body of her grandfather to the center of it and began to clean his wounds. Then she placed something in his mouth.

"What is that?" Ana asked.

"A small jade bead in the shape of the yaguar and some maize. It will be a long journey." She leaned down and rolled him carefully into the cotton wrappings. Then she stood up and asked Ana solemnly, "Where is your mate?"

"I don't know. He killed the other shifter and just...left."

Sanchia's eyes widened and she muttered something Ana didn't understand. She continued to speak in fluent Mayan as far as Ana could tell and put her hands together in prayer. Fear permeated Ana's heart and her muscles tightened. Balam had described the act of absorbing another shifter through death like a sickness. What did that mean for Chance? It was all she could do to keep herself from hysterics.

Balam's granddaughter caught her attention and said, "Carry this end. We will take him home."

Sanchia grabbed hold of the wrapped end containing Balam's feet, and Ana lifted the other end. He was heavy but she had enough strength. His home wasn't very far so it didn't take them long, even with intermittent stops to set him down so they could rest.

When they arrived at the cenote, Ana wondered where they were taking him but didn't stop to ask questions. They traveled along the wooden walkway to the limestone stairs. Just as Ana began to question how they were going to carry him upstairs, Sanchia stopped and set his feet down and motioned for her to do the same. Then she turned, faced the rock wall and opened a three by two foot door.

All the times she had passed by it, she had never acknowledged the worn wooden portal. When it stood open, she peered in and saw a narrow black hole. It appeared to have no end. To her side, Sanchia had removed something new from her satchel and set it on the ledge beside the opening. Ana winced when she realized the woman had lit what she had set down. A small plume of white smoke curled through the air. The aroma was sweet and spicy. She knew she had smelled it before and thought back to the wedding party when they had met Sanchia.

"Please," the woman said as she leaned down and picked up her end of Balam's wrapped body.

Ana helped lift him and Sanchia set his feet into the darkened portal. She motioned for Ana to push the rest of him in, which was challenging because the fabric kept snagging on the stone. When only his cotton-encased head could be seen from the opening, his granddaughter placed a red terra cotta bowl over it and shut the door.

Sanchia's eyes closed and her hands lifted in prayer once again. "I pray you find rest in Heaven, Balam, my ancestor."

The sound of streaming water echoed off the cave walls. Numb and confused, Ana stared at the gateway of his resting spot and waited, hoping Balam would speak up, and give her the direction she needed.

She suddenly remembered Markus. "What about the other shifter? What should we do with his body? He died in yaguar form."

"Is the body far?"

"No."

Sanchia lifted her pack over her shoulder and said, "Take me to him."

Balam's granddaughter held Ana's hand along the walk to the ravine and it was the only thing that kept her from turning back. She didn't want to see Markus's body again and his dull, lifeless eyes.

When they arrived, Sanchia rifled through her bag and withdrew a knife. Ana stepped back and stuttered. "What's that for?"

"The yaguar must be preserved. Balam is not here to pass it down to our descendants. It is my duty now."

Ana quickly turned away once she saw Sanchia hunch over the large cat with her blade, getting to work severing its paw off. As Ana stood there shaking, she thought of the talon Niyol had given Chance, an item that had been passed down through many generations so the thunderbird would never be lost. It had been the key for him to unlock the thunderbird mapping. Although she understood why one might keep a relic like this she wished she were somewhere else. Anywhere else.

"Ana."

She cautiously looked over her shoulder and saw Sanchia tucking something into her bag that was wrapped in cotton.

"Go get that branch." Sanchia pointed near a cluster of trees.

Ana scurried over to retrieve the thick bough and dragged it back. They slid one end under the massive body of the yaguar and used the lever to roll him into the murky water. When Markus's body submerged and dipped from view Ana gave a sigh of relief.

"What about the body? Will anyone find it?" she asked.

Sanchia shook her head. "No. No one will find it, not out here."

"Come child, it is time for you to collect your belongings. We must go."

Ana's legs carried her back to the house somehow. All she could think about was how much she didn't want to go. She wasn't ready. If Chance came back, he'd come here looking for her. Anyway, where would she go? Back home to Idaho—without Chance? What would she say to his parents? Sanchia gently coaxed Ana upstairs and her leaden feet moved despite her hesitance.

When she was a child and upset, she would sit on the floor and completely shut down. Her mom told her stories about how she would stop communicating with everyone. No one would be able to get through to her. She wouldn't smile, speak, nod or move for anyone.

Life always seemed to be just out of her control. She hadn't chosen to be born with heart defects or to have an absent dad. She hadn't chosen to have heart surgeries, but she'd had them anyway. She'd had no choice. Now, just as things had turned around for her, when she'd finally gotten the second chance she'd always dreamt of, everything had fallen apart. All she wanted to do now was sit down and be left alone.

Sanchia moved around the house, placing important

items into her satchel and enclosing larger pieces in a blanket. She shooed Ana up to her bedroom, where she plopped down on the bed and tucked her pillow under her head. She was exhausted. Her day had started early that morning when Balam's plans of a tracking test for Chance had gone terribly wrong. She was mentally and physically bankrupt.

Sleep came to her, softly, like a baby blanket laid on a dreaming cherub.

Chapter 38

Turquoise water shimmered in the sunlight, the color of the Aegean Sea. Almost unnatural, yet beautiful. Snow-tipped mountains reflected off its placid surface and a sharp breeze brushed her hair across her face.

A familiar song filled the air. Ana couldn't tell if it was a woman singing or if it was birdsong but she wanted to hold her breath so she could hear everything uninterrupted. She felt safe and welcomed.

Ana, if you are ready, I am here for you.

Ana woke with a start.

The woman's voice had been so clear in her mind. She expected to see someone standing in her room but she was alone. Ana rubbed her eyes and stretched. Her feet drifted to the floor and she groaned as she stood. She was unsure of how much time had passed but figured Sanchia would be waiting on her.

Without enthusiasm, she folded and tucked away all of her belongings into her travel pack. Then she swaddled Balam's gift to her, the golden snake hairpiece, and hid it away at the center of the bag. Her toiletries and personal effects were soon packed and all traces of her visit disappeared. She carefully made the bed because she wanted everything in its place, a form of thanks to Balam for what he'd done for her and Chance.

She left her room and stood in Chance's doorway. Her hand went to her neck and touched the pendants he'd left behind. He felt close to her, somehow. She had a piece of him with her. Even though she knew what the result would be, she tried calling him. The phone went straight to voicemail.

"Chance, it's me. Where did you go? Please call me—"

"Ana?" Sanchia's voice echoed up from the lower level.

Ana palmed her phone, turned and walked slowly down the stairs, like a death march. When she entered the living space she saw a few items missing and then noticed Sanchia. In her arms, she held a blanket that was filled and tied in a knot.

"It is time to leave. Are you ready?"

Ana took a deep breath but it didn't make her any more relaxed or prepared for whatever came next. "Yes."

She stared at every section of the room. Memories met her at every turn. The fire where Balam had taught her to make Mayan hot chocolate, the couch on which she and Chance had stayed up late listening to stories and where Chance had been tattooed with his *nagual*. Ana traced her fingers on the grain of the hand-hewn table where they had eaten their meals. It pained her to leave this place. Mostly because she was leaving without her soul mate.

On their way out, Sanchia led the way. Ana remained fixed on her footfalls and kept her head down. It was approaching early evening now according to her watch but the storm clouds had begun to disperse. Freshly washed leaves and foliage stood out like bright green emeralds against their russet trunks and branches.

Movement caught her eye. A monkey stared down at her from the crook of a tree. It chattered and sprang higher into the canopy, disappearing from sight. Her focus returned to the trail and Sanchia's footsteps.

A soft whimper to her left made her pause mid-stride. She looked and discovered a pair of brown eyes gazing at her from under a palm frond. A familiar scruffy face lifted its snout and the stray turned away, its tail wagging as it went. The dog trotted a short distance and stopped. It gave a yip and peered at her.

Everything clicked for Ana. She knew what she needed to do, even though it scared her.

"Sanchia? I don't think I'm going back with you," Ana said and slipped out her cell phone. "Do you have a phone? What is your number in case I need to contact you?"

Sanchia stopped and frowned, clearly confused. "Why not, Ana?"

"I think I have somewhere else to go. I will come back if I need to but I want your number so I can check in with you." *And to check to see if Chance comes back.*

The elderly woman rattled off numbers, which she entered into her phone. When she was done, Ana gave her a big hug and said, "Thank you for everything, Sanchia."

"Good luck, Ana. Be safe," Sanchia said and watched Ana wander off the trail.

She wasn't sure of anything right now but for whatever reason, she decided to trust her instincts. Ana waved at her friend as she stepped through the labyrinth of trees to where the dog waited for her.

Ana muttered. "I am trusting you. Please don't hurt me."

The shaggy stray licked her hand and pranced off, with Ana following close behind. They walked for about ten minutes before the canine slipped behind an enormous Ceiba tree with a trunk that was at least four arm lengths around.

What stepped around the other side was not a dog but a woman. She was securing a long piece of blue fabric around her body and tying it at her neck, the way Ana had seen Hawaiians do it. She was stunning, beautiful.

"Thank you for your trust, Ana. I am Lifen."

Long, straight black hair tumbled down past her shoulders, outlining her pale oval face. Ana thought she appeared to be middle-aged, but she had an ageless quality. Her skin seemed flawless, like fresh cream.

Ana couldn't move. She was unsure of what to do so instead she asked the first thing that came to mind. "Have you been following me?"

Lifen's lips turned up into a gentle smile and she said, "I have checked in on you from time to time, yes. Through your travels."

"Why?"

"I first felt your presence many months ago. There are not many like us, Ana. It is important to have a guide, especially when you are young—to know and understand better what you are. And to have protection."

What was she talking about? This was just too much for one day. It made her want to stomp right back to

Balam's house and hide under the covers of her bed.

"I'm sorry but how do you know what I am? How would you know? *I* don't even know."

Lifen settled onto a large stone, adjusted her wrap and said, "The ancient line of power that flows through the gifted manifests itself in different ways in men and women. Men can shape their energy, molding their bodies like clay, and women can affect energy in others' bodies to heal. Some shifters have been able to harness their energy to attempt healing although it does not come natural, and some healers have been known to shapeshift but there are often complications. I can feel what you are because I, too, have both powers."

Did she just say I'm a healer AND a shifter? After all those times she'd considered Chance lucky to be able to fly through the sky and shift into any kind of animal at a whim, she'd never dreamed it would happen to her. When he'd healed her, it was more than she could have asked for. Had he done more for her than just healing her body?

"About four months ago my boyfriend Chance saved my life with his powers. My heart stopped and he healed me, dying in the process. Lucky for him, his grandfather gave his life to save him."

Lifen nodded solemnly and looked up into the trees where a cluster of birds began to chirp and rustle the leaves. She returned her gaze to Ana and said, "When your mate healed you, he gave himself to you. He planted his seed of power within you, giving you his shapeshifting ability and awakening your feminine healing energies. It was only a matter of time before the seed took root and bloomed. I felt that happen for you yesterday. That is when I chose to come back for you. I knew you would need me. I sensed you were in trouble but am thankful to find you safe now."

Ana shuffled her shoes and stared at the impressions in the mud. She didn't want to talk about this. Talking about it would make it real and she still couldn't accept it. "Chance's cousin Markus tracked us down and attacked him and Balam, Chance's shifting teacher and great-grandfather. I tried to help—to stop it—but Markus killed Balam. And Chance was only trying to save my life. He shouldn't have—again. Chance killed Markus and then he just...flew off."

"You and I both live a tragedy. I am sorry for your loss, young one." Lifen pinched her lips and bowed her head. Then she stood, moved forward two steps with her hand outstretched and said, "We must get you away from here in case he changes his mind and comes back for you. You cannot trust him if he is infected."

"What do you mean?"

"The one you love is still there, but if what you say is true, he has been infected by the poison that is the downfall of all shifters. You must not be near him as young and weak as you are. His temptation—the voices will be too strong."

She couldn't help it. Tears streamed down her face as she thought about Chance suffering—all for her. How could she sit back and let him self-destruct? There had to be something she could do. Anything.

"But what about Chance?" She sniffled as she wiped her tears away.

"Nothing now. You must help yourself before you can help him."

"So, there's a way?" Ana asked hopefully.

Lifen nodded but doubt filled her eyes. "It is time you came to meet your new family. There are other youngsters there. A place for learning."

The snow-tipped mountains and the picturesque lake... "Is it in the mountains? I think I've dreamt about it," Ana said.

"It is. And it is waiting for you now."

Ana hesitated, stepped forward and grasped Lifen's hand. Her new mentor gave it a squeeze and led her through the misty jungle.

She didn't know if she was making the right choice and she wasn't entirely sure if she should trust Lifen, but she decided to trust her instincts, which were telling her it was the right choice for now.

Anything that could bring her back to Chance and into his arms. She had only one purpose now. To save him, even if it was from himself.

THE END

Look out for Book III of The Shapeshifter Chronicles

To get updates on upcoming book releases please visit
<u>www.theshapeshifterchronicles.com</u>
& sign-up for Natasha Brown's newsletter

Mayan Hot Chocolate Recipe

Ingredients:

3 cups boiling water
1 to 2 cinnamon sticks
8 ounces bittersweet Maya Kakaw or Xocoalt (chocolate paste) **OR**
3 tablets Mexican unsweetened chocolate, cut into small pieces
2 tablespoons of wild honey, or to taste
1 pinch of dried red chili (start with a pinch and increase to taste)

Directions:

In a large saucepan over medium-high heat, add the cinnamon sticks to boiling water. Cook until liquid is reduced to 2 1/2 cups. Remove cinnamon sticks. Remove from heat and stir in the chocolate pieces, chili, and wild pure honey. Make sure water isn't so hot that it causes the chocolate to seize up. Mix well and whisk constantly until chocolate is melted. Return to very low heat if needed to melt chocolate thoroughly. Remove from heat. Whisk vigorously to create a light foam effect.

*My thanks to Michaelene McElroy for her recipe contribution

About the Author

 Natasha Brown lives in Colorado with her family and is busily trying to write the start of a new middle grade series. She enjoys talking with students about the rewards of writing and strives to inspire them to follow their hearts.

To follow Natasha, you can find her here-
Twitter- @writersd3sk
Facebook-   https://www.facebook.com/pages/Natasha-Brown/261525383920497
www.theshapeshifterchronicles.com

Made in the USA
Lexington, KY
23 February 2014